LOST
LITTLE
GIRL

LOST LITTLE GIRL

A JACKSON GAMBLE NOVEL

GREGORY STOUT

LEVEL
BEST BOOKS

Author Photo Credit: Ted Schnepf

First edition

ISBN: 978-1-68512-045-0

Cover art by Level Best Designs

This book was professionally typeset on Reedsy.
Find out more at reedsy.com

For Carol. Here it is at last.

Praise for LOST LITTLE GIRL

"With *Lost Little Girl*, get ready to meet your newest favorite detective, Jackson Gamble. He's a PI with an ironic view of the world, an equal ease in strip clubs and executive offices, and an openness to falling in love. Greg Stout makes Gamble's Nashville, Tennessee as gritty and vivid—a character in its own right—as Lew Archer's Los Angeles. Can't wait for the sequel!" — Mark Levenson, author of *The Hidden Saint*

Chapter One

The first time I laid eyes on Delsey Lee Hawkins was on a cool, crisp Wednesday afternoon in early October. I found her waiting for me when I got back from lunch, sitting on the couch in the small reception area I keep in the outer office. When I walked in, she was thumbing through a dog-eared, pocket-sized edition of the Bible and humming tunelessly to herself.

She looked to be about fifty years old, give or take a page of the calendar. She was dressed neatly, but not expensively, in a conservative navy-blue dress, thick stockings, sensible black, low-heeled shoes, and a lightweight tan raincoat that had been worn well past the point where a trip to the dry cleaners would have done it any appreciable good. She had a plain leather handbag which she had tucked tightly under her arm, as if it were a living thing that might try to make a break for it if she loosened her grip even for a moment. Her hands were strong and red-knuckled and looked as though they'd done their share, and then some, of dishes, diapers, windows, and floors. She wore a gold wedding band and tiny gold pierced earrings. Her iron-gray hair was cut short and curled into tight little ringlets that framed her face the way lily pads surround a pool of quiet water.

When she heard me come in, she looked up expectantly before pausing to mark her place in her Bible. I smiled and said, "Good afternoon."

She scanned me up and down like a person who'd been warned to expect the worst and was somehow still disappointed. "Are you Jackson Gamble? Jackson Gamble, the private detective?" She spoke with a nasal, east Tennessee twang. The tone of her question made it sound as if scarcely a day in her life went by that she failed to encounter one or more individuals named Jackson Gamble, each engaged in a different line of endeavor. I assured her that I was, indeed, Jackson Gamble, the private detective.

The corners of her mouth turned sharply downward. "Then Mr. Gamble, you should know that I have been waiting here to see you since eleven-thirty this morning. It is now," she paused, snapped open her purse, extracted a large turnip watch, and consulted it disapprovingly, "one thirty-five and I am late getting back to work. May I ask just what kind of a business it is you're running here?"

I decided that a blow-by-blow description of my long, liquid lunch and the lady who helped me drink it wasn't quite the explanation she was looking for. Instead, I said, diplomatically, "One that requires me to be out of the office a great deal of the time, I'm afraid. That's why I have an answering service."

She acted unimpressed. "Looks to me like what you need is a good secretary."

"You're probably right," I told her. "The job's open if you're interested." When that got no reaction other than an even stonier stare, I said, "Do you want to come inside where we can talk?"

"I suppose I'd better, or I'll be here all day." She slipped her Bible into her coat pocket and got stiffly to her feet. I unlocked the door to the inner office and went in ahead of her. I flipped on the lights and pulled the customer's chair around so it faced my desk.

"Can I hang up your coat for you?"

"I'll keep it, thank you," she said, sounding very much as if she feared that if she handed it to me, I might not give it back.

I sat down behind my desk, unlocked the middle drawer, and took out a notepad and a pencil. She crossed her ankles and fidgeted uncomfortably in her chair.

"Would you like a cup of coffee?" I offered. "I'll have to make it, but it'll just take a minute."

"No, thank you." She let her eyes drift slowly around the room, like an auctioneer pricing the fixtures for a going-out-of-business sale. Taken together, they wouldn't have attracted many bidders. In addition to my desk and the chairs in which we were sitting, I could number among my assets a computer, a printer, a bookcase crammed with paperback novels that kept me occupied during slow business days, and a couple of battered, second-hand file cabinets that held all I had to show for my nine years in the private detective business. On the wall above the cabinets hung a framed copy of my license and a reproduction of a Pennsylvania Railroad calendar that had been issued during the 1940s and that matched the days of the current year. For reasons I no longer remember, I get a new one just like it in the mail every year.

The silence finally got loud enough for her, and she gave a short, self-conscious laugh. "Well, now that I'm here, I'm not sure where to begin."

"Maybe you could tell me your name?" I suggested.

"It's Hawkins. Delsey Lee Hawkins."

I wrote that down. "That would be Mrs. Hawkins?"

"Mrs. Jericho Hawkins, that's correct," she nodded.

"All right. What seems to be the problem, Mrs. Hawkins?"

"It's my daughter, Gabrielle. She's—Mr. Gamble, do you carry a gun? When you work, I mean?"

"It depends on the situation. Why, what kind of trouble is your daughter in?"

"She's been kidnapped."

I laid my pencil down and looked across my desk at her. She looked back at me levelly.

I said, "Kidnapped?"

"That is what I said, Mr. Gamble. You heard me correctly."

"Yes, I'm sure I did. I'm just wondering if that's what you really meant, because if it is—"

"I meant what I said."

"Because if it is," I continued, "then I'm afraid I don't understand what you're doing sitting here talking to a private investigator. Kidnapping is a very serious crime, Mrs. Hawkins. If a minor child is involved, it's a federal offense. You can get life just for trying it. If you really believe your daughter's

3

been kidnapped, then you need to get in touch with the police or the FBI."

"I've already tried that."

"And?"

"They weren't interested."

"Not interested?"

She looked at me with some irritation. "Mr. Gamble, is there something wrong with your hearing? Would you like me to talk louder?"

"My hearing is fine," I assured her. "It's just that I'm having trouble understanding—Mrs. Hawkins, how old is your daughter?"

"Fourteen. She'll be fifteen next month."

"And how long ago was she, uh, abducted?"

"It's been two weeks ago this coming Saturday."

"I see." I leaned back in my chair and chewed on that. I tried to imagine all the likely scenarios that the parent of a fourteen-year-old girl would characterize as kidnap, but that the police would brush off with as little concern as they apparently had. I could only think of one that made any sense.

"Let me ask you something," I said, "and please don't take this the wrong way, but I have to ask. Is it possible that your daughter might have just run away from home for some reason or other? I mean, has anyone contacted you demanding money in exchange for her return?"

She said icily, "Nobody has to 'contact' me, Mr. Gamble. My daughter is a good and proper Christian girl who wouldn't up and leave home without somebody forcing her to do it. Now you call that whatever you like, but I call it kidnapping."

"Kids run away every day, Mrs. Hawkins, without anybody forcing them to do it. Even good and proper Christian ones."

She gathered her tired raincoat around her and made a move to get up. "I can see I'm just taking up your time, Mr. Gamble. I'm sorry. I didn't mean to be a bother to you."

"You aren't bothering me, Mrs. Hawkins. This is how I make my living. Look, why don't you let me get a little more information about this—this situation, and then we can try to figure out whether there's anything I can

4

do for you."

"Does that mean you might not be able to do anything at all?" she challenged. "What kind of a detective are you, anyway?"

I bit my tongue. "A reasonably honest one, as it so happens. I'm not going to take your money or make you any promises about what I can or cannot do until I have a better idea what your problem is. Now if you want, we can sit here the rest of the afternoon and argue about how I do my job or you can let me get some information, and then we can go from there."

She squirmed in her chair again and pulled her handbag more tightly against her body. "My baby's gone. Somebody took her. What more is there to tell?"

"Well, how about if you tell me your address."

"3633 Newsome Street."

I wrote that down. "That's here, in Nashville?"

"That's right."

"You mentioned earlier you were on your lunch break. Where do you work, Mrs. Hawkins?"

"Baptist Hospital, in the admissions office."

"Do you have any other children besides Gabrielle?"

She smiled a tiny smile of inward satisfaction. "There's just my son, Jericho, Junior."

"Does he live at home, too?"

"No. He's in the army, in South Korea. He's been there going on a year, now."

"Okay." I made a couple more notes. "Let's talk about Gabrielle. Has she ever done anything like this before? Even just to stay overnight someplace, maybe at a friend's house, without telling you?"

"Never. She wouldn't do that."

"Not even once? You're absolutely sure about that?"

"Of course, I'm sure. Don't you believe me?"

"I don't disbelieve you, Mrs. Hawkins. I'm just trying to get things straight in my own mind. Now, the night she left home, a week ago Saturday, you said?"

"That's right."

"What happened?"

"I don't know what you mean."

"Okay," I said. "Was she behaving in an unusual manner? You know, did she seem nervous, or fidgety, anything like that? Had she been spending a lot of time on the telephone, or texting more than usual?"

"Not that I noticed, but then, when she's home from school she stays in her room most of the time. I couldn't really say for sure what she's up to in there."

I was starting to feel like I was trying to punch my way through a wall of mashed potatoes. "Let's get back to the night she disappeared. How did she get out of the house without you noticing?"

"Oh, I noticed, all right. I just didn't think anything of it. Gabrielle said she wanted to spend the night at her girlfriend's house. I couldn't see the harm in it, so I told her to go ahead as long as she promised to be back in time for Sunday school. Then she went into her room and packed a few things in an overnight bag and left."

"What time was that?"

"It was just about seven-thirty."

"Did you see what she took with her?"

"No. But I know she never got to Ginger's house. She just walked out the door and—disappeared."

"Just like that? None of your neighbors saw her talking to anybody in the street or in a car or anything?"

"The police checked on that. From what they tell me, nobody saw anything." She paused, as if to reset the scene in her mind.

"So, she walked to her friend's house. She didn't get a ride."

"If she got into a car, nobody saw. It was raining a little that night, and it was right around dark, so I guess there weren't too many folks outside who would have seen anything."

"What about during the last few days before she left? Did she get any visitors or new friends you might not have met before?"

"No."

"Okay. Was she having any trouble at school? Teacher trouble, for instance? Or did she have an argument with you or your husband that could have upset her?"

She hesitated for a second. "Not that I can think of."

"Well, think hard. It could be important."

She took a deep breath. "Mr. Gamble, I'm not a complete fool. I know what you're getting at. The police asked a lot of the same kinds of questions. They think Gabrielle just ran away, and I can tell by the way you're talking, so do you."

A single tear spilled out of the corner of her eye and ran slowly downward through the furrows of her cheek. "But she didn't run away. She's just a little girl. She's my daughter, and I know her better than to think she'd do a thing like that."

She shook her head doggedly, as if to force the idea out of her mind. "Somebody evil took her away. Somebody who means to hurt her or kill her or force her to do terrible things. And nobody will believe me, and I don't understand why."

I put a comforting look on my face and started to say something about how it didn't make any difference what the police or I or anyone else believed. Gabrielle was gone and nobody was questioning that. The important thing, I started to tell her, was not how she got that way, but what we were going to do about getting her back.

But I didn't say any of that, because before I got a chance, she said in a suddenly firm, accusatory voice, "Mr. Gamble, have you been born again?"

"I'm sorry?"

"Have you been born again? Are you a Christian?"

The question caught me off guard. "I was brought up Catholic, Mrs. Hawkins. I don't know if that qualifies me as a Christian for your purposes or not."

"Do you believe it's possible for the Lord God to speak directly to His children here on earth?"

"I don't know." I spread my hands helplessly. "Where are we going with this?"

7

"Mr. Gamble, all my life, I've put my faith and trust in the Lord Jesus Christ, in the sure knowledge that he would take care of me and those that I love in times of trouble. I was brought up that way and I've tried to raise my own children to hold that same conviction. The Lord knows, though, it hasn't been easy.

"Since Gabrielle first disappeared, I've prayed day and night, asking Jesus if he took her away from me as a punishment for some sin I might have committed during my lifetime."

"And has he answered you?"

She stuck her chin out defiantly. "You may laugh, Mr. Gamble, but yes, I believe he has. In fact, after my experience the other night, I'm convinced of it."

I said, "What happened the other night?"

"I had—well, you see—I've had a revelation."

Chapter Two

What followed can only be described as a long, awkward silence. I stared uneasily at my new client, not having the slightest idea what to say. She looked back with a kind of wobbly-kneed bravado, like a woman determined to speak her piece, and, having at last spoken it, expecting to be roundly ridiculed for her trouble.

Finally, I cleared my throat. "You're saying you had a revelation from God?"

She brightened for a second. Then, imagining she was being set up for a punch line, let her face go slack again.

"I won't say that's where it came from, but yes, that's what it was like. I guess you must think that's pretty silly, mustn't you?"

"It's a little outside my experience," I admitted. "Without knowing more about it, I'm not sure what I think. Did you tell that story to the police?"

"I tried, yesterday morning."

"What did they say?"

"Oh, they were very polite. But the long and short of it was that they thought I was just some crazy old lady. They said without something more definite to go on, there wasn't much more they could do than what they were already doing."

"There's something to that," I told her. But if she heard, she gave no indication.

"They told me hundreds, even thousands, of children run away from home every year, just here in Tennessee alone. They said the best thing for me to do would be to go home and try not to worry, that Gabrielle was probably all right and that she'd likely come home all by herself once she got whatever was eating her out of her system. Meantime, they'd keep looking for her.

"But Mr. Gamble," she protested, her voice cracking like ice on a frozen river in springtime, "she's not all right. I know it. I saw her."

"In your revelation, you mean?"

"That's right."

"You want to tell me about it?"

She looked at me earnestly. "You won't laugh at me?"

"I won't laugh."

"Well—it was like a dream. Only it was more vivid than any dream I've ever had. It was very late at night. I was in bed, but I don't think I was sleeping. Or maybe I was, but then I heard Gabrielle's voice, very clearly, calling my name. I know I couldn't have been sleeping then, because I sat straight up in bed. All at once, I could see her, plain as I see you now. She was in a thick mist, and the mist kept swirling around her. She called my name and tried to run toward me, but every time she did, someone or something would drag her farther away." Delsey's hands tightened in a death grip on the arms of her chair, as though she were fighting to keep from being pulled back herself into the dark mist of her own terrible nightmare.

"It was Satan himself pulling her back into that mist, Mr. Gamble. Satan or one of his agents here on earth, just like it tells in the Scriptures. And unless we do something, I'll never see Gabrielle again." She was trembling uncontrollably.

"Please, Mr. Gamble, you're my last hope. I'll pay anything, do anything, only please don't let anybody take Gabrielle away from me. Don't let them take my baby girl."

And with that, she broke down completely, her body convulsing with violent, despairing sobs. It was as though all the heartsickness and terror of the past ten days was venting itself at last, in one tearful rush. The sound she was making was the kind of wailing noise you sometimes hear at a hospital when the doctor tells the family that the patient did not survive the operation, or at the conclusion of a graveside service when those left behind realize their loved one is gone forever.

I turned in my chair and looked out the window, thinking that if I left her to herself for a few minutes she would cry herself out. When she showed no sign of letting up, I got up and went out into the hall to the water fountain. I pulled a paper cup out of the dispenser and filled it with water. Then I went back into the office and set the cup on the edge of the desk in front of her. I found a box of tissues in my bottom desk drawer and set that next to the cup of water. After that, I sat back down and waited. And I felt lousy. Lousy that I lived in a world where kids like Gabrielle Hawkins could break a mother's heart with such an apparent lack of concern, and lousy that mine was a business that unfailingly ended up attracting the detritus to my office door. Because no matter what Delsey Hawkins dreamed, or hallucinated, or had had "revealed" to her, there was very little question in my mind that Gabrielle was a runaway, pure and simple. And whatever she had been thinking about on that Saturday night she took off, I wouldn't have given sucker's odds it had anything to do with love for her poor old mom and dad.

After another minute, Delsey began to calm down. The torrential weeping tapered off to intermittent snuffling, then stopped altogether. She took a Kleenex, wiped her eyes, and blew her nose. Then she took a sip of water and wiped her eyes again.

I smiled encouragingly. "Okay now?"

She nodded. "I think so, yes. I don't know what came over me. I don't usually do that in front of strangers."

"Don't worry about it. You want some more water?"

She shook her head, no.

"Do you think you can handle a few more questions?"

"I think so."

"Okay, then let me ask you this. Do you or your husband have any enemies who might see abducting your daughter as a way of getting even with you for something you might have said or done in the past? Anything at all, even if it's something small?"

"Mister Gamble, I work in a hospital. My husband is a minister, a man of faith. What could we possibly do to provoke someone to hurt our child?"

"I don't know," I said. "Sometimes matters of faith can be a touchy subject.

11

Time was people were tortured or even burned alive for what some claimed were heretical beliefs."

"Our church is not like that," she said, with a firmness that surprised me. "We believe in the literal teaching of the Bible. That is hardly cause for anyone to hate us."

I decided that arguing that point would only drag us further into the weeds. "Delsey, I have to ask you something. If you don't want to, you don't have to answer, but if you do, I'd appreciate your honesty."

"Ask your question, Mr. Gamble. I have no secrets."

"Just this. Why isn't your husband here with you?"

"What do you mean?"

"Well, you didn't say you were separated, or divorced, so I assume your husband is aware of the situation and shares your concerns. That means unless he's disabled or doesn't care about your daughter for some reason, he could have come along today if he had wanted to. I'm just wondering why he didn't." And then I had a thought. "Or could it be he doesn't know you're here?"

"He doesn't know. He would have never let me come if he did."

I started to say "Wouldn't let you?" then remembered that my technique of repeating her statements back to her as a means of obtaining clarification was one that she found irritating.

"Can I ask why not?"

She was quiet for a moment, as if searching for the right words to answer the question. "My husband is a preacher of the Gospel. He's pastor of the Divine Light Pentecostal Congregation, in Antioch. It's a small congregation, and very conservative in its teachings."

"So, what are you telling me, that the church has an injunction against hiring private investigators?"

"Not in so many words, no. But we do believe that when bad luck befalls us, it's God's will, and we have no choice but to bear the burden he gives us. According to what the Book of Job teaches, Gabrielle's disappearance is just another part of God's plan. When and if she comes back home again is also in his plan."

But there was more to it than that, I knew, even if Delsey couldn't or wouldn't put it into words. People from the Appalachian region are of Scots-Irish descent, and whether they call themselves "hillbillies," "hill people" or some other self-referential term, they tend to harbor an innate distrust, and sometimes even a hostility toward outsiders, which included even a Missouri native like me. And for good reason. They have seen their mountains stripped of timber and coal for construction and to fire the mills and furnaces of Ohio and Pennsylvania. And then they stood by helplessly as, one by one, the companies that supported them and their families pulled stakes or merged with foreign companies, in the process taking away their jobs, their pensions, and their self-respect and leaving them with nothing except broken promises and chronic diseases like black lung. Handing over any amount of their hard-earned money to a stranger, even in the direst emergency, was simply not something people like Jericho and Delsey Lee Hawkins would be inclined to do. Nor if they did, would it be something the members of their community would view favorably.

"So then, until God decides to give you a helping hand, you're just supposed to sit around and worry yourself to death, is that it?"

"And pray. God knows, I've done that, Mr. Gamble. I've prayed until I've worn my knees bloody. And I know that by coming here, I'm going against the will of my husband and the teachings of my church, but I can't let my daughter just vanish from the face of the earth without a fight. I can't, and I won't, and I don't care anymore who knows it or what they think about it."

"The Lord helps those who help themselves, Delsey."

"The Bible doesn't say that, Mr. Gamble. You're just making fun of me."

"Not at all. Based on what you've told me, I'd say it took real courage for you to come here today."

She gave me a weak smile. "Thank you for that, Mr. Gamble. I don't know that Jericho would agree, but it's nice of you to say so, just the same."

I said, "Are Gabrielle and your husband close?"

She hesitated just for a moment. "I wouldn't say close, exactly. Jericho isn't someone who allows himself to be close to anybody, except, of course, to the Lord. Oh, he loves his children, make no mistake. And he loves me too, in his way. He just doesn't find showing it an easy thing to do."

She sighed. "I suppose in that respect, Jericho has to have walked a very lonely path all these years. That's a sad testament to a man's calling to the service of the Lord, don't you think? After all, what's to be gained preaching the good news of the Gospel if you never allow yourself to experience love in your own life?"

I leaned forward in my chair and rubbed my eyes. I couldn't be sure if it was from having to sit and listen to the sorry saga of the Hawkins family, or if the too-many margaritas from lunch were finally catching up with me. But all at once, I felt dead tired, and no longer even remotely interested in getting drawn into a maudlin philosophical discourse with the saddest Hawkins of them all.

"I'd like to get back to Gabrielle," I said, trying to get things moving again. "You said when she left the house, she was planning to spend the night with a girlfriend. What was her name, Ginger?"

"Ginger Aldrich, yes. She and Gabrielle go to school together, in the ninth grade. Ginger lives at the other end of the block from us."

"Okay." I made a note of the name on my desk pad. "What I was going to ask you is, when did you actually find out Gabrielle didn't spend the night with Ginger? Was it that night, or the next day?"

"It was the next morning. As I told you, I made her promise to be home in time for nine o'clock Sunday school. That's where the young folks go when the grown-ups are attending services. When it got to be eight-thirty and she still wasn't home, I called Ginger's house to hurry her along."

"And what happened?"

"Ginger said she didn't know anything about Gabrielle planning to spend the night. She said that was the first she'd heard of it. I tell you, Mr. Gamble, when she told me that I liked to fall over dead right there on the kitchen floor."

"So, as far as anybody can prove, Gabrielle never went to Ginger's house?"

"That's what Ginger says."

"And that's what she told the police?"

"Yes."

14

"What do you make of that?"

The question seemed to confuse her. "I guess I don't rightly know what to make of it. I'm sure Ginger isn't telling the truth, if that's what you mean."

"Can you think of any reason why she would lie?"

"Not right off, but I know that's what she's doing. Maybe she's afraid of getting involved with the police. Kids can be that way sometimes."

I nodded. I knew that mentality all too well. And I knew it wasn't limited exclusively to kids, either.

"Is it possible you might have misunderstood where she said she was going? Maybe she said she was going to spend the night with somebody else instead?"

"There isn't anybody else, Mr. Gamble. Gabrielle hasn't got any other friends living close by except for Ginger. And even if she did, that doesn't explain where she is now."

"How about boyfriends? Was your daughter dating anybody who could have picked her up in a car, maybe after she got down the block and out of sight?"

She threw me a look of undisguised horror. "Absolutely not! Gabrielle's been told any number of times there'll be no dating until she's sixteen. As I have already explained to you, she is a good Christian girl."

"Right, I remember we talked about that. Did you happen to bring along a photo of Gabrielle?"

"Yes, I have it here." She reached into her purse and handed me a three-by-five color image, the kind they make from school picture-day photos. It showed a stunningly pretty young girl with long, dark hair that had been carefully teased to make her look like a *Cosmopolitan* cover girl. She had wide brown eyes, high cheekbones, and wore a pouty expression that was as close to sexy as I guessed a fourteen-going-on-fifteen-year-old could come. I supposed she must have inherited her looks from her old man. She didn't look anything in the world like the sad-faced lady sitting across the desk from me.

"Can I keep this for a while?"

"Do whatever you need to. Are you going to be able to find her?"

"It depends. If she's still in the city, then yes, I probably can, although with the head start she's got, it might take a little time. If she's left town altogether, then I don't know what to tell you, except that it'll be a lot more difficult. And it could get expensive."

She bobbed her head animatedly, like a kid who had been expecting a "no" from mom and pop and was surprised and delighted to get a "maybe" instead. Then the word "expensive" registered and her expression got serious again.

"I didn't bring very much money with me, I'm afraid. I didn't know how much to bring, and I get nervous walking around with a lot of cash in my purse."

"I understand."

"Oh, but that doesn't mean I won't pay you," she added quickly. "If you'd like, we can go over to the bank right now. I'll get you whatever you need."

"How much did you bring?"

"About two hundred dollars."

"That's fine for now. Let me have a hundred, as a retainer. My rate's three hundred a day, plus expenses. I'll work on the hundred against expenses until I have a better idea what I'm up against. After that, we can decide whether you want me to keep going."

She opened her purse and counted out three twenties and four tens. As she passed the bills across the desk, I caught sight of a small automatic pistol in her open bag. She saw me staring at it and quickly snapped the purse shut again.

"Are you sure that will be enough?"

I wrote out a receipt for the money and gave it to her. "For the time being it'll be fine. If I need more, I'll let you know. And by the way, do you have a permit to be carrying that gun?"

"I didn't know I needed one."

"You do. And another thing. If you've got cash in your purse, then you ought to carry your gun in your pocket. You're a lot more apt to get your purse snatched than you are to get your pocket picked. Your gun won't give you much protection if somebody else is running down the street with it."

"Oh, I don't think I'd ever use it. It belongs to Jericho. I don't know if it

16

even works. I just brought it along so I'd feel safe."

From me? I wanted to ask, but I let it go. "In that case, you'd be safer without it."

"I'll remember that." She started up out of her chair. "Is there anything else I can tell you?"

"Just a couple more things. I need to know where Gabrielle goes to school."

"Woodcrest High School, on Glenrose Avenue."

"Is there somebody there I can ask about her?"

"Well, all her teachers know her. They can tell you what a good student she was—she is."

"That's not what I'm looking for. I was thinking more along the lines of a counselor or a dean who might know whether she was having any special problems."

Delsey thought for a moment. "There's a Miss Totten, I think her name is, who is her adviser is this semester. You could try her."

"Good." I wrote the name down. "The other thing is, I need to stop by your house later today. I want to get a look around Gabrielle's bedroom to see whether she left anything behind that might give me an idea where to start looking."

"All right, but would after supper be soon enough? Jericho will be at evening services, and I've already defied him once just coming here. There's no call to throw it in his face if I don't have to. Most Wednesdays he goes to evening services by himself, so I have the house to myself from seven until about ten. If you can come then, he won't know you've even been there."

"Seven o'clock will be okay," I said. "Meantime, if I need to reach you, is it a problem if I call you at work?"

"No. Just dial the main number and ask for admissions." She rose and buttoned her coat to leave.

"Mr. Gamble, may I say something to you? Something personal?"

"I can't wait," I said.

"Well, I just want to say—I want you to know, Mr. Gamble, that in spite of your worldly and sometimes cynical ways, I believe you are a righteous man, and godlier than you would ever admit even to yourself. And I believe

17

I have made the right choice coming to you."

I hoped she was right about that and said so.

Chapter Three

After Delsey left, I propped my feet up on my desk and took another look at the photo of Gabrielle Hawkins her mother had given me. I tried to imagine myself in her position: an uncommonly pretty girl of almost fifteen years, on the run from a stiflingly religious and apparently unhappy life at home. Where would I go, I asked myself, and what would I do when I got there?

The possibilities, I knew, weren't good. Which was why I had made a point of not mentioning any of them to Delsey. Most kids who run away from home don't get very far. And a good portion of them wind up back on their own front porches within a few days, hungry, tired, broke, and desperately in need of a hug and a bath and a good night's sleep. The others, the ones who choose to leave for good, or who are driven off by parents who can't, or won't take care of them, typically head for cities like Atlanta or New Orleans. They go there in hope of finding a way to support themselves, and, just maybe, a better life than the one they left behind. But for most of the thousands of runaways who disappear for good every year, that's not the way it turns out.

A few kids, the lucky ones, make their way into a private or publicly-supported shelter for runaways, where there are responsible people to take care of them, no questions asked, until they can get their act together and either go back home or make some kind of permanent arrangement for themselves. For the rest, the future is a lot less promising. Prostitution, crime, drugs, pornography, and violent death at the hands of people who are unspeakably evil are the depressingly regular stops along the line. The fact that Gabrielle had already been gone longer than a week suggested strongly that one of these was probably the direction she was heading. Delsey, I knew, wouldn't want to hear that. No mother ever does.

I got the telephone number for the Woodcrest Consolidated High School and put in a call to Ms. Margaret Totten in the guidance office. When she came on the line, I explained briefly who I was, and what I wanted to talk to her about. She sounded busy but agreed to give me a few minutes if I could get there before three o'clock. I thanked her and said that would be fine.

I locked the office and walked outside into the sunshine of a perfect autumn afternoon. A little cool for the first week of October, maybe, but still pretty enough to make me wish that for one more day at least, I had never heard of Gabrielle, Delsey Lee, and Jericho Hawkins. For a few moments, I just stood on the sidewalk, breathing the crisp, clean air and feeling good to be alive.

Twenty minutes later, I was sitting in my car in front of Woodcrest High School, feeling a lot less good. Woodcrest was the kind of place that could do that: an old, crumbling hulk of a Coolidge-era school building, with graffiti-marred walls and grimy windows protected from rock-throwing vandals by heavy wire mesh screens. In the afternoon shadows, it squatted like some impenetrable citadel of gloom squarely in the middle of an equally old, gray, used-up section of the city known as Jacktown.

In the years following the end of World War II, Jacktown was the kind of neighborhood people called "working class." Then, it represented a respectable rung for families on the economic ladder between the four-flats and rooming houses north of the river to the security and comparative gentility of newer, middle-class developments like Priest Lake Park or Hickory Valley in the south. That was then. No more. The inexorable dynamics of time, neglect, and demographics have seen to that. Today, the preferred term for Jacktown, and other crapped-out neighborhoods like it, is "transitional." It's a nice-sounding word that sociologists have invented to avoid having to call them what they are: slums.

I got out of the car and looked around at what was little more than a brooding mélange of potholed streets, peeling frame houses, dried-up lawns, and that most peculiar of Southern phenomena, rusted-out cars and pickup trucks perched on cinder blocks in the side yards. It made me understand, with sobering clarity, what it must really be like to be hanging onto respectability by a slender thread. It also gave me a first-hand look at what Gabrielle Hawkins was running away from.

A steely-eyed security man stopped me just inside the front door of the high school and asked me to state my business. He called on an intercom to confirm my appointment before giving me directions to the guidance office and a yellow plastic clip-on badge that said VISITOR.

I set off through the vestibule, past the obligatory dusty glass case filled with tarnished gold and silver athletic trophies. Next to that was a wood and brass plaque engraved with the names of alums who had died during the seemingly endless and frequently pointless wars in which the country had been involved since World War II. A memorial, it seemed, to lessons not yet learned.

Past the vestibule I turned right and headed down a long, sparsely illuminated corridor that was lined on both sides by orderly ranks of steel lockers, several with derogatory racial or sexual slurs scratched into the paint. Every fifty feet or so, the hallway was punctuated by a windowless classroom door. One of the doors was propped open with a wooden wedge, probably a fire code violation. As I passed by, I paused to give a listen to what was going on inside.

A balding, middle-aged man wearing faded blue jeans and a corduroy sport coat two sizes too large for him was pointing with a yardstick to something written on a dry-erase board. I couldn't read it from where I stood, but the nut of his presentation seemed to be that communism was a pre-industrial phenomenon, whereas fascism was post-industrial. It sounded reasonable to me. I couldn't have argued the case one way or the other.

An exquisitely bored-looking kid sitting near the door looked over and spotted me standing in the hallway. I smiled and gave him a thumbs-up salute of encouragement. He curled his lip in a better-than-average impersonation of Kurt Russell playing Elvis Presley and returned the salute with his middle finger. I moved on, feeling over the hill and totally out of place.

I found the guidance office around the next corner. A pretty, petite woman who introduced herself as Margaret Totten met me at the door. She was about thirty-five, with penetrating blue eyes, short blond hair, and a compact, well-proportioned figure. She wore dark blue slacks with matching shoes and an ivory-colored blouse with three-quarter length sleeves. She gave me a no-nonsense handshake and led me into a tiny, cluttered cubicle at the end of a row with three more similar, but empty cubicles.

Just to get the conversational ball rolling, I said, "Are you the only one on duty this time of day, or what?"

She gave me a look of weary patience, as if the subject were a sore spot with her. "I'm the only one on duty, period. Last year, there were two of us. Before that there were four." Then she added, "The conservatives are in charge these days. They'd rather spend money on penitentiaries than education, or haven't you heard?"

"It was in all the papers," I reminded her. "That's a nice outfit you're wearing. Mind if I ask where you hide your gun?"

The temperature inside the cubicle seemed to drop about twenty degrees. "Is that a pass, Mr. Gamble, or just your idea of a witty remark? It's hard to tell these days, you know."

"Call it a weak attempt at humor, Ms. Totten. No offense intended."

She looked at me closely, like a cat trying to decide whether to pounce or let the object of its attention go on its way. After another moment, she seemed to make up her mind and conceded a tight smile.

"Well, then, none taken. And anyway, it's not as rough and ready around here as you might think. Most of our security measures are intended to keep outsiders on the outside, where they belong, and not in the hallways selling drugs and causing trouble. The students themselves are mostly good kids when you get to know them. They just need encouragement and somebody to pay a little more attention to them."

"Or maybe a little less?"

"Is there a meaning in that, or is your sense of humor showing again?"

"No, I was thinking about Gabrielle Hawkins. I got the impression from her mother that a kid could hardly want for any more encouragement and attention than what she gets, at least from her mother. It didn't seem to do her much good."

"Ah, yes." She drummed her fingernails on the edge of her desk. "You wanted to talk about our young runaway. Perhaps before we go any further, you'd better let me see some identification."

I handed her my photo I.D. She glanced at it briefly before giving it back again.

"You know, I believe you're the first private detective I've run across in all the time I've been here. Juvenile officers, absolutely, we get them all the time. Same with welfare department people, and even immigration agents. But never a private eye. I wouldn't have guessed anybody living in this part of town could even afford to hire one."

"It's a slow time of the year," I said. "Right now, I'm having a special."

"Also," she said, "what with you not actually working for any law enforcement agency, I'm not sure I'm even allowed to divulge any information on any student here."

"Call her mother if you need permission to talk to me. I've got her number if you want it."

She thought about that. "Or maybe I should invite you to speak at our next career day. I'll bet some of our students would find you fascinating. What would you think about that?"

I couldn't tell from her tone whether she was putting me on or just being plain snotty. In this business, it's not always easy to tell the difference.

"Send me the date and I'll put it on my calendar. Meantime, since I seem to be taking you away from something you'd rather be doing, maybe you could give me a little more information about Gabrielle so I can let you get back to it."

"Well, you were a bit vague on the telephone earlier. What exactly is it you're looking for?"

"At this point, anything you can tell me. Like, for example, do you know of any reason why Gabrielle would have wanted to run away from home?"

She looked as if she wanted to laugh out loud. "Let me ask you something, Mr. Gamble. When you drove over here just now, did you have a bucket over your head or did you actually look out the window? Because if you looked, you saw more reasons than I could begin to enumerate why somebody would want to run away."

"Yeah, there's that," I agreed. "But I was hoping for something more specific. See, one of the complications I've got with this case is that Gabrielle's mother has the idea her daughter has been kidnapped."

"Kidnapped?"

"That's pretty much what I said when I heard it. Evidently, Delsey had a dream or a vision or something the other night that convinced her Gabrielle was being held by somebody against her will. She called it a revelation."

"Well, I hope you didn't take her seriously."

"Why shouldn't I? You think people with money are the only ones who have kids that go missing? Check out your milk carton while you're having your Grape Nuts tomorrow morning."

"That's not what I mean and you know it. Delsey comes from fundamentalist people, from the mountains up near Kingsport. It's very common among unsophisticated people to place literal interpretations upon dreams. Did she tell you they're charismatics, and that they drink strychnine and pass live rattlesnakes around during their services? It's one of the ways they test their faith, you know. They believe if the snake bites them or they take the poison and they die, it's because their belief in the healing power of God wasn't strong enough to protect them."

"'They will pick up serpents with their hands, and when they drink deadly poison, it will not harm them at all; they will place their hands upon sick people and they will get well.' It's from the sixteenth chapter of Mark, in the Bible."

"Oh, please, you can't be serious. You're taking Delsey Hawkins's money on the pretext of investigating a bad dream?"

I said, "I'm a private investigator, Ms. Totten, not an evangelist. And I'm not taking her money under any pretext, except that of finding her daughter. I only mentioned the kidnap angle on the off-chance that there might be something to it."

"Absolutely not. The entire idea is preposterous."

"Okay, then, forget I mentioned it. Let's talk about Gabrielle. Was she—is she having any special problems here at school that you're aware of?"

"If she is, they haven't been serious enough to come to my attention," she said. "After you called, I pulled her file, just to be certain I had my information straight." She opened a manila folder on her desk and briefly consulted the contents.

"As far as Woodcrest High School is concerned, Gabrielle Hawkins is your basic, plain vanilla student. Not a druggie, no attendance problems, just an average, C-plus kind of a kid. I'd have to say she doesn't have as many friends as a lot of other girls her age, and except for trying out for a part in the school play, not much on extracurricular activities. I remember once she told me she'd like to be an actress."

She paused and spread her hands in front of her. "Other than that, I don't think there's a great deal I can tell you. I hate having to admit it, but with the budget situation the way it is, except for students who are either star performers or chronic bad actors, I don't have time anymore to get to know any of them the way I'd like to."

"That's funny," I said. "Delsey seems to think you know Gabrielle pretty well."

"I met her and her mother one time during the summer when she was getting enrolled and I've talked to her a few times since then. By default, since there's nobody left but me, I'm her adviser. If Delsey wants to take that to mean I know her well, then I guess I know her well."

"Right, got it. Does she have a boyfriend, you know, some high school hero who could talk her into an extended romantic getaway?"

"If she does, it's news to me. And anyway, if there were another student here at Woodcrest who's missed as many days as Gabrielle, I'd know about it."

"Well then, what about outside school, or at home? Would you know whether there's anything seriously wrong there that she might want to run away from?"

"Apart from the usual pressures of being fourteen and female, I wouldn't have any idea. That is, unless you want to count Jericho."

"You know Jericho?"

"I know him well. Gabrielle is not the first of the Hawkins children to pass through the hallowed halls of dear old Woodcrest."

I started to ask another question, but the agitated flicker in Margaret Totten's eyes told me she had something more she wanted to say. I kept my mouth shut and waited for her to spill it.

"Mister Gamble, I've been a counselor at this high school for going on seven years. And during that time, I've had a chance to meet a lot of parents, as you might well imagine. Sometimes I meet them under good circumstances, other times, not so good. But the thing that always strikes me is how much alike most of them are. They're blue-collar types, generally with no more than a high-school diploma, working jobs that barely pay enough to let them keep body and soul together.

"So, you say, okay, what's wrong with that? And the answer is, nothing at all. By and large, they're decent people who hope their kids will grow up to amount to something more than they did themselves. Jericho Hawkins, though, is like nobody else I've ever met. He is without a doubt, the most closed-minded, self-righteous man who ever called himself a minister of God. Next to him, Pat Robertson sounds like Howard Stern."

"What are you telling me? That Gabrielle's run away because her old man is a young earther who actually believes the world is six thousand years old?"

She dropped her eyes, a little self-consciously. "No, of course not. It was just something—I don't know, I thought it needed to be said, that's all."

"Happy I could be here to listen."

She shook her head, as if trying to bring her thoughts into clearer focus. "He refused to call the police after Gabrielle disappeared, you know. The only reason he finally agreed to do it was because I informed him that state law requires her to attend school until the age of sixteen. That, plus as a counselor, I am a designated reporter. That means I'm legally obligated to advise juvenile authorities of suspected abuse or other circumstances that might endanger a child. If he didn't call, I told him I'd report her as a truant and him for parental neglect."

"That explains one thing, then," I said. "Delsey told me Jericho didn't know she'd come to see me. I wondered why he sat still for the cops when he wouldn't allow her to hire a private investigator."

"You mean apart from the fact that she doesn't have much money? You know, I don't understand why Delsey stays with him. It has to be a joyless existence."

"Maybe she hasn't gotten around to having her consciousness raised yet," I ventured. "Or maybe she just takes being married seriously. There are still a few people around who do that, I'm told."

She made a noise that could have been a laugh. "Are you married, Mr. Gamble?"

"No."

"Ever been?"

"Oh, I get it. This is where I'm supposed to say, Gee, Ms. Totten, you've got a point there. I guess I don't know what the hell I'm talking about. But the thing you have to keep in mind before you begin passing judgment on Delsey is that people don't always walk out on a way of life because it's unpleasant. They also have to have someplace else to go. You evidently thought you did. Maybe Delsey not so much."

"That's a bit presumptuous of you, Mr. Gamble, don't you think? Or am I really as transparent as that?"

"Not enough to worry about. But when you've been in my line of work for a few years, you develop a pretty good ear for where people are coming from."

"Yes," she said coolly. "I can see where you'd have had the opportunity to get a first-hand look at more than your share of disastrous marriages, wouldn't you?"

"I don't do that kind of work, Ms. Totten. Not anymore."

"Well, just the same, I suppose for my own good, I'd better try to confine my comments to the subject at hand. Or have you finished asking your questions?"

"Almost," I said, hoping to avoid provoking another flare-up. "The night Gabrielle disappeared she told her mother she was going to stay overnight with a girlfriend named Ginger Aldrich. Can I assume you already know about that?"

She picked at an invisible spot of lint on her blouse. "The police mentioned that when I spoke to them, yes."

"Then you must also know that when the cops questioned Ginger, she denied knowing anything about Gabrielle's plans. Now the obvious question, it seems to me, is which story is the right one?"

"At this point, what difference does it make?"

"It depends," I said, "maybe none. If Ginger was telling the truth, and I'm starting to have a lot of trouble believing she was, then the answer is no difference at all. But if she was lying, it might mean she had a pretty good idea Gabrielle was getting ready to take off for parts unknown, if not that night, then soon. And if that is the case, maybe she also knows where Gabrielle was planning to go, or with whom."

"Well, there's an easy way to find out about that," she said, reaching for the telephone. "Let's ask Ginger."

Chapter Four

It took about five minutes for Ginger Aldrich to get from her last period study hall to the guidance office. The way Margaret Totten and I were hitting it off, it felt more like five lifetimes. She passed the time by rattling and shuffling papers distractedly around her desk. I stared at the institutional green walls of the cubicle and tried to remember whether there was anything I had seen or read recently that might help me communicate with a fifteen-year-old girl in the age of Tik-Tok and Snapchat. Nothing much came to me.

When Ginger finally arrived, she was flushed and out of breath, as if she had run the entire way. She was a pretty girl, not nearly in a league with Gabrielle Hawkins, but still in the team picture, in a green-eyed, freckle-faced kind of way. She wore blue jeans obligatorily torn in strategic places, red high-top sneakers, and a black-and-gold Vanderbilt football jersey with the number sixty-nine stitched on the front. Her red hair was parted on one side and hung down her back almost to her waist.

When she came into the office, she looked uncertainly back and forth at Margaret Totten and me, then smiled shyly into the empty space between us.

"You wanted to see me, Miss Totten?"

"Yes, I did, Ginger. Come in." She gestured at the other visitor's chair. "Sit down, won't you?"

She waited until Ginger got settled, then nodded in my direction. "Ginger, this is Mr. Gamble. He is a private investigator who is helping the police look for your friend Gabrielle. I told him you wouldn't mind if he asked you

29

some questions."

Ginger eyed me suspiciously, as if she minded very much.

"Are you really a private detective?"

"I sure am. Do you want to see my identification?"

"I guess not. But I already talked to the police."

I said, "I know you did, Ginger, and I'm sorry to have to be asking you these same questions all over again. But the problem is, the police are pretty busy, and they don't seem to be having much luck finding Gabrielle. What's more, since the time you talked to them, they've probably had a dozen more missing person cases come in, and that's on top of the ones they were already investigating."

"Does that mean they aren't looking for her anymore?"

"No, not at all. It just means they don't have the manpower to keep working on any one case full time. Gabrielle's parents are very worried, and since they haven't heard anything, they hired me to help out."

She screwed her face into a look of derision. "Is that what they told you? Because if it is, that's a lie."

"What's a lie, Ginger?"

"Gabrielle's parents being worried about her. If they're so worried about Gabrielle now, how come they were always yelling at her and picking on her while she was still around?"

"I don't know. What did they pick on her about?"

"Everything. How she dressed, how she fixed her hair, who her friends were, what kind of music she listened to on the radio. Sometimes it seemed like they didn't like anything about Gabrielle at all. So how come now they're so worried all of a sudden?"

"I don't have an answer for that, Ginger. Sometimes, even when people love one another, they have a hard time getting along together. They just aren't able to share their feelings very well."

She gave an exaggerated shrug of her shoulders, as if to say that was just the kind of bullshit answer she would have expected from someone born at around the time the dinosaurs walked. I couldn't blame her. It sounded like a bullshit answer to me, too. I wished I had a better one.

30

I said, "Ginger, when was the last time you saw Gabrielle?"

She wrinkled her forehead in thought. "It was, let's see, it must have been about two weeks ago, right before she...right before she left."

She let the thought hang in mid-air, as if unsure of the proper word to put to the deed.

"Was that here at school, or someplace else?"

"It was at school. We had lunch together in the cafeteria."

"Did you talk about anything special?"

"Not really, just the usual stuff, homework, clothes, teachers, that kind of thing. You know."

I might have known once, but I doubted that I did any more. "When you talked, did she seem okay to you?"

Ginger wiggled uncomfortably in the molded plastic visitor's chair. "Okay?"

"You know. Was she nervous, upset, unhappy, spaced out?"

"Oh. No, she seemed okay to me."

"Then she didn't say anything to give you the idea she was planning to run away, or maybe just that she might have wanted to run away?"

She said, without hesitation, "Nothing at all."

"You seem very sure of that, Ginger."

"You'd be sure too if you had as many people ask you that question as I have."

I smiled encouragingly. "I probably would at that. The night Gabrielle left she told her mother she was going to spend the night at your house—"

"I don't know anything about that," she cut me off. "I already told the police that."

"I know you did, and I'm not saying different. I was just wondering whether you can think of any reason why she would have said that's where she was going."

She gave me another shrug, which I took this time to mean that she considered my question a stupid one. "I guess she probably figured that was the only way she could get out of the house."

"That makes sense," I agreed, "but why you? Why not tell her mother she was staying with one of her other friends?"

Another shrug. "I guess maybe because we live close. That way her parents wouldn't have to drive her, and nobody would have to come and pick her up."

That answer came a bit too easily, as if it had been rehearsed ahead of time. Rather than try to drill down, I decided to change directions. "Ginger, from what I've been hearing, you're Gabrielle's best friend. You probably know her better than anybody, maybe even better in some ways than her mother and father."

"I guess so."

"Okay, so since that's so, and she wasn't coming to your house, then where do you think she was really going? Is it possible she has a boyfriend she was planning to see that night?"

Her voice went up an octave. "I don't know."

"Well, does she have a boyfriend at all?"

"I already told you, I don't know." Then she added, by way of explanation, "Gabrielle doesn't like to talk about that kind of stuff."

"What kind of stuff is that, Ginger?"

Her eyes slid toward the floor. "You know."

"You mean sex? Gabrielle doesn't like to talk about sex?"

"That's right."

Margaret Totten shot me a look that said I was getting very close to taking this line of questioning too far. I gave her a short nod to indicate I understood.

"Okay, then let's talk about something else. Since Gabrielle left home, have you been in touch with her? I mean, just about everybody in the world is running around all day long with a phone in his hand. Has she called you, or sent you a text to let you know where she's staying?"

"No."

"Doesn't that seem odd? After all, you're her best friend. Wouldn't she want you to know that she's okay?"

"I don't know. Running away is odd. Maybe she hasn't found a place to stay yet."

"Do you have any idea where she might be looking?"

"No."

"Or what she might be doing?"

"What do you mean? Doing what?"

"You know, something to support herself. She has to eat. She needs someplace to live, that kind of thing."

"Working, I guess."

"At what?"

"How do I know?"

"Well, what could she do? What is she good at that would pay her enough to live on?"

She appeared to give the question some thought, as if it hadn't occurred to her before that moment.

"She could be—I don't know, she could be a waitress or something, couldn't she?"

"Not in this state, no. Not without a work permit." I turned to Margaret Totten. "Gabrielle didn't have a work permit from school, did she?"

"No, she didn't."

"Well then, that's not it," I said. "Anything else you can think of?"

"No. I mean, I guess not. I don't know."

I said, "Ginger, is Gabrielle doing drugs?"

She looked up sharply. "Of course not."

"You seem pretty sure. Did the police ask you about that, too?"

"Yes, and I told them the same thing. Gabrielle is my friend, and if she was doing drugs, I'd know it. It's not something you can hide. Besides, what difference does it make if all you're trying to do is make her come back home to Delsey and Jericho?"

I sighed. "Ginger, I know you're at an age when you more or less automatically tune out a lot of what the adults around you are saying, and sometimes that's not a bad idea. But I'm going to talk to you like an adult now, and I'm going to ask you to listen very carefully to what I'm about to tell you. Not because I'm older than you, or because I think I'm smarter, or even because I'm trying to scare you. I want you to listen because it's important to Gabrielle. And because it's the truth."

She didn't say anything to that.

I said, "Okay?"

She kept her eyes riveted to the floor. "Okay."

I looked over at Margaret Totten. She was staring back at me hard enough to burn holes in my shirt. I knew I was on thin ice, getting thinner.

I said, "I've got a picture of Gabrielle that her mother gave me. Have you seen it?" I took the photo out of my jacket pocket and showed it to her. She lifted her eyes long enough to glance at it and give me a short nod.

"Gabrielle is a very lovely girl," I went on. "In fact, for somebody her age, she's about as pretty as any girl I've ever seen."

"So?"

"So, nothing, except that there are lots of other people who would be apt to think the same thing about her. People who hang around bus stations and shopping malls and playgrounds looking for pretty girls just like Gabrielle. Looking for boys, too. Do you know the kind of people I'm talking about?"

"Perverts."

"Perverts, yes. Sometimes they're also called chicken hawks and pimps. You understand where this is heading?"

"'Course I do. I watch television."

"Then you should know people like what we're talking about are especially interested in young girls. Particularly girls who are pretty like Gabrielle, and who look more grown up than they actually are."

"What are you saying, you think she's a whore now?" This time she didn't give me the courtesy of a shrug. "That's really stupid. Gabrielle would never do anything like that."

"Oh yes, she would," I said, more calmly than I felt. "She'd do it in a heartbeat if she were shot full of enough dope, or if she'd been beaten up or raped enough times that she didn't care about herself anymore. It happens all the time, Ginger. And it doesn't take nearly as long as you might think. Didn't the police tell you that when you talked to them?"

"No, and I don't believe you now!" Her face got red and she began to tear up. "I think you're making this up."

"I wish you were right, Ginger, but I'm not. This isn't television. I don't like it any more than you do, but I'm telling you the way things are because you need to understand how important it is that I find Gabrielle."

Nobody said anything. Margaret Totten held her breath. Ginger kept staring at the floor, her long hair masking her face like a fine amber veil.

I said gently, "Here's what I think happened that Saturday night, Ginger. You tell me if I'm wrong. I think Gabrielle told you she was planning to run away from home, and that she was going to use staying overnight with you as a cover for getting out of the house. I also think she told you, or at least you have a pretty good idea, where she was planning to go, or who she was going with. I think she would have had to tell you that much because she needed your help, and she knew she could count on you not to tell anybody else. Does that sound about right so far?"

She shook her head determinedly. "No!"

I leaned over and put my hand on her shoulder. "Gabrielle was right to trust you, Ginger. You're a good friend and you know how to keep your mouth shut. But you're going to have to be an even better friend now, and tell us what you know, because now you understand that Gabrielle could be in very serious trouble. That's why Mr. and Mrs. Hawkins are so worried. You may not think they're the best parents in the world, and maybe they're not, but that doesn't mean they don't love Gabrielle, or that they want to see something like what I've just described to you happen to her. The question is, do you?"

Margaret Totten finally found her voice. "Ginger, if you know where Gabrielle is, you have to tell us. You're a smart girl. You know what could happen to her. What might have already happened."

Ginger looked indecisively at us both, and I thought for just a second that I might have gotten through to her. Then, like a long-distance runner struggling for one more kick late in the race, she seemed to reach deep inside herself for a last measure of resolve.

"I'm sorry, Miss Totten. I really am. I wish there was something I could tell you, but I don't have any idea where Gabrielle went or where she is now. Besides, for all anybody knows for sure, she might not have gone anyplace at all. I mean, maybe Delsey and Jericho just killed her and buried her in the back yard or something. Gabrielle always said they were crazy enough to do that, you know."

If it was a hole card intended to throw us off track, it was a good one.

"Ginger!" Margaret Totten exclaimed. "That's a terrible thing to say! Mister and Mrs. Hawkins are worried sick about Gabrielle. They want to bring her back home. That's why they hired Mr. Gamble."

"I'm sorry, Miss Totten," she said, not sounding sorry at all. "I was only telling you what Gabrielle told me. I didn't mean anything by it."

Time hung heavily in the air, like smoke from a dying fire. Then Margaret said, "I think that's all for now, Ginger, unless Mr. Gamble has any other questions." The way she said it made it clear that I did not.

I said I was finished, for now.

Margaret smiled doubtfully at Ginger. "Let me sign your hall pass, then, and you can go. We can talk some more later, if you feel like it." She took the slip of paper, scribbled her initials on the bottom, and handed it back.

I took out one of my cards. "Ginger, if you should happen to remember anything later on about Gabrielle that you think might be important, would you let Miss Totten know, or else give me a call? I'd really appreciate it."

She nodded and said she'd be sure to do that. But right then, I wouldn't have bet my P.I. license on it.

Chapter Five

I t was almost four-thirty when I finished talking with Margaret Totten and Ginger Aldrich and drove away from Woodcrest High School. I thought about offering Ginger a ride home, but then realized that, things being the way they are these days, that would be a bad idea. Margaret Totten sensed what I was thinking and offered to give Ginger a lift, since the last buses had left half an hour earlier. So instead, with time to spare before I was due at Delsey's house, I decided to make myself useful.

Many years ago, Nashville had a Union Station that was served by passenger trains of the Louisville & Nashville and the Nashville, Chattanooga & St. Louis railroads. L&N and NC&StL trains could take travelers to such far-flung places as Chicago or Atlanta, New Orleans or Florida, or even New York City aboard trains with colorful names like the *Humming Bird* or the *South Wind* or the *Dixie Flyer*. In those days people could ride in Pullman sleepers and take their meals in elegant dining cars where they would be served with great courtesy by porters and waiters and stewards schooled to provide the utmost in customer satisfaction. It was too good to last.

Except for the elderly and those fearful of flying, by the 1960s the public had largely stopped riding trains, and so the government gave us Amtrak. That left Nashville with a single service between Chicago and Florida that had an inordinate amount of trouble staying on time and on the track. That train disappeared for good in 1979. After that, our magnificent Union Station stood abandoned and decaying for many more years until it was finally repurposed and turned into a boutique hotel offering upscale accommodations and facilities for over-the-top weddings. That meant for an underage, unaccompanied runaway like Gabrielle Hawkins, her only means of getting out of town were the airport, where it would be impossible for her

to get through security without identification, or the bus station, which is where I made my next stop.

I spent ten minutes' worth of Delsey's money showing Gabrielle's photo to half a dozen pairs of glassy eyes behind the ticket windows and the lunch counter. Not surprisingly, all I got for my trouble was exercise. Try showing a photo of almost anybody to the man or woman behind any big city ticket counter and see what kind of a response you get. Unless the subject bears a marked resemblance to Freddie Krueger or the Creature from the Black Lagoon, odds are you're going to come up emptier than a politician's promise. Like picking locks with a hairpin, it's something that works better on television than in real life.

From the bus station, I drove to a nearby CVS pharmacy where I ordered two dozen more prints of Gabrielle's picture. The kid who waited on me said I could have them after four o'clock the following afternoon. For another sawbuck, I got him to make it first thing in the morning.

When I got back to the office, I found a customer in the waiting room, warming the same seat Delsey Hawkins had occupied twenty-four hours earlier. His name was Douglas Dahlberg. He was tall and thin and dressed like a man accustomed to buying his clothes at Goodwill resale outlets. He wore a dark blue watch cap, a scraggly beard, and hair that just touched the epaulets of his Army surplus field jacket. I would have put his age at between thirty-five and forty-five. He claimed to be a songwriter. And he had a very unusual problem.

"Hank Williams has been stealing my songs."

"I see," I said, wondering what I had done to deserve first Delsey and now Mr. Dahlberg. "Would we be talking Hank, Junior, or Hank, Senior?"

"Senior, of course," he replied in a tone of voice that said I should have known better than to ask. "Anybody can tell the kid's material doesn't sound anything like mine."

"Mr. Dahlberg," I reminded him, "Hank Williams is dead. He has been since New Year's Day, nineteen fifty-three. You're not old enough to have written anything that long ago."

"That's exactly what I'm trying to tell you!" He peered at me across the desk through wire-rimmed glasses with bottle-bottom lenses. "I've only been writing songs for thirteen years, so how could somebody who's been dead that long possibly have written them first?" He reached into his coat pocket and took out a harmonica. "Here, listen," he said and began playing. He wasn't half bad, and it only took a couple of bars before I recognized the melody.

"See what I mean?"

"'Your Cheatin' Heart,'" I said.

"Oh sure, that's what they want everybody to believe," he snorted. "Actually, I wrote that song ten years ago. I call it 'Blue Moon over Kentucky.'"

"I think Bill Monroe might have beaten you to that one," I said, though I knew I was standing on fairly shaky ground. Being a former drummer from a spectacularly unsuccessful rock and roll garage band from Kansas City, I didn't know enough about country music to put a cork in a jug of moonshine.

"Look, Mr. Dahlberg, I'm getting very confused here," I began.

"There's nothing to be confused about," he cut me off in mid-thought. "This is my music. Somebody else takes the credit and winds up with the money, but I write the songs."

I started to tell him I knew for a fact that was a sappy Barry Manilow song from the nineteen-seventies, then decided throwing that tidbit out on the table would only muddy the waters more.

I sighed. "Mr. Dahlberg, what do you want me to do?"

It was exactly the question he was waiting for. "I want you to believe me, that's all. I just need somebody to believe I'm telling the truth."

"Fair enough," I said, enlightenment coming to me at last. I leaned over my desk and said, sincerely, "Mr. Dahlberg, I believe you wrote every song you claim to have written, same as George Harrison did with 'My Sweet Lord.' I also believe that you didn't consciously copy them from anybody else. I haven't heard them, but I am also willing to bet that these are very beautiful songs, and if Hank or Mother Maybelle or anyone else wrote something else that sounds a lot like them, it just proves you're on the right track and need to keep trying."

He blinked at me twice before allowing himself a hopeful smile. "You're serious?"

"Like a hundred-car pileup."

"Thank you." The smile he gave me this time split his face from ear to ear. "How much do I owe you?"

"Twenty dollars," I told him, "but not until you sell your first song. Until then, just keep plugging away. I know you're going to be a big success."

He thanked me again and shook my hand a dozen more times before I could chase him out the door. When I was sure he was safely on the elevator, I went down the hall to the soft drink machine and treated myself to a Diet Coke. No less than my just reward, I told myself, for one small, but significant, contribution to the human condition.

I killed the next hour catching up on paperwork and paying some bills that were starting to curl around the edges with age. By six-thirty, I'd had enough of that. I locked the office, phoned the answering service to let them know I was leaving and drove back to Jacktown.

The streetlights were coming on when I turned onto Newsome Street and found Delsey's address. It was a house pretty much typical of the neighborhood: A five-room, postwar frame job with a postage-stamp yard surrounded by a rickety picket fence. Along one side, a rutted gravel driveway wandered drunkenly toward a one-car garage in the back. Next to the walk, late-season marigolds clung tenaciously to life in beds that hadn't been cultivated in weeks.

Like a swaybacked plow horse on its last legs, a dozen-year-old Dodge sagged at the curb on tired springs. It was painted a dark color, blue, or maybe black, with no chrome or other trim to relieve its somber livery. It was just the sort of transportation I figured the shepherd of a none-too-prosperous flock would be apt to own. I drove down to the end of the block, made a u-turn in the intersection and parked on the opposite side of the street, two houses down from the Hawkins place.

Five minutes later, the front door opened, and a man came out. He wore a white shirt, buttoned to the neck with no tie, gray pants, and a dark windbreaker. He had wavy salt-and-pepper hair, a chin you could hang a fire bucket on, and high, prominent cheekbones. As he paused beneath the porch light to zip his jacket, I could see he was tall and angular and looked to be about the same age as Delsey. He turned for a moment in the doorway and said something into the house, then climbed into the Dodge and drove off trailing a dense cloud of oil smoke. I waited ten more minutes to be sure he wasn't just running down to Pep Boys for a pint of motor honey and then crossed the street to the house.

I pressed the doorbell, and, when nothing happened, realized the problem and rapped noisily on the screen door. After a moment, Delsey's face appeared in the window. She squinted at me through the glass, then nodded in recognition and threw back the lock.

She admitted me into a tiny front room that was decorated with a mixed bag of furniture and accessories that offered allegiance to neither style nor period. A worn Mediterranean couch squatted along the back wall. Facing the couch were two contemporary armchairs that had not been formally introduced, and a maple rocker with a bright floral seat cushion. A discount-store reproduction of Leonardo's *Last Supper* hung above the couch along with a framed enlargement of the photo of Gabrielle that Delsey had given me, and another picture of a sharp-faced young man dressed in a military uniform. That had to be Jericho, Junior. Likenesses of Delsey and Jericho, Senior, were nowhere to be found. I wondered whether the Divine Light Congregation had a problem with that too, or if Delsey and Jericho had come to a mutual realization that they had seen more than enough of one another, and didn't need portraits to remind themselves of what they looked like.

Delsey had a look on her face that was part hopeful and part apprehensive, as if she'd been praying that I'd have news for her, but wasn't sure she wanted to hear what it was. It was the same look people in the hospital wear when the surgeon comes in to tell them whether the growth he's just cut out is malignant or benign. She also looked like she'd been crying again.

I said, "How are you doing, Delsey? You holding up okay?"

She forced a tight smile. "I'm all right. I just haven't gotten used to coming home to an empty house yet. Before, when Gaby was here…" She let the thought trail sadly off before shifting mental gears.

"I'm sorry, Mr. Gamble, I just realized I'm being very thoughtless. Can I offer you something to eat or drink, or would you like to sit down for a while?"

"Not now, thanks. I want to look around Gabrielle's room first. After that, we can talk for a few minutes."

She looked at me with alarm, as if something in my voice had sounded a wrong note to her. I said, "I went over to the high school this afternoon, Delsey. I talked to Miss Totten and Ginger Aldrich."

"And what did she tell you?"

"If you're asking about Ginger, she didn't tell me anything. She claimed not to have any idea what Gabrielle might have had in mind when she left."

She gave me a fearsome scowl. "That little devil. And I suppose she stood there in front of God and everybody else and told you she didn't know where my Gaby is."

"I don't know who else was listening, but yeah, that's pretty much what she said. My guess is, you're right. She knows something, but she acts like she's scared to death to say what it is."

"Wasn't there something you could have done to make her tell?"

"Well, I could have beaten it out of her, but I hate to use brass knuckles on a fourteen-year-old kid in front of a witness. Better to grab her in the alley after dark."

When that got no reaction other than an empty stare, I said, "Look, Delsey, I understand you're worried, but getting information out of people who aren't ready to give it up isn't the easiest thing. If Ginger knows something that'll help us find Gabrielle, the way to get it isn't by frightening her."

"Then what are we going to do?"

"I've got extra prints of Gabrielle's photo coming. Tomorrow, I'll start passing them around where they're likely to get the most attention. Meantime, I'd like to take a look around Gabrielle's room. I know it's a long shot, but she might have left something behind that could give us an idea where she was going."

"I've been through that room a dozen times, Mr. Gamble. As the Lord is my witness, there just isn't anything in there."

"Then it won't hurt if we try once more, will it?"

She looked doubtful but didn't make an issue of it. "Her room is at the other end of the hall," she said, pointing. "Come on, I'll show you."

She walked ahead of me into a small room at the back of the house and switched on the light. It was a kid's room, neater than I expected, but otherwise unremarkable. It had a double bed with a chenille spread, a single nightstand, a dresser, and a desk. Above the desk was a shelf with a handful of books and magazines and some stuffed animals, including Opus, the comic-strip penguin. There was also a live animal stretched out on the bed, a large gray tiger cat that eyed me suspiciously before jumping down onto the floor and bounding out of the room.

"That's Gaby's cat," Delsey told me. "His name is Stanley. He ain't much on meeting new folks."

"What a relief," I said. "I thought it might be personal."

I continued looking around. On top of the dresser was a plastic rack filled with music CDs by groups that I doubted Delsey and Jericho would have cared much for if they ever read the lyrics. The closet and hallway doors were papered over with posters of rock-and-roll singers, including, so help me, Johnny Cash dressed in black, Kurt Cobain, Freddie Mercury, and a stripped-to-the-waist Jim Morrison leering at an audience hidden just beyond the footlights.

Rebels one and all, I thought. How appropriate.

I crossed to the dresser and pulled open the top drawer. Inside were kid-sized bras and underpants, most a lot sexier than the industrial-strength lingerie I remembered from my fumbling-in-the-back-seat days, and a few pairs of pantyhose that had gotten tangled limply together like a nest of hibernating snakes. I wondered, did young girls wear those anymore? Did any woman?

I said, "Did the police look around in here?"

"Yes, and they left things a mess. It took me the rest of the day to straighten up after they were finished." Then, wistfully, she added, "When Gabrielle gets back, I want everything to be just as it was before she left."

I doubted whether that would turn out to be the case. "Do you remember the name of the officer you spoke with?"

"Yes. It was Sutton. Detective Sutton."

"Carl Sutton? A big guy, black, keeps a pipe in his front coat pocket?"

"That's the one. Do you know him?"

"A little." I knew Carl Sutton, all right, and better than just a little. As police work goes, the runaway unit of youth services is not one of your high-profile assignments. And contrary to what some people might think, tracking down missing children does not involve driving all over the county hunting for the child in question. Rather it is a coordinated effort with state and federal investigators, multiple telephone hotline services, community outreach organizations, and other designated reporters.

Following a preliminary investigation to determine whether a child has been abducted by a divorced parent, absorbed into a street gang, spirited away by a lovesick teacher, coach, or other misguided third party, or victimized by a sexual predator or a killer of children, the search settles into a "watch and wait and hope" that the kid turns up in one piece and ready to go home or into counseling. Carl Sutton, I knew, was good at his job. He was conscientious, thorough, and treated every case as if it were the Lindbergh kidnapping.

"He's a good cop, and a good man," I told Delsey. "You couldn't ask for anyone better."

"I pray you're right, Mr. Gamble."

"Is Sutton the one you told about your revelation?"

"Yes."

"Have you talked to him other than that?"

"I talk to him every day. I think he'd probably just as soon I didn't, but so far he's been too nice to tell me not to."

"What is he nice enough to tell you?"

"He just keeps saying not to give up hope, and that something will turn up soon." She paused for a moment, as if weighing the odds for such an outcome. "I know he means well, but I'm beginning to wish he'd stop saying it. It's getting so even I don't believe it anymore."

I knew what she meant, but didn't see any point in going back over plowed ground. I went quickly through the rest of the dresser without finding anything more than sweaters, scarves, blouses, and nightgowns. There were no diaries filled with secret plans, no airline or bus ticket receipts, and no letters from faraway places with strange sounding names. I continued to search, drawing more blanks in the closet, the desk, and under the bed, and the bookshelf didn't look too promising, either. Just a few drugstore paperback romances, some Nancy Drew mysteries that Gabrielle probably inherited from Delsey and never read and a stack of teenage movie and music fan magazines. There was also a vinyl-covered three-ring binder that looked like a photo album.

I took one down and began leafing through it. Sure enough, it was filled with grainy, amateur-quality snapshots that appeared to have been printed from digital images. There were photos of big brother Jericho and Delsey at home. There were outdoor scenes from around Nashville. There were pictures taken at birthday and slumber parties, and a few middle-school picture-day photos of boys and girls I assumed were Gabrielle's classmates. Still no photos of the old man, though.

And then I had a thought. I remembered when I had asked Gabrielle's friend Ginger whether she understood what I meant when I mentioned the possibility that Gabrielle might have fallen into the hands of a sexual predator: *Of course, I do,* she'd said. *I watch television.* So, if Ginger watched TV, maybe Gabrielle did, too. And if she did, then she might have an idea where to hide something she didn't want found.

I went back to the dresser and the desk, this time pulling each of the drawers all the way out and feeling underneath. And I got lucky. I found what I was looking for under the middle drawer of the desk: a small manila envelope taped to the bottom. I tore it loose and extracted the pictures it contained. Composition-wise they weren't very good, but for my purposes, they were good enough.

He was in his mid-to late-twenties. He looked like a side man in an airport hotel country and western band. In the first photo, he was sitting by himself on what were obviously the steps of the Parthenon in Centennial Park. He was wearing faded Levis, a tan leather jacket, cowboy boots, and sunglasses with mirrored lenses. He was skinny enough to have been made out of pipe cleaners. His hair was sandy brown and his face was partly covered with the type of stubbly beard that is much in fashion these days. A cigarette hung lazily from the corner of his mouth.

In a second photo, he was sitting in the same location, but this time with a woman of approximately the same age, also visibly underweight, with stringy blond hair and a pale complexion. I supposed she could have been his wife or perhaps just his girlfriend. She was looking directly at the camera, but not smiling. In the third, the woman was absent and Gabrielle had taken her place. The two were sitting close together, both smiling into the camera, his arm wrapped possessively around her shoulder. She was wearing a yellow shell and a short denim skirt. I couldn't quite read the expression on her face, but if I had to guess I would say it was a mix of contentment plus a pinch of apprehension, as if she were happy with what was happening, but a little scared as well.

I walked over to where Delsey was sitting on the bed and held out two photos for her to see, the one that showed the man by himself, and the one where he was sitting with the woman. I said, "I know this isn't a very good picture, but I wonder if you can tell me whether you've ever seen these people before. Maybe they live in the neighborhood here, or maybe they're members of your husband's congregation?"

She studied the image intently for a moment and then shook her head. "I don't think I've ever seen them before."

"You're sure? I'm especially interested in this man here. Could he be a neighbor, or maybe somebody your son used to hang out with?"

"My son never had friends who looked like that," she said, missing the point by a city block. "Why, who is he?"

I showed her the third picture. "I was thinking more about your daughter, Delsey."

"Gabrielle?" Her eyes widened as she took in the implications the photo presented. "Are you saying you think these people had something to do with her disappearance?"

"That's what I'm going to try to find out. They're obviously too old to be her classmates and you say they aren't anybody you know, so who are they? And more to the point, what's her relationship with them?"

"Maybe they're the ones who kidnapped her," she said, her voice rising excitedly. "Maybe the man in this picture is the one you should be looking for. Find him and you'll find my Gabrielle."

"I'll find him," I told her. "But I doubt very much, and you might as well get it through your head, too, that Gabrielle wasn't kidnapped by this man or anybody else. If she's with him now, it's because she wants to be."

"How can you know that?"

"Because when Gabrielle left here last Saturday, I don't think she had any intention of spending the night at Ginger's house. You know as well as I do, that was just a story that she and Ginger cooked up so she could get out of the house."

"I don't believe that," she said stubbornly. "Where did you get a notion like that?"

"Nothing else makes sense, Delsey, unless you can think of some other reason for Gabrielle keeping these photos hidden."

"But what possible interest could he have in Gabrielle? He must be at least ten years older than she is."

I slid the pictures back into the envelope and put it in my jacket pocket. "Do you need me to tell you the answer to that?"

She was silent for a moment. "You're talking about sex, aren't you? That's what this is all about."

"Among other things, yes. Let's hope this guy is just somebody who gets his kicks having young girls as arm candy. At least then he won't hurt her. What really worries me is that he might be a pornographer or a pimp or even worse." It sounded bad and I knew it. I just couldn't think of a way to sugarcoat it.

I said, "Look, Delsey, when I took this case, I told you I'd try to find your daughter, and I will do my best. But something you're going to have to face is the very real possibility that when I do, she may very well be a lot different kid from the little girl who left here ten days ago. You might not even want her back."

I stopped to let her think that over for a moment. "Do you understand what I'm talking about?"

She said stiffly, "I understand perfectly, Mr. Gamble. But I want you to know, no matter what she might have done, nothing has changed. Gabrielle is my little girl and her place is here with me. Your job is to bring her back. What happens after that is in the hands of the good Lord."

Chapter Six

The room seemed to get very still and small, as if all the life had suddenly been sucked out of it. Maybe it was just the last of the twilight outside dissolving into darkness, but all at once, I felt an overwhelming urge to be someplace else.

I looked over at Delsey, sitting on the edge of the bed. Her eyes were like dark pools of sadness that seemed to have no bottom. I said, "You have anything to eat today?"

She looked at me blankly. "What?"

"I asked you whether you had anything to eat today. Did you have any lunch this afternoon?"

"Oh. No. I mean, I went straight back to work after I left your office. I had the hours to make up, and anyway, I haven't been feeling very hungry lately."

"How about supper? You had any supper yet?"

"No. I was getting set to fix something, but I didn't know for sure what time you were coming."

I said, "I think I'd like something to drink now, if the offer is still good."

She got up from the bed and smoothed the spread back into place. "I've got some instant coffee. If you can wait, I'll fix you a cup."

I followed her into the kitchen. "Got anything cold? I'm not feeling much like coffee."

She nodded. "There should be something in the refrigerator. Let me look."

"I'll get it. You sit down."

I pulled open the refrigerator door, took out a can of Diet Coke, and set it on the counter. Then I rummaged around a little more and finally came up with a package of sliced ham, a carton of eggs, a small green pepper, a quart of milk, and a tub of whipped butter. I found an iron skillet hanging on a rack over the stove.

While Delsey watched, fascinated, I sliced the ham and part of the pepper and threw them both into the skillet with some butter. I let that fry for a few minutes, then broke a couple of eggs and dumped them in on top of the ham, scrambling the whole shebang together into a half-assed omelet. When it looked done, I scooped it onto a plate, salted and peppered it, and set the plate, a fork, and a glass of milk in front of her.

"What's this for?"

"What does it look like?" I asked. "It's for you to eat." I popped open the tab on the Coke can and sat down across from her.

"You may not feel so chipper now, but that's no excuse for running yourself into the ground. It won't do any good for me to bring Gabrielle back home if you're going to be a basket case yourself when I get her here."

"I expect you're right," she said, without much conviction. She stared at the plate for a moment before tasting a bite of pseudo-omelet. "This is very good."

I grinned. "You don't need to sound so surprised. Most of the world's great chefs are men."

"Oh, I know that. It's just that my Jericho's never been able to cook much of anything, and Jericho, Junior, he ain't any better."

"You must have really spoiled them, then. I never met a man who couldn't fry ham and eggs in a pinch."

"I spoil everybody," she said matter-of-factly. "First, I spoiled my husband and my son, and then I spoiled Gabrielle. That's how come she's in all this trouble now."

"I wouldn't hog all the credit if I were you. Gabrielle is plenty old enough to know what's right and what isn't."

"You don't have any children, do you, Mr. Gamble?"

I sighed. "This is the second time today somebody's used that line on me, Delsey. The answer is no, I don't. But I don't have to have a coffee mug that reads 'World's Greatest Dad' to know there's no percentage in feeling guilty about trouble your kid has gotten into all by herself."

"That's not what I'm talking about. It's more than that. I knew Gabrielle had to be up to something, the way she was being so evasive about where she was going and who she was seeing the past few weeks. But I didn't want to admit she might be getting herself in over her head, so I just told myself whatever she was doing was only a phase she was going through, and let her keep at it until she got it out of her system. If I'd taken a firmer hand when I had the chance, maybe I could have stopped her from leaving home."

"Gabrielle has two parents," I reminded her.

"I'm her mother. It says in the Bible it's my job to nurture the family." She doodled on the table cloth with the tines of her fork. "But it's so hard, especially when you can't be watching every minute. You want to trust your children, to give them as much freedom as you can. I just never dreamed she could be sleeping with a grown man, or getting ready to do something as foolish as running away with him." Her eyes searched mine, looking for something—I didn't know what—that would help her keep from having to acknowledge what we both knew was the truth.

"That is what she was doing, isn't it? She's been sleeping with him?"

"Your eggs are getting cold, Delsey."

Obediently, she took another forkful. But her eyes rested heavily on mine. I felt their weight like wet sandbags.

I said, "Yeah, that's probably what she's doing. What do you want me to tell you? It's not the smartest thing, but it doesn't have to be the end of the world, either. It just depends on how you and Jericho decide to handle it after she gets back."

We sat quietly for a few minutes after that. Delsey pushed her food dispiritedly around her plate, taking small bites at long intervals. I sipped my Diet Coke and wondered, without really wanting to know, what it would be like to find out your fourteen-year-old daughter is playing house with a man twice her age. Gabrielle wasn't my kid, wasn't anything more than another face in another photograph.

And yet...

During my time with the cops and now working on my own, I have encountered lowlifes of just about every stripe, including murderers, rapists, carjackers, muggers, prostitutes and pimps, wife-beaters, flim-flam men—you name it. One and all, they more or less come with the territory, and after a while, you become numb to it all. But in my mind, at least, there is a special circle in hell for abusers of children, and I knew when I found Gabrielle, I would have to be very careful how I would deal with the man in the photo, if, in fact, he had harmed her.

Delsey took a sip of her milk. "You know, Mr. Gamble, I was just thinking what a strange thing it is. Here I only walked into your office a few hours ago and already you know more about me and my life than friends I've known for years."

"Not really," I told her. "All I know is you're a woman with a daughter who's gone missing from home. Other than that, I don't know what things make you happy or sad, or whether you like chocolate or vanilla ice cream, or if you voted for a Republican or a Democrat in the last election."

"Well, you still know more about me than I do about you. How long have you been a private detective?"

"Almost nine years."

"What did you do before that?"

"I was with the police. I spent three years as a uniformed patrolman. Then I made detective third grade and got loaned out part-time to the district attorney's office. I was there for three more years. Before that, I was in college."

"That's how you know Lieutenant Sutton, then. Why did you leave the police department?"

"If I get this one right, do we move on to the lightning round?"

She flushed. "I'm sorry. Shouldn't I be asking you these things?"

"No, it's okay. It's just that I hardly ever meet anybody who's interested in hearing the answers. But since you brought it up, I probably wouldn't have quit at all if I'd gotten assigned to narcotics or homicide or something straightforward like that."

"That's the kind of answer I would have expected to get from Gaby."

I laughed. "Okay, then, think of it this way. The district attorney is an elected official, so although it pretends not to be, at its heart the D.A.'s office is a political operation. It's a place where sometimes as much work goes into making deals to get guilty people off as it does into gathering evidence to put them into jail. Oftentimes, the only difference is whether they've got the money or the right hooks into city hall, or the state capitol, or within the police department itself. I don't know, probably it was naive of me, but I never figured that was what being a cop should be all about. At least, that wasn't the reason I got into law enforcement."

"And now you don't have to make deals anymore, is that it?"

"I wish that were true. I still have to make them. But now and then I have the option of deciding for myself where and when I do it. With the cops, my choices were a lot more limited."

"I'm not sure I see where there's very much difference."

"Maybe there isn't any. Or maybe I'm just more comfortable drawing my boundaries where I decide they belong, instead of where somebody else tells me they have to be. Besides, without my police pension I still had thirty-odd years to go before my Social Security kicked in, and I couldn't see spending them selling used cars or standing behind the counter in some hardware store."

She nodded, unconvinced. "So where do you go from here? To find the man in the photograph, I mean?"

I took another swallow of my soda. "The first thing is to find out who he is. Once I do that, it'll be fairly easy to track him down."

"And when you do, then what?"

"Then I talk to him and see what he's got to say."

She put her fork down on her plate. "I don't understand. If he has Gabrielle with him, what else is there talk about?"

"Well, that's just it. If she is with him, then there's nothing to talk about. But for all we know now, this guy could be some celebrity neither of us recognizes, or a friend of a friend and Gabrielle just wanted her picture taken with him. If that's the case, I'll talk to him and find out if there's anything he can tell me. But if he's got your daughter or if he knows where she is or if he's done anything to hurt her, I'll make him wish he'd never laid eyes on her."

"Are you going to ask the police to help you?"

"Not right away. I think for the moment I'd rather have them continue to pursue their own leads rather than having me send them off in a direction I'm already going. Before we do that, I'd like to give them a little more to go on than just a couple of snapshots."

"What else do they need?"

"A name would help. So would a better photograph, or a witness who might have seen him with Gabrielle. Look, Delsey, I know how you feel, believe me. If I could bring her home tonight, she'd already be here. But unless we get lucky, that's not the way it's going to happen. You've just got to give me time to work this out my own way."

"Give you time." She played my words slowly back to me, like a tape recorder running at half-speed. "Give you time. Everybody wants time. That's what Jericho keeps telling me, and Lieutenant Sutton, and now you.

"I want you to know, Mr. Gamble, that I am fifty-four years old. I'm no longer a young woman, and there are no more children in my future. Only the ones I already have. As it is, Gabrielle being born to me as late in my life as she was is a miracle." She reached across the table and took hold of my hand. The strength in her grip was astonishing.

"Take all the time you need to do your job the way it should be done, and don't take any shortcuts to save money for a foolish woman who is old enough to know the need for patience. But if it turns out in the end that Gabrielle cannot be found, or if she's dead, or broken beyond healing in her heart and spirit, then you should also know that in all of eternity there will not be enough time to make my life worth living again."

I couldn't think of anything to add to that. I finished the last of my drink, said I'd be in touch, and let myself out, reminding Delsey to bolt the lock after me. The night air was clear and getting colder, and I could see my breath glowing like foxfire in the orange light of the rising moon. The soft days of autumn were melting away. Before many more days passed, there would be a frost, and then the last of the flowers clinging to life next to the walk would be gone, too.

Chapter Seven

Morning brought overcast skies and a persistent drizzle that threatened, with a little encouragement from a cold wind out of the north, to turn into sleet. The birds and squirrels that normally chattered away in the trees outside my bedroom window seemed to be sleeping in, so that the loudest outside noise was coming from gelid raindrops falling on the unraked leaves in my front yard. I fought the urge to crawl back under the covers for a good half-hour before I dragged myself out of bed to shave, shower, and drive downtown to the office.

The news on the car radio was filled with the usual inconsequentials. A two-headed calf was born on a farm south of Tullahoma. A singing dentist living in Memphis was being given even odds of winning the November mayoral election, and although warmer weather was expected by the weekend, the experts were predicting this winter would be the coldest since the record year of 1951. Nobody mentioned a little girl named Gabrielle Hawkins, who was going on twelve days away from home without word of her whereabouts, and whose mother was nearly out of her mind with worry.

I parked my robin-egg blue '64 Thunderbird in my regular spot at the U-Save across the street from my office. The 'Bird was a relic from an era when the country was still grieving over the assassination of President Kennedy and the Beatles were taking the AM airwaves by storm. It had come into my possession several years earlier, signed over by a client who was temporarily short of funds. I was coincidentally without wheels, having run off the road in an ice storm, and a deal was struck. Our agreement was that the client could reclaim the Thunderbird for the amount of the original debt whenever he could scrape it together. In the meantime, I was responsible for the care and feeding of the beast and would be free to drive it as much as I wanted. About a year ago, the arrangement became permanent, as the client had died without ever settling his account. And since the title to the Thunderbird had been endorsed over to me the day we shook hands, I became the new owner. That changed the car's status from a lovingly maintained garage queen to daily driver. The old boat burns oil like a diesel locomotive and the front bucket seat on the driver's side is showing some wear. But 10W-30 is cheap, and except for those minor faults, she's as solid as the day she was built.

I buzzed the call bell and rode the elevator up to the seventh floor. I unlocked the waiting room door and flipped on the lights. There was a small pile of mail on the floor beneath the slot. I picked it up and let myself into my private think-tank to check it out. I could have saved myself the trouble. A breathless mailgram from Publisher's Clearing House advised me that I, Mr. Jack Gumball, might already be the winner of ONE MILLION DOLLARS! Another, less upbeat notice from the landlord reminded me that if my rent check wasn't in the mail by the twenty-first, next month I would be plying my trade from other premises.

The sound of the waiting room door opening and closing kept me from dwelling on the prospect of that. A moment passed, and then a face I had seen only fourteen hours earlier appeared in the doorway. Its owner was still dressed in a white shirt, buttoned at the collar, with no tie, and black pants. The windbreaker from the night before had been replaced by a shiny suit coat that might have matched the pants once, but didn't any longer. The sleeves of the shirt and the coat were too short by inches, exposing bony wrists and hands lined like highway maps with thick, blue veins. The hands were clutching a leather-bound copy of the Bible, and I thought for just a moment that he might use it to hit me on the head.

Without speaking, he walked slowly toward me until he was standing right in front of the desk. I looked up into a deeply furrowed face with coal-black eyes that glittered with opalescent intensity, like Bela Lugosi's in the Tod Browning version of *Dracula*. The routine I was getting now wasn't nearly as good. Stick him in a bare-walls meeting hall with a clutch of six-foot diamondbacks slithering around his neck, and he could probably scare the holy hell out of even the most devout follower of the cross. Here in my office, the effect was considerably diminished, and I had to struggle to put away a yawn.

"Something I can do for you, brother?" I asked.

"I do not visit with deceitful men, nor do I consort with hypocrites. I abhor the assembly of evildoers and refuse to sit with the wicked."

"Well then, you've come to the right place. The assembly of evildoers is one floor up. Down here, we just take care of minor fuckups."

He drew himself up on the balls of his feet so that he looked half a head taller than he was. "Do you know who I am?"

"Elmer Gantry? The Reverend Mister Black? Give me a hint."

"Laugh if it makes you feel superior, Mr. Gamble, but I'll thank you not to ridicule the Lord's work."

"The Lord's work," I echoed. "Is rubbing noses with timber rattlers what passes for the Lord's work these days, Reverend Hawkins? Or would letting your daughter disappear into the wind be closer to what your faith calls for?"

"Then you know who I am. And since you know, you have no call to blaspheme," he said softly. He spoke with perfect diction, as if he were reading from Scripture, but with a definite accent that came straight from the mountains of east Tennessee.

"And you've got no call to come sailing into my office to lay some third-rate fire-and-brimstone routine on me, either. Acts like that went out with Billy Sunday, or haven't you been keeping up with your PTL Club?"

"A man who wallows like a hog in the garbage of other people's lives scarcely seems suited to pronounce judgment on those who serve a higher calling."

"Now that's perfect," I said. "That's just perfect. For a second there, before you opened your mouth, I was hoping that some of what I've heard about you might be wrong, and there would be something about you I could like, or at least that we might be able to have a civil conversation. But I guess that'd be asking too much of anybody who'd let his own daughter vanish off the face of the earth without lifting a finger to get her back."

"What's done is done. The Psalms tell us even from birth, the wicked go astray. We are warned to let them disappear, like the water that flows into the distance."

"And Matthew says, 'Suffer the children to come to me, for the kingdom of heaven and earth belongs to such as these.'" I leaned back in my chair to keep from getting a cramp in my neck looking up at him.

"Look, Reverend, we can stay here and lob Bible verses back and forth for the rest of the day, but the fact is, I'm kind of busy right now with more temporal matters. If you've got something on your mind, I wish you'd save us both some time and just say what it is."

He shook his head disdainfully. "I hoped you might be a man who would listen to reason, but I can see that I was wrong. Yesterday my wife paid you a hundred dollars to look for our daughter. Last night she allowed you to enter our home. In both cases, she meant well, but she was wrong to do both of those things, and she has been encouraged to see the error of her ways."

"And now you're going to show me the error of mine?" I was almost salivating at the prospect of that, but he wasn't about to be suckered into throwing me any raw meat.

"You are not of our faith and cannot be blamed for your ignorance. Therefore, no harm has been done and I bear you no ill will. But now I must tell you that your work where our daughter is concerned is finished. You can keep the money my wife has given you as compensation for your trouble, but you are to stop what you're doing right now, and not try to contact either of us again. Is that clear?"

"It's clear, all right, but it's not your call. Your wife hired me, and until she fires me, I stay on the case."

"You are provoking me, Mr. Gamble. The Bible cautions that only a fool provokes the godly."

"Give it a rest, Reverend. What are you going to do, call down the lightning to strike me dead? My business is finding people who have gone missing, which your daughter certainly has. She's not some kid playing hooky from school. If you don't care what happens to her, that's fine with me. Your wife does, though, and for reasons that I doubt you'd be able to understand, so do I."

"You'll be getting no more money from us."

"There are other compensations," I said.

"Nor any help, either."

"I just love a mystery, don't you?" I stood up and leaned across my desk until we were nearly nose-to-nose. "We don't seem to be communicating very well here, sir, so let me see if I can make my position completely clear. You have annoyed me in record time, and that's not easy. You have annoyed me with your sanctimonious attitude, your indifference to your daughter's welfare, and with the way you think you can walk in here and insult my intelligence by trying to frighten me with some fundamentalist mumbo-jumbo you've lifted completely out of context to fit your own purposes.

He opened his mouth to say something, but I kept on plowing straight ahead.

"Well, okay, you've had your say. Now here's mine. Whether you like it or not, or whether you pay me or not, I'm on the case. And until your wife says otherwise, and maybe even after that, if I can find a client, I'm staying on the case."

"That would be unwise."

"Unwise why?" I spread my hands in frustration. "I'm not understanding this, Reverend. Do you mean to stand there and tell me you don't care what happens to your daughter? Do you have any idea what happens to minor children who run away from home without a safe place to go or money to support themselves? Especially young girls who are as grown-up looking as Gabrielle?"

"I detect a note of lust in your voice, Mr. Gamble. It does not reflect well upon you."

It took me a moment to process what he was saying, and then his meaning sank in. "We're done here, Reverend. And if you say one more word, just one more word at all, I'm going to come around this desk and hammer you into the floor like a carpet tack. Now I strongly suggest you smarten up and get out of here before I lose my temper and do it anyway."

I sat down again and pretended to read some papers that were scattered on top of my desk. A moment later, I heard the door open and close again, and when I looked up, he was gone.

I waited five minutes for the blood to stop pounding in my ears. Then I walked across the hall to the washroom and splashed cold water on my face. It helped, but only a little, and by the time I got back to my desk, I could feel the heat boiling up from under my collar all over again.

I was looking out the window, still grinding my teeth the way my dentist tells me not to when the telephone rang. I snatched it out of its cradle on the second ring and growled something into the mouthpiece that doesn't bear repeating.

The female voice at the other end said, "Mr. Gamble, this is Maggie Totten, at Woodcrest High School."

"What a relief," I said. "For a minute there, I thought I'd had all the excitement I was going to get for one morning."

Her voice stayed neutral. "We have a temper today."

"We have a temper every day, Ms. Totten. Some days, we just stash it away in places where we have trouble finding it again."

"It must be a real business builder for you," she said. "I tried to call earlier, but I got your answering service instead. They said I could leave a message."

"I'd hate to think I was paying them for nothing."

"Well, obviously, my feminine charm is wasted on you this morning, so let me just get to the point." There was a silence on the line that was just long enough for her to switch the phone from one ear to the other.

"The reason I called is that I have Ginger Aldrich sitting in my office right now. Apparently, she's had a change of heart since yesterday and wants to talk to you about Gabrielle. She won't tell me what it is, but from the look on her face, I'd say it was important."

"I'll be there in fifteen minutes," I said and hit the door on the dead run.

Chapter Eight

On the face of it, nothing much had changed from the day before. We were the same three people sitting in the same government-green office, trying our best to find the words that lay just beyond our reach. Margaret Totten wore maroon slacks today, with a gray satin blouse. Ginger Aldrich wore the same jeans and sneakers and an orange-and-white Tennessee sweatshirt, a cross-state switch in allegiance from the black-and-gold of yesterday's Vanderbilt jersey. I might or might not have changed shirts. When everything you own is button-down and blue, it's hard to tell the difference.

After a few clumsy nice-to-see-you-agains, I cut to the chase. "Ginger, Ms. Totten tells me you may have remembered something about Gabrielle."

She fidgeted in her chair. "Could we just talk alone?"

No way was I going to sit in a closed room with a fifteen-year-old girl. "I think we both owe it to Miss Totten to trust her, Ginger. She's as worried about Gabrielle as you and me."

"And anyway, Ginger," Margaret said, "it's against the rules for me to leave you alone with someone from outside the school."

"Are you going to tell my parents? Or the police?"

"That depends upon what you tell me. I'm not here to make trouble for you. All I want is to find Gabrielle and bring her home. Unless you tell me that she's tied to the railroad tracks and the train is due any minute, what we talk about here is strictly between you and me and Ms. Totten."

"I just don't want anybody else to find out that—that I lied."

"Nobody's going to find out anything, Ginger. What you tell us stays right here in this room." I let a harder edge slip into my voice. "But if you lie to us again, and Gabrielle winds up dead because you knew something and didn't tell us, then that's on you. And whether or not anybody else finds out, you'll live with that the rest of your life. Do you understand?"

When her only response was a small movement with her hands I said again, a bit more emphatically, "Do you understand?"

"Yes."

"All right, then," I said, "just so we're clear. What do you have to tell us?"

"Well…I don't know where Gabrielle went. But there's this guy she might be with. He might know where she is. Her parents don't know about him. She was supposed to be meeting him that night. She said they were going to go away someplace together, to live. But I think that was mostly her idea, because I've seen him around since then, and he had another woman with him. So that means Gabrielle must be…someplace else. And besides, like you said, I haven't heard from her and I think I would have if she was okay."

I showed her the picture I had taken from Gabrielle's room. "Are these the people we're talking about?"

Her eyes widened. "Where did you get that?"

I let her question pass. "Is this the man Gabrielle was supposed to be meeting with the night she disappeared?"

She nodded. Progress at last. I sighed an inward sigh of relief and said, "Does this guy have a name?"

"It's Bobby something-or-other. I don't think he said his last name."

"What about this woman here? Does she have a name?"

"I guess so, but I never heard what it was."

I looked at her, hard.

"Honest."

"Who took these pictures, you?"

"Yes. I used the camera on my phone. I sent them to my email and when I got home, I printed them out and gave them to Gabrielle."

"Are there any more of them still in your camera, or are these three all there were?"

"These are all."

"Okay." I put the photos down on Margaret Totten's desk. "You said before you'd seen Bobby with another woman since the time Gabrielle left home. Is the woman in this picture the one he was with?"

"Yes."

"Besides the time in the park, when did you see her with Bobby?"

"It was a couple days ago."

"Can you be more precise? Are we talking Tuesday, or over the weekend, or what?"

"It was this week. Monday, I think."

"All right, good," I said. "Where were you?"

"I was in the car with my mom. We were going shopping. We drove past a filling station. He was putting gas in his truck. The woman was sitting in the front seat."

"And you're sure it was Bobby? How were you able to recognize him if you were in a moving car and he was pumping gas into his truck?"

"His truck is special. It has four wheels in the back. I think those are called dualies. And it has a special paint job. I haven't seen any other ones like it. It's bright red, with four doors and silver stripes on the hood and a camper top over the back. Bobby said it's fixed up on the inside, too, with a mattress and a stereo and stuff. He said he could live in it if he had to. He let us ride in it once. That's when we met him the first time. We were walking home from school and he stopped and offered to drive us home."

"But then he didn't take you straight home."

"Not right away. He drove us around for a while and then we ended up at the park. I was a little scared at first because I didn't know what he might do. But then I thought, he's got this lady with him, and what can happen with her around? All we did was hang around the park for a few minutes and I took these pictures and then he dropped us off."

"So then other than at the park and that one time outside the gas station, have you seen her or Bobby anywhere else? Like, for instance, maybe one of them might live someplace near where you or Gabrielle live?"

"No."

"Okay," I said. "We're doing great. I just have a couple more questions, and then we're done."

"It's all right. I want to help."

"I know you do, Ginger, and I appreciate it. After you went to the park with Bobby and the lady, did you go anywhere else, like stop for ice cream or a soda?"

"No."

"Or maybe he took you to where he lives?"

She shook her head. "We just rode around. We didn't stop anywhere. Then I told him I had to get home because I was going to be late. Gabrielle was getting worried, too. She was afraid if she got home late her mom and dad might start asking questions about where she was. Bobby said okay and then he took us over to Winford Street and dropped us off. That way nobody we knew would see us getting out of the truck. We walked home from there."

"When you were at the park, other than when you took your pictures, did you talk to anybody else? Even just for a minute?"

"We didn't see anybody else."

"By any chance, did he talk about where he lived, or where he works?"

"No, he never said anything about that. He just talked big about how he was a movie producer." She laughed derisively. "He didn't look very much like a producer to me."

"No? What did he look like? Physically, I mean?"

She looked at me, confused. "You can see for yourself. You've got his picture."

"Pictures don't always tell the whole story, Ginger. I'd be willing to bet even seeing him only the one time, you probably noticed something about him that's not in the photo."

"Well, he doesn't have any scars or anything, if that's what you mean. He's tall, though, I remember that. Taller than you, I would say, but real skinny and pale, like if he'd been sick or something. He has dark brown hair, but I don't know what color his eyes are. He had on sunglasses the day I met him." She frowned at the recollection. "I didn't like him very much."

"Why not?"

"Because, I don't know how to say it any other way, he was an asshole."

She shifted her eyes toward Margaret Totten, expecting to be told to watch her language. When Margaret said nothing, Ginger continued.

"He kept acting like he was a real important person, and like he was doing Gabrielle and me some kind of a favor just being with us. Gabrielle, though, she seemed to think he was the greatest thing ever. But I don't know what she liked so much about him, especially since it seemed like he already had a girlfriend."

"Did you tell her that?"

"Later on, I tried to, but I don't think she was listening. She has to figure that out for herself. It's her life, you know?"

That was exactly what had me worried. "How old would you say Bobby is, Ginger?"

"Not as old as you; maybe twenty-five or thirty. It's hard to tell for sure." She gave an indulgent smile, as if to say that, to her generation, anybody over thirty was a prospect for an AARP membership.

"Did either Bobby or his girlfriend give you the impression they were on drugs?"

"They could have been, I guess. I don't know. He seemed nervous and he was smoking the whole time. I was afraid the smell would get on my clothes and then my mom would ask me where I had been.

"The woman acted different, like she was falling asleep. She didn't talk at all except when Gabrielle asked me to take everybody's picture."

"What did she say then?"

"She said 'leave me out of it,' but he grabbed her by the arm and made her sit on the steps with him. She wasn't happy about it, though."

"Did she seem like she was afraid of him? Like maybe she thought he might hurt her?"

"She might have, I guess. I don't know."

Margaret Totten spoke up. "Ginger, Mr. Gamble asked you about this yesterday, but I'd like you to think about it again. Is it possible that Gabrielle had met Bobby before the day he took the two of you for a ride in his truck?"

"I thought about that. Probably she must have, because I don't know why else he would have stopped to give us a ride. I mean, who does that?"

I could have told her, but I kept quiet and let Margaret ask her questions.

"Do you think she's been sneaking out of the house to meet with him?"

"I don't think she could have gotten away with that, but I'm pretty sure she's been talking to him on the phone. She told me he said he liked to hang out at some bar down on Broadway and that when she was a little older, he'd take her there and show her a good time. I don't remember the name. It had diamonds or something like that in the name."

I said, "Was it the Rhinestone Cowgirl?"

"Yeah," she said, "that was it, the Rhinestone Cowgirl. I doubt if he could actually get her in there, though. I mean, you have to be twenty-one just to get into a place like that, don't you?"

"You have to look twenty-one, anyway," I said. "Is there anything else you can tell me about Bobby?"

"Not that I can think of. Like I said, I only just met him that one time." She looked at me earnestly. "Mr. Gamble?"

"What is it?"

"Now that I've told you—now that you know about Bobby, do you think Gabrielle's okay?"

"I don't know enough yet to give you an answer, Ginger," I said. "I hope so. You've met him. I haven't. Until we find her, all we can do is think positive thoughts."

"Well, when you find her? She'll know I talked to you."

"Yeah, she probably will."

"Would you tell her I did it because she's my friend? And because I was scared for her? Would you do that for me?"

"I think you should tell her that yourself, Ginger. I think it would mean a lot more to her hearing it from you."

Chapter Nine

I t was as good an exit line as anybody could ask for. I didn't have any more questions for Ginger and said so. Margaret initialed her hall pass and excused her.

After Ginger was gone, Margaret turned to me. I got the feeling something had upset her. "What do you make of that?"

"I'm not sure. Either we got the right story this time, or we just heard Plan B that she and Gabrielle cooked up in case somebody wasn't buying the original story."

"Do you think she was lying again?"

"No, I think this time she was telling the truth, or at least as much of it as she could without getting herself into trouble. She's been walking around for the last few days with a lot of guilt on account of Gabrielle. Sooner or later, she was going to have to let go of it. It was just a matter of her finding the right person to hear what she had to say."

There was a beat. "And the right person just happened to be you," she said, turning suddenly cool again. "God, I wish I understood what it is that makes you men think the way you do. Don't you think you were a little over the top, frightening her like that? I mean, are you really that insensitive?"

And there it was. I said, "Why do I get the feeling this is where I came in? Look, Margaret, there's something we need to get straight. Here at school, in your world, you want to assume the best about the kids you work with. I understand that. I even applaud it. Yours is a caring profession. Because of that, you don't want to accept that kids sometimes do terrible things, with terrible consequences. You tell yourself they just made a mistake, or it's somebody else's fault, or they come from a shitty home environment, so we'll let what they did slide this time. Then you go to a staff meeting or you bring in a consultant and they tell you, you know, you're right, these kids aren't so bad. They just need a little more love and attention and they'll turn out fine.

"But the fact is, about half the crimes in this country are committed by children, and the hurt they inflict on others is not an abstraction. Some teenager with a sad story hurts, or kills, somebody else, because he needed money to buy drugs or to make his bones with some street gang, or just because he's having a bad day and somebody looked at him wrong.

"Your consultants don't tell you the whole story about girls barely old enough to get a driver's license who end up tricking on street corners because it's the only way to keep their pimp from beating them half to death with a coat hanger or carving their initials in them with a straight razor. I've seen plenty of it, Margaret. I lived it and worked it every day when I was with the cops, and nine years later I'm still up to my ears in it. So, if I come across as insensitive when I'm trying to get information from somebody like Ginger Aldrich, it's not because I'm insensitive. I just don't have the luxury of sparing some teenager's psyche, even a nice girl like Ginger when she's obviously lying like she was the other day. I'm too busy trying to save another little girl from winding up dead in some alley dumpster."

She leaned back in her chair and was quiet for several minutes. The clock on the wall ticked past eleven twenty-nine toward half-past the hour. Outside the guidance office, a bell rang, and in another moment, the corridor was flooded with the youthful racket of teenaged voices, shuffling feet, and lockers banging open and shut. We sat looking at one another, saying nothing, until the hallway outside her office was quiet once more.

Margaret said, "You don't like me very much, do you?"

"I haven't decided yet. I think maybe I do, but you don't make it easy."

"No, I suppose I don't. But there's something I didn't tell you before. Something you should know before you make up your mind."

"I'm listening."

"How do I start?" She paused to take a breath. "Before I got into guidance

68

work, I was a teacher. Not here at Woodcrest, at another high school in another part of the city. A better part of the city, you might say. The houses were bigger and the cars were newer. In those days I was Mrs. Michael Pomeroy.

"Anyway, it was a Friday afternoon, and I had been working late, grading papers. When I was leaving to go home, a couple of boys—they couldn't have been more than sixteen or seventeen—tried to grab my purse, and when I wouldn't let go, they pushed me down a flight of stairs. I was knocked unconscious, of course. The custodian found me a few minutes later and called for an ambulance. I had a few broken bones; my right arm, my collarbone; a fractured skull. But I was also pregnant at the time. She would have been our first child, but because of what happened, I lost the baby. Later, my husband and I learned that because of complications from the miscarriage, there wouldn't be any more chances for having children. The boys that pushed me weren't in any of my classes, but I knew who they were, so when the police came to see me in the hospital, I identified them and said I wanted to press charges.

"Of course, the boys had a different story. They said I had been making sexual advances toward them, that I grabbed one of them and started kissing him. He said when he tried to push me away, I fell down the stairs. In other words, it was an accident, but it was still my fault.

"His friend swore that yes, that was the way it happened. They were both from good families, and neither of them had a police record, so there was never a trial or even much of an investigation. Just an informal hearing. I don't know what the judge thought, or whose version of the story he actually believed, but when it was over, the boys each got six months of court supervision and community service. I got an indefinite medical leave and a six-figure settlement because the school district thought I'd sue for wrongful discharge if they tried to fire me, which I know is what they wanted to do. Then, after I signed, they transferred me here. I'm pretty sure they hoped that once I got a look at this place, I'd quit."

"Why didn't you?"

"Because I was stubborn, I guess, and I wasn't about to let the district off that easily. Anyway, Michael and I had been married about a year when all this happened. At first, he tried to be supportive, but I think finally he found it impossible to live with the certainty that there would be no children in our future. He never said so, but after a while, I began to think that he had it in the back of his head that there was something to those boys' version of what happened, or that I had acted in a way that encouraged them.

"After that, we just started drifting apart. Six months later, he served me with papers. The whole time after I came home from the hospital, we hardly ever even slept in the same bed. He said he thought I'd rest better if I had the bed to myself, but I knew that wasn't what it was. Toward the end, I don't think he even touched me." She shook her head sadly. "After the divorce, I went back to using my maiden name. I just wanted him out of my life."

I didn't know how to respond to that, so I kept quiet and waited.

"Can you understand I needed him to touch me? Not for sex, just to be close. Just to let me know that he still loved me and that I wasn't dirty or depraved, or guilty of anything more than being in the wrong place at the wrong time. That was all I wanted." She looked at me earnestly. "I'm telling you this because I want you to understand that I have no illusions about who some of these kids are, or what they're capable of doing. But that doesn't mean that I shouldn't try to help the ones I can, does it?"

"I'm sorry, Margaret," I said, unhelpfully. "I am a fool."

"Sometimes, probably, yes," she said, showing me the barest hint of a smile. "But in this case, it's not your fault. It was me that married Michael Pomeroy, not you."

"I get that, but that's only half of it. The worst part is that I'm sitting here dragging up bad memories for you and raking Ginger over the coals, and before the week is over it probably isn't going to make any difference."

"I don't understand."

"It isn't going to make any difference," I said, "because by tomorrow morning I won't have a client." Without waiting for her to ask another question, I sketched in the sequence of events since the previous afternoon, starting with how I'd come to find the photos that were hidden in Gabrielle's desk and ending with the visit I'd been paid earlier that morning by Jericho

Hawkins.

"This is tragic," she said when I was finished. "Do you think Delsey is going to ask you to stop looking for Gabrielle?"

"I don't think she has much choice. She's a strong woman. I give her credit for that, but she sees herself as subservient to Jericho, especially since he's not only her husband, he's also her pastor. If he says he made her see the error of her ways, I'd be inclined to take him at his word."

"Do you think he'd hurt her?"

"No. He's a bully, and self-righteous as hell, but he doesn't strike me as violent. More likely he threatened her with the wrath of the Old Testament God. I don't know, but I'm pretty sure she'll be calling me off any time now."

"And having to drop the case would really make that much difference to you?"

"When you put it that way," I said, "it makes it sound like all I'm interested in is the money, or to prove something to myself. Maybe there's something to that, because finding people is what I do, and I'm good at it. But there's something about this case that's gotten me hooked. Maybe it's because Gabrielle Hawkins sounds like a good kid who's gone from being stuck in a bad situation to running away into a worse one, and nobody seems interested in helping her. Not her old man, not the cops, and until today, not even her best friend. Nobody seems to care about her much except her mother, and now me. I just don't want to let her slip away, Margaret, and unless I do it, nobody else is going to do anything to help her."

"I'll help her, Gamble," Margaret said. "You and I will help her together." She picked up her pencil and tapped it on the edge of her desk.

"The problem, as I understand it, is that technically, Jericho Hawkins can't throw you off the case because he didn't hire you in the first place. But Delsey can, and if she does, you have no legal standing to keep looking for Gabrielle, is that it?"

"About it. The state says I have to have a client."

"Well, would I do?"

"Would you do what?"

"Would I do as a client? What if I hired you? I have a right to do that, don't

I, as a concerned citizen? I mean, I can't hire you on behalf of the school district, but I can on my own, can't I? Suppose I paid you, I don't know, how much do you get for looking for lost little girls?"

"Three hundred a day plus expenses, standard rate," I said, following her lead. "But like I told you yesterday, this week I'm having a special. For you, the price is dinner. With me. Out. Tomorrow night, say, at eight o'clock. That is, unless you're already seeing somebody. I guess I should have asked about that first."

"I thought you didn't like me."

I gave her a wide smile. "I've had an epiphany."

"Well, I can't, not tomorrow," she said, and then quickly added, "I have an engagement with some friends I can't get out of. But Saturday night is okay. If you can keep from starving to death until then, you've got a date. And you've got a client."

It was the best offer I'd had all week. I wrote down her address and phone number, and got the hell out of her office before I said something else stupid to make her change her mind.

When I got back to my car, I realized that there was nothing else I could do at that particular moment about finding Gabrielle. And so, with time on my hands, I decided to take a ride over to Centennial Park and cruise past the Parthenon. I wasn't really counting on finding anything there that would help me find Gabrielle, but I did think it was possible I might run across somebody who could point me in the direction of Gabrielle's Bobby or the woman who sat with them that day on the steps of the Parthenon.

As its name suggests, the Parthenon in Centennial Park is a full-scale concrete replica of the original Parthenon in Athens, Greece. It was designed by a former Confederate army officer and was built in 1897 as part of Tennessee's Centennial Exposition. In the present day, it serves as an art museum and an occasional movie prop, and houses an impressive 42-foot-tall re-creation of the statue of *Athena Parthenos*. Today, however, I wasn't interested in classical Greek architecture or statues of mythical goddesses. There was a little girl gone missing and a couple of people I needed to find who might know where she was.

I left Woodcrest High School and drove out West End Avenue to the park. I was thinking about the last time I was there, on business. I was just over three years on the job and a newly-minted detective. We got a tip that a witness we had been trying to locate liked to go to the park early in the morning and feed popcorn to the geese. Quite by accident, the guy had overheard a bit of conversation that took place in a bar between two lowlifes who had been arrested for murder, largely on the testimony of this witness. Problem was, before one of the lowlifes bonded out, he had made noises about making sure the witness didn't appear at the grand jury hearing. After a meeting between the cops and the A.D.A. assigned to the case, it was decided to put the witness into protective custody, at least until after the hearing.

My partner Wanda and I drove out to the park early the next morning to pick up the goose man and keep him under wraps until the hearing, which was scheduled for the following week. Sure enough, just after sunrise, we found him sitting on a bench near the park lagoon with a bag of popcorn on the seat next to him. A half-dozen geese were gathered around his feet, honking and squawking, demanding their accustomed handout. That day they missed their breakfast, however. As we approached our guy, we could see that he was slumped slightly over to one side and that he wasn't moving. We thought at first maybe he had dozed off, or that he'd had a heart attack. But instead, what we found was a dead man with an old-fashioned icepick shoved all the way up to the handle into his right ear. With no witness to testify, the hearing was postponed, the indictment never came and the two scumbags walked free. And that might have been the end of it, except, after booking it out of Tennessee, the pair embarked on a multi-state crime spree through Arkansas, Louisiana, and Texas, where they shot and killed a 7-11 counterman outside Fort Worth.

Thanks to video cameras inside the store and on the pump island where they filled the tank of their stolen Ford pickup, they were apprehended in El Paso and brought back to Fort Worth for trial. Texas is a state that is not in the least bit queasy about handing down the death penalty, and the Tarrant County prosecutors wasted no time swinging for the fences. Three years later, the two came to the end of the line at the point of a needle at the Texas

State Penitentiary in Huntsville.

On this day there were no corpses resting on park benches, nor was anyone hanging around the Parthenon. On a warm summer day, the wide lawn there is crowded with tourists, Frisbee players, sunbathers, couples holding hands, and people sitting on the steps eating their lunches or puffing on a fat boy. However, in the waning light of this chilly and wet afternoon, there was nobody doing anything, just a few squirrels chasing each other around, chattering away, and having the time of their lives scrounging for acorns. Maybe they had an idea where I might find a pretty girl named Gabrielle, but if they did, they weren't in a mood to tell me.

Chapter Ten

In 1974, Los Angeles-based songwriter Larry Weiss wrote a song called "Rhinestone Cowboy," and recorded it on an album entitled *Black and Blue Suite*. The song, which was about a past-his-prime performer hoping to hold on to fame for just a while longer, met with only modest success for Weiss. However, popular country-western singer Glen Campbell, who was touring in Australia late that same year, heard it on the radio, and upon returning to the United States, pitched it to Capitol Records. The Campbell version became a crossover smash, holding the number one position for three consecutive weeks on the Billboard Hot Country Singles chart and two weeks at number one on the Hot 100 list. For the year 1975, it wound up being the number-two hit single across all markets.

Sensing an opportunity to cash in on the song's popularity, a Nashville entrepreneur named Tommy Gillis, who was suspected by local law enforcement to have ties to organized crime, opened a nightclub the following year, using the name Rhinestone Cowgirl. The gender-bender was necessary because the "Rhinestone Cowboy" title was copyrighted, and because it didn't quite fit the club's *raison d'etre*, which was as a tuck-a-buck bar serving watered-down liquor and featuring a revolving stage populated by B-list pole dancers who weren't hired for their ability to discuss the teachings of Thomas Aquinas.

As it has been since the day the doors opened, the biggest part of the Cowgirl's clientele is made up of businessmen traveling on expense accounts and local college boys who manage to bluff their way past the bouncer with unconvincingly altered ID cards wrapped in folding money. For adventurous patrons with deeper pockets, lap dances are available for a small extra charge. Private dances, which involve very little dancing, but lots of full-body contact, can also be had, most major credit cards accepted. And despite the club's immediate and continuing success, for reasons that nobody has ever been able to quite figure out, Tommy Gillis went missing a year or so after the grand opening and later turned up dead in a back-alley dumpster, minus his hands and feet.

Ginger Aldrich had told Margaret Totten and me that the Rhinestone Cowgirl was a place Gabrielle's boyfriend Bobby, last name unknown, had promised to take her to show her a good time. I couldn't imagine why anyone would think that a fourteen-year-old girl would be interested in pole dancing, but a lead is a lead. And so, that night I decided to wander down to the Cowgirl to show around the photos Gabrielle had hidden in her room. My hope was that somebody might recognize either Bobby or the woman he'd had with him and furnish me with a full name.

Taking my time, it was about a ten-minute walk from where I had parked my car on Fifth, near Ryman Auditorium, to the corner of Third and Broadway. Considering that it was after ten o'clock on an out-of-season weekday night in the heart of the Bible Belt, there was a fair number of people out on the street. In the neon daylight of Lower Broad, they made for an interesting study in contrasts.

Some were expensively dressed, master-of-the-universe corporate types, letting off a little steam after a tough day of negotiating some big deal destined to change the course of American enterprise for decades to come. Mixed in were wide-eyed, country-mouse tourists, getting an up-close look at big city nightlife. And there was also a healthy smattering of others, including uniformed police, tired hookers with swollen feet and smudged lipstick, blue jean-clad college kids who might or might not have been old enough to legally buy a drink, and a cadre of down-and-outers stumbling toward a clean bed at one of the rescue missions that dot the area. In exchange for a mumbled prayer and a soon-to-be-forgotten pledge to start walking the straight and narrow, these luckless individuals could count on a shower and a clean bed tonight, and a hot breakfast in the morning.

And then there was the handful of hard-eyed individuals who seemed to be doing nothing more than standing around watching everybody else. These, I knew, were plainclothes vice cops. Their function was to make sure that anybody who wanted to have his or her taste of sin, however tentative, could do so without being mugged, raped, or otherwise getting into trouble and making the wrong kind of headlines. It is the unwritten rule of tourist traps. Raise all the hell you want, go back home and tell all your friends and neighbors about it, but whatever you do, keep it off the six o'clock news so we don't have to crack down and spoil everyone else's fun.

It was between shows when I got to the Rhinestone Cowgirl. The revolving stage was dark and motionless and the only music playing was an old Johnny Cash song, "Cocaine Blues," blasting from the jukebox. The place was about half filled. Most of the patrons were men who looked like traveling salesmen, but also a few couples who had either wandered in by accident or else were trying for a jump start getting into the mood before heading home or back to their hotels. I paid my ten-dollar cover charge and was admitted by a bouncer who looked strong enough to yank a telephone pole out of the ground and then snap it across his knee just to prove his breakfast that morning had stuck to his ribs. I found a seat at an unoccupied table for two next to a group of noisy corporate types who seemed intent on having a night of high-jinks on the company's nickel. They were arguing spiritedly about where would be the best place for their upcoming five-day golf outing, which, I guessed qualified their discussion as a tax-deductible business meeting.

Three "hostesses," with apparent time on their hands before the next show, were hanging near the bar. All were dressed in matching costumes: a tiny white imitation leather skirt on the bottom and an equally immodest white vest made out of the same *faux* leather up top. Their outfits were trimmed with blue fringe around the hem of the skirt and the top of the vest, and accessorized with a white ten-gallon hat, a pair of white boots, and a blue rhinestone choker around the neck. Taken as a package, they looked like Dallas Cowboys cheerleaders who had stuck around beyond their sell-by dates.

The youngest of the three, a black girl with incongruously bleached blonde hair, was smoking a cigarette and doing her best not to make eye contact with any of the customers. Another, a white girl with coal-black hair accented with a bride-of-Frankenstein yellow-orange streak, was grinning contentedly to herself and swaying gently back in forth in time to music that only she could hear. Her arms, legs, and neck were decorated with enough ink to print a Sunday newspaper, including a brightly colored bird nesting in a bough of deep green leaves on her shoulder, a teddy bear cavorting on her left breast, and what appeared to be a praying Virgin Mary just below her hip. But it was the third hostess who spotted me first and drifted over to take my order. She was a tall, nicely-shaped brunette with blue eyes tending to violet, and impossibly long legs that looked even longer beneath her barely-legal skirt.

I smiled up at her.

She blinked once and said, "Fuck you, Gamble."

"It's good to see you, too, Carly."

"I thought I told you after last time I didn't want you coming around me anymore."

"No," I said, shaking my head. "You said not to call you. There's a difference."

"Not as far as I'm concerned, there isn't. What are you doing here, anyway? I thought you were seeing somebody."

"It didn't work out."

"Right. That's pretty much the story of your life, isn't it?"

I flinched a little at that. The somebody she was referring to was a songwriter named Cathleen Courtney, whom I had been dating regularly before one of her compositions struck the mother lode and she was offered a job in Los Angeles to work for one of the big West Coast recording companies. Our parting had been painful and prolonged, and we tried for a while to stay in touch. I even flew out to L.A. once, over a long weekend, but almost from the moment wheels hit the runway, we both realized things just weren't the same. When she dropped me back at LAX for my return flight, we exchanged promises to keep in touch, but it was half-hearted, and the phone calls and emails soon dried up.

Before I could think of an answer to Carly's question, one of the junior executive types sitting at the table opposite me banged his empty beer mug on the table and said in a too-loud voice, "Hey, honey, how about a little service over here?"

She eyed him coldly. "I'll be right with you, sir, if you can just hold on a minute." She turned the same icy look on me. "I'll ask you again. Why are you here?"

"Thought I'd take in the show," I said. "And I wanted to talk to you for a minute if you've got time for an old friend."

She started to say something in reply, probably like, "what friend," or maybe "fuck you" again, when the loudmouthed guy at the next table leaned over and tugged roughly at the hem of her skirt. "You working here, sweetheart, or are you just figuring out a hookup for later with this old boy?"

It was a small thing, really, grabbing at Carly and talking to her the way he did. Just the kind of thoughtless violation that must happen to waitresses a thousand times a day in restaurants and lounges all over the world. It was also none of my business, but all the same, it made me angry. Maybe because it had been a long day and I was getting tired, or maybe because Carly Barrett was a friend, and, for a season in my life, something more than that. Whatever the case, I wasn't going to let it go.

Without really thinking about what I was doing, I reached out quickly and took hold of the man's wrist, jerking him halfway out of his chair in the process. Then I squeezed hard, digging my thumb into the soft space between the two bones in his forearm. He gave a short yelp of pain and tried to pull away, but I tightened my grip and gave the arm a sharp twist.

On reflection, I would have to admit it was a foolish thing to do, especially since I had no idea who the man was, or whether he and the other three men with him might be made members of the Gambino crime family. And as any cop can tell you, cemeteries are filled to the fences with people who got there ahead of time by sticking their noses into affairs that were none of their concern. But I wasn't thinking about that just then. I was too angry for that kind of introspection. The man's three table companions went wide-eyed with surprise, but none of them said anything or made a move for a piece.

I pulled the mouthy bastard toward me so he could hear without my having to raise my voice and said, "Some advice for you, friend. You want to keep using that hand to push a pencil or jerk off or whatever it is you do with it you'd better keep it away from places it doesn't belong." Then I gave his arm another twist for good measure, and let him go.

I turned back to Carly. She gave me a look of mild amusement, as if what I had done was just the kind of behavior that she would have expected from me, but she said nothing. I said, "I'll take a bottle of beer now, Carly. Stella if you have it. And I imagine these gentlemen will be wanting their check."

"They're all caught up," she said. "We don't run tabs here." Then she turned and walked back to the bar. While she was gone, I got up and walked over to the jukebox. I browsed through the titles until I found a couple of songs I liked, dropped in some quarters, and pushed the necessary buttons.

The first licks of Vince Gill's "Sweet Thing" were just rising when I returned to my table. My Stella was there waiting, and so was Carly, seated in the chair opposite mine. The adjoining table was now empty, its former occupants no doubt agreeing amongst themselves that whoever had coined the term Southern Hospitality hadn't gotten the inspiration hanging around the Rhinestone Cowgirl on a weeknight night. I sat down, took a swallow of my beer, and grinned at Carly.

"I guess now you're going to tell me that what I did was an atavistic male response to a perceived invasion of his territory and that I ought to be ashamed of myself."

She leaned forward in her chair, cupping her face in her hands and exposing a fair amount of cleavage above the top of her costume. "Actually, I was going to say I was hoping you might rip his arm off and beat him to death with the bloody stump. And Gamble, I apologize for what I said before. About your breakup, I mean. I heard what happened with you and—I'm sorry—what was her name?"

"Cathleen. Cathleen Courtney."

"Cathleen, that's right. Well, anyway, I heard from a mutual friend, never mind who, about how she took off on you and I'm sorry for rubbing it in. I guess I just didn't think I'd react that badly seeing you again."

"You weren't rubbing it in. Besides, she didn't exactly take off. She got a job offer from a record company in California and she accepted. She invited me to come with her, and I said I'd think about it, but it never happened. I suppose I never quite saw myself as a PI in Los Angeles. Too much like a cliché."

She smiled at what must have been her mental picture of that. "Not you," she said, "not hardly. You're glued in much too tight right where you are, saving this Southern-fried Sodom from a fate it so richly deserves. You're also too hardheaded to admit how much seeing her go must have hurt you."

I didn't know how to respond to that. But our conversation was drifting into an uncomfortable place that I didn't want to revisit. I'd spent enough time there already.

"Yeah, well, that sort of brings me around to the reason I came by tonight. There are a couple people I'm looking for and I thought you might be able to help me find one of them."

She abruptly sat up straight and gave me a look as if I had slapped her across the face. "You must think I'm incredibly stupid."

"Why would I think that?"

"Because all of a sudden I think I'm incredibly stupid. I mean ricochet romance is one thing. I can live with that. I sat down here thinking, maybe even hoping a little, that you'd come to see me like you used to, and all the time you're just putting in another day's work. What, are you going to bill some client for the beer and the conversation?"

"I never said I was doing anything else."

"No," she said softly. "I guess you didn't at that. You've always been honest that way, haven't you?"

"What do you want me to tell you, Carly? We were good together for a while, and then it ended. I thought we both agreed on that."

"Agreed, yeah, I suppose we did." She glanced back over her shoulder in the direction of the stage. It was still darkened, but there were the shadowy figures of stagehands moving around on it, rearranging props and lights for the next show. Other customers were coming through the door as well, and the place was beginning to fill up ahead of the last show for the night.

"Look, it's going to be pretty noisy in here in a couple of minutes and I'm going to have to get back to work. If there's something you want to ask me, you'd better do it now, otherwise the boss will expect me to charge you for a lap dance."

I considered the prospect of that, then took out the picture of Bobby and placed it on the table where Carly could see it. "This guy here," I said, pointing. "I need to talk to him. He's in his twenties, tall and thin. He wears sunglasses with mirrored lenses. It's possible he's some kind of movie producer, or at least he talks like one. It's also possible he's selling drugs. Word is, he likes to hang out down here on Lower Broad. Maybe he's been in here a time or two."

She glanced briefly at the photo. "I don't know. We get a lot of guys come in here looking like that. What else have you got?"

"Right here." I took out the picture of Gabrielle and placed it on the table next to the first one. "Her name is Gabrielle."

"She's beautiful. Who is she?"

"She's a teenaged girl who's gone missing and her mother wants her back." I tapped my finger on the first photo. "I have reason to believe this guy here might know where she is."

"But you don't know his name?"

"His first name is Bobby. That's all I got."

She said, "Bobby?" and I could almost hear the wheels turning in the back of her head. "Let me take another look. Could he have had a beard that he shaved off?"

"I don't know, I've never seen the guy. This is all I've got to go on."

"Because if he did," she went on, "then he might be somebody who used to go with a friend of mine. This isn't a very good picture, so I'm not a hundred percent sure. I only saw him a couple of times, but if he's the guy I'm thinking about, his name is Bobby. What made me remember was the sunglasses. I never saw him take them off. He said his eyes were sensitive to bright light."

"But you don't remember his last name?"

She nodded. "I do. His name is Fury. Bobby Fury."

"Fury? Really?"

"Well, actually it's Furillo. He had some idea about going into the movie business and he thought Fury made him sound more like an action hero, so that's the name he's been using."

"You said he was seeing a friend of yours. What's her name?"

"Michelle. Michelle Reddick, but she goes by Mickey."

I showed her the last of the three pictures. "Is this Mickey?"

She stared at it for a moment, then shook her head slowly. "It looks like her, and yet it doesn't. The Mickey I know looks, well, better than that. This woman looks like she's been living on the street. I mean, her face is all drawn and if it is Mickey, she's lost a lot of weight." And then a thought came to her. "You mentioned before you thought Bobby might be selling drugs. Could he have gotten her hooked on something?"

"I don't know. You've met him, I haven't. When was the last time you saw him?"

"Not for a while. He came in here one night a couple months ago. Mickey was working here at the time, and he was drunk and pissed off at her about something. He started yelling at her and smacked her a couple times before the manager heard the ruckus and threw him out the back door, head first. Mickey didn't come to work the next day or the day after that, and when she did come back, she had some bad bruises that we had to cover up with makeup. It was right after that she broke up with him."

"These pictures weren't taken more than a couple weeks ago. Could she have gotten back together with him?"

"Maybe. I don't know. You'll have to ask her."

"I will. You said Mickey works here?"

"She did, but she got fired for showing up late for work once too often. That's always been her problem. She's unreliable. Of course, when she was still working here, she was better looking, but even so, after a while, she got a reputation. I don't know what she's doing now. You know, people start checking references. None of the good places will even talk to her anymore."

"You mean good places like this?"

"It's a living," she said, frowning, and I knew I had crossed a line. "Is there anything else?"

"Only if you've got an address for Mickey, or maybe a phone number? Right now, she's the only lead I've got."

"Well, I'm not a hundred percent sure where she is now, because most of the time she stays with whatever man is willing to take her in. Usually, it doesn't last very long, and then she goes off the rails and has to find somebody else. But the last I heard, which was after she broke up with Bobby, she had an apartment over by the old airport. I don't know the number, or if she's living there with somebody else, but she's in the third building you come to after you pull in the parking lot. Her place is on the second floor."

"Okay."

I jotted down the information in my notebook and took a last swallow of my beer. There was nothing left to talk about, and it was time to go. The jukebox had stopped playing and colored stage lights were coming up ahead of the next show. I put my hand out across the table. "Listen, Carly, I'm sorry about what I said. And maybe if you're free some evening....."

She pulled her own hand back. "Don't worry about it. We both said things we shouldn't have. I guess that's part of why we're not together anymore. Fact is, I met myself a real nice guy not too long ago. He comes by all the time to keep me company, except when he's on the road like he is tonight. But he's got a good job and he treats me nice, and, well, like you said, what else can I tell you?"

"How about, it was good seeing you again?"

"Oh, it was, Gamble. It really was. And I hope if you get back this way you get the chance to meet my guy. I think you'd like him."

"I'm sure I would," I said. But she was already walking away.

I took out my wallet and dropped a twenty on the table. Then I got up and started walking. I didn't stop until I got back to the parking lot where I'd left my car. Once there, I toyed with the idea of taking a run past the apartment where Mickey Reddick was supposed to be staying. Then I looked at my watch and decided to let it go. It was almost midnight, not the best time to be ringing the doorbells of strange women.

Mickey could wait until tomorrow.

Chapter Eleven

The next morning, I got to the office a few minutes early. I was expecting to find a message from Delsey, informing me that she had changed her mind about hiring me to find Gabrielle and that my services would no longer be required. I had laid awake long into the night, mentally composing an airtight argument I could use to persuade her not to drop the case. However, as it turned out, I never had to use it, as there was no message, meaning that either Jericho had changed his own mind—which seemed unlikely—or else Delsey had decided that getting her daughter back home safe and sound was more important than acquiescing to her husband's dictates. Either way, no message meant I was still on the job, and that I had work to do.

I put in a call to Carl Sutton at Metro PD headquarters to find out what progress, if any, he had made with his own search for Gabrielle Hawkins. After two days on the case with only the slimmest of leads and no quick way to track down Bobby Fury, I figured now it was time to talk directly to cops. Chances were, if Bobby had a record of prior arrests, the police might at least have an LKA, a last known address, I could use as a place to start. Carl agreed to see me, but said he was covered up at the moment and that he thought he'd be free if I could stop by around ten. That gave me time to stop by the CVS to pick up the duplicate pictures of Gabrielle that I had requested the day before.

After I finished with Carl, my plan was to spend the afternoon handing the photos around at the bus station, women's shelters, youth hostels, the Salvation Army, and anywhere else where an underage girl on her own with

85

no money and no opportunity for meaningful employment might turn up looking for a meal and a safe place to spend the night. Before I did that, however, I needed to talk to Mickey Reddick, in hopes she might be able to give me a lead on where I might find her former boyfriend Bobby Fury. Between Carl Sutton and Mickey Reddick, I was counting on one of them knowing something.

After a doughnut and a Diet Coke at Dunkin, I drove over to police headquarters. I found Sutton in his office, shuffling through a stack of paper and muttering darkly to himself. When he saw me, he waved me into his visitor's chair.

"So," I said. "How are things?"

"Good question," he said, leaning back heavily in his chair. "What do you say we run it down. I'm black and I'm living in Tennessee. I'm thirty-five pounds overweight, I'm diabetic and I've got six more years before I can even think about drawing my pension."

"Living the dream," I said.

"Something like that. Did I mention I've got two kids in college?"

"I knew that. Someday if you're lucky they'll be supporting you."

"I wish." He paused long enough to straighten the papers he had been working on. "You're here because you want to find out what we've turned up on that Hawkins kid, right?"

"I'll take from that Delsey already called you this morning."

"She calls first thing, every morning. How much are they paying you?"

"They aren't. Delsey hired me, but she doesn't have any money to speak of, so I'm working gratis for now. If something else comes along that has a chance of earning me an actual fee, I might have to quit looking. Meantime, I'm just crashing around hoping I might scare a rabbit out from under a bush. Plus, I've got photos. This afternoon, I'm planning to spread them around where they might do some good."

"In other words, you've got nothing. Same as us."

I shrugged. "I've got these." I showed him the photos I'd found in Gabrielle's bedroom.

He looked at them for a long moment. "Where'd these come from?"

86

"They were taped to the bottom of a drawer in her bedroom. Next time, maybe look a little harder."

"So, the kid was clever. Who knew?"

"I wonder. Take a look at this one." I showed him the picture of Bobby and Mickey together. "Do you know whether either one of these two has ever been in the system?"

"I could tell you better if we had names to go with the faces."

"The guy is Bobby, probably Robert, Furillo, but he goes by Fury. The woman is Michelle, also known as Mickey, Reddick."

"That's all we need," he said, typing the names into his computer. He waited a moment while the computer ran its search, then turned the monitor halfway around so we could both see it.

"Here we go, Michelle, AKA Mickey, Reddick. She's something of a known quantity. In the last five years, she's been picked up for shoplifting, possession of a controlled substance, prostitution, and passing bad checks. Suspended sentences in each instance except for the bad checks. Public defender got her off with just restitution plus probation, so she's never been inside except for a couple of overnighters waiting for arraignment."

"Somebody bail her out?"

"ROR, it says here. Judge must have been in a good mood, or else he was banging her."

"How long ago was that?"

"Just about a year. She's been clean since then, so more power to her."

"Not much of a public enemy, then. What have you got on her boyfriend?"

"Let's take a look. Okay, behind door number two we've got Mister Bobby Fury." A few keystrokes later we had our answer. "Ah, here he is. Robert James Furillo, age twenty-eight. He's got a record going back at least ten years. Before that, some juvenile stuff, but those records are sealed. After that, we're looking at vandalism, dismissed after community service, underage drinking, dismissed, public urination, dismissed, and DUI plus driving without insurance. That one resulted in a five-hundred-dollar fine and license suspended for six months. There's more shit like this, but all in all, I'd say he's just a minor league fuckup. Oh, no, wait a minute. Here we have a couple of arrests for assault. Both times, beat up a woman, both times charges dropped when the victim declined to press charges. You suppose he threatened them?"

"Or else they kissed and made up, no surprise," I said. "Was either one of those women Mickey Reddick, by any chance?"

"Doesn't say, just that the county attorney decided that without corroborating testimony there was insufficient evidence to go chasing after a misdemeanor assault charge. The last couple years, there's been nothing, so maybe he's cleaned up his act." He tapped the end of his pencil against his front teeth. "You like him for this runaway of yours?"

"She was seen with him at least twice. I figure it's worth a conversation."

"I suppose so, unless she turns up first. You do know, though, her mother's claiming this was a kidnap."

"Do you believe that?"

"Let me ask you first. Did you meet her old man?"

"Once. He turned up in my office yesterday. He put on an Old Testament act, like he thought he could turn me into a pillar of salt."

"Right, the guy's a nut job, probably next to impossible to live with. That's why I don't think she was grabbed," he said. "Otherwise, I'd have called in reinforcements first thing. I think the kid just plain ran away. Only problem is, once she's in the wind like she is now, almost anything is possible. My guess, though, is that without any money or valid identification, she won't be able to get very far."

"There's something else we need to think about," I said. "What I heard, Bobby supposedly told Gabrielle and her girlfriend he was in the business of making movies."

"And you're thinking what, porn? That's not good."

"She's a good-looking kid, Carl. Internet porn is a big business."

"It's legal," he said, "and it's easy money. All you need is a basement or a back yard or a motel room and a camcorder. Hell, on just one website alone there are links to more than thirty-six million videos, and more show up every day. Child pornography, though, that's another story. It's even more profitable than adult porn, but it's illegal as hell and it's very risky. Let's hope our boy is just looking for a good time, or maybe he hasn't done anything at all." He shrugged. "For all we know he's into educational films. You know, 'I really like this boy but he wants to go all the way, and I'm afraid if I say no, I'll lose him.'"

"I remember those from health class. They were a hoot."

Sutton stood up and put his coat on. He unlocked his desk drawer, took out his service weapon, and clipped the gun and holster to his belt.

"Going somewhere?" I asked.

"Take a ride with me."

"Where are we going?"

"I thought we could get some fresh air. Who knows, maybe we'll get a lead on our little princess."

We rode down in the elevator to the underground parking area and climbed into Sutton's cruiser, a plain white Ford Crown Vic that looked to be well past its retirement date. The paint was scratched, the carpet was dirty and the inside smelled of spilled coffee, tobacco smoke, and puke, all unsuccessfully perfumed over with liberal applications of Lysol.

Sutton read my thoughts. "This baby's coming up on four years old, which, if it was a prowl car or a state police vehicle would already be into its second life as a gypsy cab. Missing Persons, though, we don't drive the cars hard and we don't put on a lot of miles. Plus, the guys at the garage keep the oil changed and the antifreeze fresh, so we get the hand-me-downs, like this creampuff. The smell, though, there's not much they can do about that."

He was quiet as we left the police parking garage and drove downtown. We made a couple of turns before pulling up in front of a windowless, blue-painted cinder block building that had only a steel door and a number painted on the wall.

"You say you've got pictures?"

I handed him one from the envelope I had picked up at the photo shop. "Back in a minute," he said. "Sit tight." He walked to the door and pressed a bell. In a moment the door opened and he went inside. Five minutes later he was back.

"What was that?" I asked.

"Women's shelter," he said. "They do their best to stay under the radar, but the ones who need help seem to be able to find it. Sometimes stray kids wander in there, too. They can't be there long, though, because they're underage. If the kid doesn't want to go home, the staff there refers them to youth services where they can stay until a more permanent placement can be made. I'd have taken you along, but they know me and my being there doesn't raise any eyebrows. You look like you could be somebody's ex-husband."

We made a few more stops like that, at the Salvation Army Mission, a Catholic church, a temporary shelter called the Oasis Center, and two rescue missions. In each instance, Sutton took one of my photos and went in alone while I waited in the car, breathing the disinfectant-laden air that filled the passenger compartment like the smell of gladiolas at a funeral home.

"Don't know how much good any of those will do," he said after the last of his solo visits. "But these are all places open twenty-four hours a day, no questions asked. If she turns up at any of them, I'll get word."

"That's if she's on her own," I said. "I'm willing to bet she isn't."

"Maybe not, but it doesn't hurt to try. Let's go. We've got two more stops I want to make."

The first was at a McDonald's on Broadway, where he ordered two Big Macs at the drive-up window. The second was at the Greyhound depot on Fifth. Sutton ignored the yellow-painted curb and parked his car in a loading zone near the front doors. He picked up the bag with the Big Macs and we went inside. At that hour, the bus station was beginning to fill with travelers awaiting the arrival of the 11:25 bus from Chicago, departing at 11:45 for Atlanta.

"I was here yesterday," I told Sutton. "Those people working the counter wouldn't notice anything unusual if the ghost of Elvis stepped up to buy a one-way ticket to Memphis."

"Not interested in them," he said. "I'm interested in that raggedy-assed fella sitting way back there in the corner pretending not to see us. His name is Hamburger. That's what we call him, anyway because that's the only thing anybody's ever seen him eat. He might've had an actual name once, but he

90

says he doesn't remember what it is, and nobody else seems to know either. But he pretty much lives here at the bus station and he sees everybody that comes through. That can sometimes be useful more often than you might think."

Sutton waited until Hamburger finally turned his head in our direction. When he did, Sutton held up the McDonald's bag so the man could see it, and then pointed directly at him. The man nodded and we walked over to the bench where he appeared to have made himself at home. He had a plump pillow propped up behind his back and a duffel bag stuffed with who-knew-what underneath the bench.

"Gamble, this here is Hamburger. Hamburger, this is my friend Jackson Gamble. He's a PI. He helps me out sometimes, same as you. If he ever comes to you looking for help, I'd consider it a favor if you'd give it to him, okay?"

Hamburger looked me over from head to toe and then nodded. "If he's okay with you, Skipper, he's aces with me."

The man Sutton called Hamburger was small and wiry, with rheumy brown eyes. He wore a gray shirt and pants, like a custodian might wear, and a heavy black overcoat dirty enough that nothing short of a slow walk through a car wash would improve its appearance. It was hard to tell how old he was. He could have been fifty or he could have been eighty. His face and hands were weather-beaten, and if he had any teeth in his head, they weren't anyplace where I could see them.

"Brought you some lunch, Hamburger," Sutton said, handing over the McDonald's bag. "You might need to ask one of the ladies over at the lunch counter to toss it into the microwave for a few seconds after we're done here."

"Don't want to bother 'em none," he said, "I can warm 'em up under the hand dryer in the washroom."

"Whatever works," Sutton said. "Do you need a couple bucks for some coffee?"

The little man shook his head. "They give it to me no charge."

"Okay. Listen, Hamburger, I told my friend Gamble here that you might be able to do him some good with a little problem he's got, if you're willing.

I told him there ain't anybody in town better with faces than you are."

"You got that right, Skipper," Hamburger nodded animatedly. "I see 'em once, I don't forget." He turned to me. "What can I do you for, Mr. Gamble?"

I took out another of the duplicate photos and showed it to him. "I was wondering if you might have seen this girl come through the bus station, say, in the last two weeks or so. She's about fifteen, but she might look a little older."

He looked at the photo, then shook his head. "This little girl ain't been through here, at least not while I was watching. If she had, I'd a sure noticed. Yes, sir, she's a pretty one. I'd a noticed."

"You're sure?"

"Sure as anybody could be. I have kind of an eye for pretty girls."

"All right, thanks," I said. I gave him one of my cards. "If you do see her, could you give me a call, or call Detective Sutton? You can reverse the charges if you need to."

He gave me a toothless grin and patted his coat pocket. "Got me a phone right here. I got more stashed away in my locker. People always seem to be leavin' 'em behind when they get on the bus, so I just pick 'em up and put 'em in my locker. Don't know how folks can be that careless, these things bein' expensive and all. There must be near a dozen in there, most with good batteries."

"You have to admire his resourcefulness," I said after we got back into the car. "It's a wonder, though, that he makes out with just an occasional Big Mac."

"I slipped two twenties into the bag," Sutton said. "He's a Desert Storm vet. I like to help him out a little when I can. I check in every week or so, make sure he's doing okay and not creating any problems for the folks at the bus station. As a favor to me, they look out for him, too. Once in a while, he spots somebody we're looking for, so he more or less earns his keep. If he eyeballs our girl, we'll know it."

"If he does," I said, "I'll buy him the best meal he's ever eaten."

Chapter Twelve

Sutton and I parted ways back at police headquarters. He went back to his desk, to do whatever cops do when they're not on the street. I drove back to the office. I parked my car in a public lot on Fourth Street and walked around the corner to a deli where I ordered pastrami on light rye, a bag of chips, and two cans of Diet Coke. Then I headed back to the office. I spread my lunch out on my desk, leaned back in my chair, and tried to piece what I knew about Gabrielle Hawkins's disappearance together into some sort of logical order.

That she was with Bobby Fury now, or had been at the time she vanished was the linchpin of my investigation. If I went with that assumption, everything made at least a modicum of sense. Gabrielle was a pretty girl, on the cusp of young womanhood. Assuming what Ginger Aldrich had told me was accurate, Gabrielle was unhappy with her home life and wanted to get away. Maybe not forever, but at least for a while, if only to see what life was like outside of Jacktown.

Bobby Fury, who likely started out as an accidental acquaintance, and who made some big noises about making movies, would have seemed to Gabrielle to be her ticket to an immeasurably more exciting life. Whether she knew that Bobby's métier was low-budget porn, if in fact that's what it was, seemed doubtful. Girls that age tend to be very self-conscious about their body image, and not at all inclined to take their clothes off in front of a camera. There would have been ways to force her into participating, but even makers of porn films need to keep records to prove their talent is of legal age. Child pornography is not a trivial offense, and I doubted whether Bobby would have wanted to risk prison time plus a lifetime jacket as a sex offender for something like that. On the other hand, of all the kinky variations of porn, and there are thousands, including S&M, amateur, gay sex, group sex, you name it, nothing is hotter or more profitable than kiddie porn—if you can get away with it.

But if making a film—any kind of film—with Gabrielle in a starring role was not what this was about, then what? I supposed it was possible Bobby had done nothing more than taken a liking to her and was giving her a place to stay, or taken her to a shelter, until she got herself sorted out. That would have been innocent enough, maybe even forgivable, if not particularly smart. Or Bobby could be a middleman whose role was to deliver girls to an unknown third party to be forced into prostitution, or to be spirited out of the country and sold into the overseas sex trade.

Finally, there was the real possibility that, whatever all this had started out to be, somewhere along the line things had gone wrong and Gabrielle was buried in a shallow grave where she would never be found. And with that, I realized that after nearly three days on the case, the trail had taken me no farther than Bobby Fury. And that meant it was time to go and see Mickey Reddick.

I gathered up the trash from my lunch and tossed it into the wastebasket before walking down the hall to the restroom to wash my hands. Then I went back to the office to lock up before heading out. When I got there, I found I had a visitor. Her name was Roberta Jeffries. Mrs. Roberta Jeffries. She was medium height, thin, wearing a man's flannel shirt, a pair of faded blue jeans, dark sunglasses, and dirty white sneakers. She might have been attractive, but I couldn't tell from her appearance at that moment. She had either taken a nasty fall down a long flight of stairs or else somebody had done a very thorough job of beating the living hell out of her. When I opened the door to the inner office so she could come through, she rose gingerly, as if every movement was cause for considerable pain.

After she was seated, I said, "How can I help you, Mrs. Jeffries?"

She took off her sunglasses and leaned toward me so I could see her face. Both eyes had been blackened; the left eye was still partly swollen shut.

There was an ugly purple bruise that extended from her hairline down to her jaw and she had a split lip that had taken half a dozen stitches to close.

"My husband William, he done this to me night before last." She spoke with some difficulty and I could see that a couple of her lower front teeth had been knocked loose just below the gum line. A partial retainer was holding them in place.

"Have you told this to the police?"

She shook her head. "It wouldn't do no good. They'd just keep him for a day or two and then they'd turn him loose. Then he'd come back and do me all over again."

"Where is your husband now, Mrs. Jeffries?"

She made a small movement with her hands and I could see that even the effort of doing that was painful. "Who knows? Gone, drunk, shacked up with some woman who don't know better than to let him through the door. But he'll come back and when he does, it'll likely start all over again."

I said, "I wish I could help you, Mrs. Jeffries, I'm afraid there isn't very much I can do. I'm not a policeman. I can talk to your husband, maybe shake him up a little, but if what you've told me is correct...."

"You sayin' you don't believe me?"

"I'm sorry. That didn't come out right. I believe you, but you really do need to go to the police. What your husband did to you is felonious assault. If you file a complaint, he'll be arrested. He won't be able to hurt you again."

She looked at me with eyes that were flat and empty of emotion, as if she were already dead and was just waiting to slip into final darkness. I'd seen that look before, too many times, and I waited for what I knew she was going to say to me next.

"I want you to kill the son of a bitch. Go find him and then shoot him down dead in the street and back your car up over him to make sure he's finished. You do that and I'll pay whatever you want."

"I'm sorry, Mrs. Jeffries," I told her. "I really can't do that."

"Figured you'd say that." She nodded her head sadly. "Then you need to talk to Wanda. She said you could help me."

I felt my stomach drop. Wanda Beaudry was a woman I'd met several years earlier when I was working with the cops. She was a couple of years older than me and was from Shreveport, Louisiana. Like me, she was relatively new on the job and was assigned part-time to the district attorney's office. We'd worked together on a few investigations, and although we'd never become sexually involved—she claimed I wasn't her type, though I never found out what that was—we eventually got to be pretty good friends. She was smart and honest on the job and warm, outgoing and funny when it was time to play. But all that changed, abruptly and forever, about two years after we had met.

One night late I got a telephone call from Wanda. She needed help. When I got to her apartment, I found her flat on the floor in much the same condition as Roberta Jeffries, only worse. The unemployed construction worker she'd been living with had gotten drunk and worked her over so thoroughly that at first, I wasn't sure whether she was going to live or die. She was an officer of the law and she carried an off-duty weapon, so why she didn't just shoot him there and then and claim self-defense, I'll never know. But then, why do the best women so often seem to find the worst men?

As carefully as I could, I put a cushion from the couch under her head and covered her with my coat. Then I called for help. While we waited for the ambulance to arrive, I held her hand and comforted her as best I could. During those few minutes, she neither spoke nor cried. She just stared at the ceiling and squeezed my hand. To the best of my knowledge, except for the time she spent in the hospital, that was the last time she had allowed any man other than me to touch her, except to shake hands.

In addition to cracked ribs and a broken arm, the beating had also shattered the orbital bone around her left eye. Although she didn't lose the eye, her vision was blurred and when she was finally able to return to work, she was reassigned to an administrative post in the personnel department. When she refused to press charges, I had a pretty good idea what was going to happen next. I just couldn't do anything to stop it. Nor, for that matter, did I want to.

It took a couple of months, but one morning the former boyfriend turned up dead, stuffed inside the firebox of a retired steam locomotive that had been donated to the city and placed behind a fence in Centennial Park. He had been shot in both kneecaps, both elbows, and then once in the back of the head. Some kids playing around the engine a week or so later noticed a smell coming from inside the firebox. They opened the butterfly doors expecting to find a dead raccoon and instead got the surprise of their lives.

From the amount of blood on his sleeves and pant legs, it was apparent that there had been a considerable amount of time between the fourth shot and the last one that finished him. And although the gun was never found, ballistics determined that the weapon used was a .22 caliber Walther that had gone missing from the police evidence locker. Though the weapon was never recovered and the evidence was circumstantial, the investigating detectives had no trouble figuring out what happened. Under the circumstances, there was no choice except to prosecute. The female A.D.A. assigned seemed not to be interested in putting a great deal of effort into prosecuting her case, and Wanda was never convicted of anything. However, her career with the police was finished. With her disability payments plus an off-the-books payoff that was more of a going-away present than a settlement to avoid a lawsuit, she enrolled at Vanderbilt and got a master's degree in sociology, then opened a shelter for battered and abused women. She's still running that shelter today, and occasionally, when she needs help with a special problem, like the one standing before me now, she gets in touch with me. And she always has the same reason. There is a score to be settled. I go along just to make sure things don't go sideways and somebody ends up getting killed.

"Wanda said I should show you the rest." Roberta Jeffries stood and unbuttoned the cuffs of her shirt. She pulled up the sleeves and showed me the ligature marks on her wrists. Then she opened the shirt and let it fall off her shoulders. Her back and breasts were marked with deep red welts as if she had been beaten with a heavy strap.

She started to unsnap the waistband of her jeans. "You want to see the rest of it?" Her face showed neither shame nor embarrassment, and I realized this was not the first time she had been down this road.

"No," I said, picking up her shirt and holding it so she could slip it back on. "Have you seen a doctor?"

"At the shelter. She says I'll be okay, I guess. But…"

"I understand," I said. "It's going to take some time. Are you staying at the shelter?"

"Got to, for now at least. If I go back home, there's no telling what William will do."

"I understand. I'll call Wanda. Things aren't ever going to be the same, but they will get better. I expect somebody's already told you that. We'll do what we can."

That seemed to be all she wanted to hear. "Wanda says I can trust you." Then she thanked me for my time, put her sunglasses back on, and left.

I waited fifteen minutes then picked up the phone. A familiar voice answered on the second ring.

I said, "It's me, Wanda."

"Did you talk to Berty?"

"You mean Mrs. Jeffries? I talked to her."

"Did she show you what he did?"

"Yes."

"All of it?"

"Enough of it."

She said, "He didn't just knock her around, Gamble, he came close to killing her. After he beat her, she couldn't stop screaming so he stuffed a rag into her mouth and whipped her with his belt until she passed out. Then he locked her in a closet and left her there all night."

I said, "It's not your fight, Wanda, you've moved on. Let the cops handle it. Your job is to help heal the victim."

"Gamble, we can't let this go. You know that."

"I'm not saying let it go. I'm just saying it's not our fight."

"I need your help. Either you get on board or I'll do it alone."

I sighed into the mouthpiece, knowing she wasn't bluffing. "When?"

"I need to check this guy out first, find out what his movements are. Once that's done, I'll give you a call."

"All right," I said. But I knew that, whatever Wanda was planning, it would not turn out well for Mr. Jeffries. And I knew I wanted no part of it.

Chapter Thirteen

After my meeting with Roberta Jeffries and my telephone conversation with Wanda Beaudry, what little enthusiasm I still had for the Gabrielle Hawkins case was quickly evaporating, replaced by a feeling of anger and revulsion. It seemed as though everything I'd experienced in the last couple of days revolved around women who had been mistreated by their men in one way or another. It made me want to just go home, go back to bed and pull the covers up over my head.

Instead, I reminded myself that there was work to be done. Gabrielle was still missing. That was a minus. On the plus side, Jericho Hawkins hadn't come back to stuff a snake down my pants. Delsey Lee Hawkins hadn't called to fire me yet, and even if she had, I still had Maggie Totten as a backup client. With that in mind, I headed out to meet with Mickey Reddick. Since fewer people these days have landlines, she wasn't listed in the telephone directory. I couldn't find a number or an address online either, but Carly had given me a fairly good idea of where Mickey lived, and being the man of action that I am, I locked the door to the inner office and headed out.

Mickey Reddick's apartment was in a complex called Kingswood. It squatted dispiritedly on several acres of rolling hillside across from the old Metro Airport site. Kingswood's most distinctive feature, apart from the mind-numbing drone of jet aircraft on final approach to BNA airport and traffic on the Interstate, was that all its buildings were phonied up on the outside to look like medieval castles, complete with plywood battlements, miniature turrets, and fanciful coats-of-arms tacked to the wall.

I followed the directions I'd gotten the previous evening and parked in front of Building Three. It was called The Glengarry, and, like all the other buildings in the complex, was a two-story job with paired outside doors at either end. For no particular reason except that it was closer to where I was parked, I tried the doors at the south end first. Luck was with me. Inside the foyer were six ground-floor apartments and a stairway leading up to six more second-floor units. I checked the mailboxes and found the name REDDICK penciled onto a plain white card taped to the box for apartment 2-B.

I climbed the stairs and rapped on 2-B's door. My knock was answered by a slightly built, dark-haired young woman wearing a baggy gray sweatshirt and a pair of cutoff blue jean shorts.

I said, "Mickey Reddick?"

She looked at me as if she had been expecting somebody else. "Maybe. Who're you?"

I studied her briefly. She had a face that said the drugs, whatever, they were, had long since stopped being fun. She was underweight. She smelled bad. Her skin was sallow and marred with acne. Her teeth were stained, and she looked years older than her actual age, which I guessed to be about twenty-five. With a lot of makeup and something done with her hair, she might have looked passable in the semi-darkness of the Cowgirl, at least as long as she kept her mouth closed. Under conventional lighting, she looked as if her remaining lifespan could be measured in months rather than decades.

"My name is Jackson Gamble. I'm a private investigator." I gave her a look at my ID. "I'd like to ask you a couple of questions if it's all right."

"Oh yeah, what about?"

"Bobby Fury. I understand he used to be a friend of yours."

Sudden fear chased the blank look from her eyes. "I don't know anybody named Bobby Fury."

"Hang on a minute." I stuck my foot into the opening so she couldn't close the door in my face. "I spoke to another friend of yours last night, somebody named Carly Barrett. The way she told it, you and Bobby used to be an item."

"Then she told it wrong, because I don't know any Carly Barrett, either. I think maybe you got me mixed up with somebody else."

I gave her a knowing grin. "You're going to have to do a lot better than that, Mickey."

"Look, mister, I don't know you and I don't know any of these people you're asking about, either. So why don't you just fuck off before I start yelling for help?" She put both hands on the door and pushed, but with my foot wedged in the way, it wasn't going anywhere.

I took a roll of the dice. "Withholding evidence in a criminal investigation is a felony, you know."

Snake eyes. "You're not a cop and this don't sound like a criminal investigation. Now I'm not fooling. I'm gonna start hollering rape if you're not out of here in two seconds."

I said, "What's the hurry, Mickey? Are you expecting a delivery this morning? Which is it, meth or crack?" I put a look of concern on my face. "Please don't tell me fentanyl. That shit will kill you."

"I don't know what you're talking about."

"Let's don't kid one another. I'm willing to bet there isn't a person who knows you're alive who doesn't also know you've got a problem. All I need from you is five minutes of your time and a little bit of information and then I'll be out of your life forever. Either that, or else we can just sit here and when your connection shows up, I'll throw him down the stairs, and then if he can get up and walk away, maybe he'll come back tomorrow. By then, you should be in pretty tough shape."

"You wouldn't do that."

I said, "You're starting to look a little shaky, Mickey. I'd say your delivery service is running late this morning."

She glared at me with undisguised hostility, then moved back out of the doorway. "All right, come on in and ask your questions. But make it fast, I—well, like you said, somebody's coming over. You need to be gone before he gets here."

I went inside the apartment and sat down on the arm of a sagging, unmade sleeper couch. Mickey sat across the room, in a plastic and aluminum lawn chair. Other than the sleeper couch and a folding TV tray that held a flickering black and white TV set, it was the only piece of furniture in the room. There were dishes in the sink and magazines on the floor. An unmistakable odor of days-old kitchen waste hung in the air.

"Love what you've done with the place," I said, gesturing expansively. "You fix this up yourself?"

"Yeah, well, I'm not planning on sticking around here too much longer. I've had about all I can take of this two-bit cracker town. Soon as I get a little money together, I'm splitting for California. I've got friends there with connections in the movie business."

"I hope it works out for you. Meantime, what are you doing for rent money these days? Carly said she's worried about you."

"I've been...I haven't been feeling good. I'm a little behind on the rent right now."

I said, "Mickey, I'm not a doctor, but I can tell you if you don't get yourself cleaned up pretty soon, you won't be around a year from now. I can put you in touch with some people who can help you, if that's what you want. The first call is the hardest, but after that, it gets easier." When she didn't respond, I said, "While you're thinking about that, why don't you tell me what you can about Bobby Fury?"

"I never said I knew him. You did."

"And I never said I believed you. Look, I heard about what happened at the Cowgirl. Under the circumstances, I can't blame you for being scared of him, or for not wanting to get mixed up with him again. But right now, I'm looking for a young girl who's missing from home. I think Bobby might have her with him, and I have a bad feeling that unless I find her soon, what Bobby did to you, he'll end up doing the same thing to her."

She jerked her head toward the kitchen. "I think there's some change on the counter in there. Why don't you use it to call somebody who gives a shit?"

"I've got a better idea, Mickey. Why don't you use it?"

"Me?" She pulled a pack of cigarettes from the pocket of her jeans. She shook one loose and lit it, coughing harshly as she did so. "Who would I call?"

102

"The little girl's mother. If you don't want to tell me what you know, maybe you could tell her. The kind of shape she's in now, I know she'd be especially grateful for your cooperation."

Without answering me directly, Mickey wedged her cigarette in the corner of her mouth and held out her right hand toward me, palm up. It was marked with a quarter-sized, angry-looking red patch, blackened in the center.

"Know what that is, Mister Detective?"

"Yep. Cigarette burn."

"You've seen 'em before?"

"I used to be a cop," I said. "I've seen a lot of things."

"The son of a bitch." She took a deep drag on her cigarette and balanced it on the arm of her chair. "Bobby did this to me. After what happened at work, I didn't see him for nearly six weeks. Then two nights ago he showed up here, acting like nothing ever happened. I told him I didn't want to see him no more."

"And that was enough to set him off?"

"Not right away. First, he tried to be all nice and kissy-face, you know, shit like that. But I knew all he wanted was a quick roll in the hay and then he'd be out the door. I knew that if I let him do me then, we'd be right back where we were before, so I pushed him away and told him if he didn't get out right now, I was going to call the police. So, he said, well, if that's the way you want it, that's fine, here's a little something you can tell them about when they get here."

She paused, as if to gather her thoughts. "I help you find him, mister, you got to promise me that when you do, you won't let him do this to anybody else ever again. You got to kill him. You got to put him deep in the ground, 'cause if you don't, he'll be right back here to do me worse."

That made two women in less than two hours who wanted me to kill their men, and for good reason. The thought came to me that I should start a subsidiary operation as a hitman for hire.

"I know some people, Mickey, and if you let them help you, I promise he won't hurt you again. Just tell me where I can find him."

She took another drag on her cigarette and exhaled the smoke forcefully in my direction. "Like I said, we haven't been exactly close for a while. But when we were still together, he was renting a place over on Antioch Pike. I don't remember the number, but it was close to the railroad bridge. The damn trains would go by there all night long. The only thing is, he might not be there anymore. Last time I was with him, he had started looking around for another place closer to the city, but I don't know if he's found anything yet. Like I said, except for the other night we haven't been in touch a whole lot lately."

"Okay, so he was looking for a place in the city. You know where?"

"No idea."

"Let's try something else." I took one of the copies I had made from the photo Delsey had given me out of my pocket and showed it to Mickey. "This is the girl I'm looking for. Have you ever seen her before?"

"She looks young. Who is she?"

"Her name is Gabrielle." I showed her another photo, this time the one I found taped to the drawer in Gabrielle's bedroom. "Maybe this will jog your memory."

She looked at it intently. "Oh, yeah, right, I remember her now. That was clear back in the summer, before Bobby and me broke up. We were driving around one day and we picked up this girl and another one, her friend, I guess, and took them to the park. The friend was taking pictures with her phone. I guess I didn't get at first this was the same girl as we saw that day. Funny thing was, now that I'm remembering this, is that Bobby seemed to know just where to look for these girls."

I nodded. "Okay, so what did you do with them after you left the park?"

"Nothing. We dropped 'em off close to where they lived and took off. Far as I know, that was the end of it."

"And Bobby never said anything about her after that?"

"No. I mean, he might have got married to her the next day, but I wouldn't know. Bobby never talked about other girls around me." She rubbed her hands against her legs where they stuck out below her cutoffs, as if she were feeling a sudden chill. I was beginning to worry if I didn't get something useful from Mickey soon, her withdrawal symptoms would make any further conversation pointless.

"Let's try something else," I said. "You mentioned Bobby was looking for a new place. Rental property in the city is generally more expensive than it is in Antioch. Why do you suppose he wants to move into the high-rent district?"

"He's been talking about making movies. He thought it would be easier to find actors who would be willing to work with him if they didn't have to come all the way out to where he was living before."

"Sounds reasonable," I agreed. "But he's going to need money to pay his talent and to buy recording equipment and get a studio set up. Does he have that kind of money?"

"He doesn't. But he's got an investor, a guy named Jack Olin. He's supposedly going to advance Bobby some money to get started."

"Where can I find Jack Olin?"

She shrugged. "I don't know. He works out of an office downtown someplace, in one of those tall buildings. I don't know which one."

"Well, then, here's another question. What interest would this Jack Olin have in bankrolling an inexperienced filmmaker?"

"Jack Olin is already in the movie business. He makes porn and puts it up on the Internet. I figured maybe he needed help making more of it."

An unwelcome idea came to me. "Would you happen to know where Jack Olin recruits his actors?"

"All over. Most of the people who do porn are pros. A lot of them like what they do. If you're good at it, it pays pretty well. You can make fifteen hundred or so for a ten-minute scene, more if it involves bondage or a gangbang or something like that." She gave me a sly look. "Are you into bondage, Mister Detective? For two hundred bucks you can tie me up and do whatever you want with me."

"Not really my jam," I said, "but I appreciate the offer. Tell me more about Jack Olin's talent. Are they all professional actors?"

"Not everybody. I know some of the girls from the Cowgirl have made videos with him. Other times they just find people where they can, you know, out-of-work musicians, people who need money, people just looking for a new high. I told Bobby I might try it, but he said, first, you know, first I'd need to get cleaned up a little bit. Said I might not look too good in a close-up."

"The camera is unforgiving," I said. I had a couple more questions I wanted to ask, but a hard knock on the door brought an end to our conversation.

She locked her eyes on the door as if Christmas morning was waiting on the other side. "My, uh, friend is here, Mr. Detective. You're gonna have to go now."

"I understand," I said. As I got up to leave, I picked up the photos I'd shown her and which she had dropped on the floor, and placed one of my cards on the kitchen counter.

"Remember what I said about people who can help you, so you don't miss any more rent payments. Else, give me a call if you want and I'll put you in touch."

On my way out, I took a careful look at the individual standing in the hallway next to Mickey's door. He wore sunglasses and a baseball cap turned backward, which made him look like nobody and everybody else at the same time.

"How's business?" I asked him.

"The fuck you care?"

"Just making conversation," I said. Then with my left hand I swatted his cap and sunglasses off his head and with my right I grabbed a fistful of his hair and slammed his head against the wall, once, and then a second time. His eyes went out of focus and he sank to his knees on the floor.

"You might want to think about raising your prices," I told him. "I hear this is a dangerous neighborhood.

Chapter Fourteen

It took a couple of phone calls before I was able to learn that Jack Olin was president of a company called J-LOW Productions and that the office was located in the Life and Casualty Building, easy walking distance from my office. It was a nice afternoon, warmer than it had been the day before and just as sunny. The sidewalks along Church Street held only a few people, who I guessed were either getting an early start on the weekend or hurrying back to the office following an afternoon meeting or a lunch date that might have run a little long. I hoped Jack Olin was the type who didn't mind putting in a full day's work, even on a Friday.

I checked the directory inside the lobby entrance of the L&C Building and found the suite number for J-LOW Productions, Inc. I rode the elevator up to the eighteenth floor and followed the arrows around to Suite 1810. It was all the way at the end of the corridor on the south side of the building. A small brass nameplate attached to the frosted glass door confirmed I was in the right place.

I pushed the door open and walked into a reception area that was large, modern, and decorated with calculated showiness. There were chrome and glass occasional tables, framed prints by Marc Chagall and Alexander Calder, and a fair-sized, modernistic sculpture that could have been a Henry Moore perched atop a mirrored pedestal. A powder blue suede sectional couch that probably cost more than the rent on my office for an entire year extended the length of one wall and part of another. The carpet was royal blue with deep, thick pile. At the end of the reception area was a desk made of oiled, natural oak. Seated there, typing at a word processor, was a luxury blonde who looked as if she had been placed there by the decorator. I let my eyes do a slow crawl. She was in her mid-twenties with blue-gray eyes and a smile that could have melted ice inside a deep freeze. She wore a tan blazer and a bright yellow satin blouse. The top three buttons had been left strategically unbuttoned. An engraved metal sign on her desk said her name was Arlene Olive.

She stopped typing and took off the recorder headset. "May I help you?"

"Let's find out," I said. "I'd like to see Jack Olin."

She let her lips compress into the tiniest of frowns and flipped open an appointment book. "Is Mr. Olin expecting you, Mister…"

"Gamble," I finished for her. And no, I'm sorry, he's not expecting me."

She shut the book again and folded her hands on top of it in a gesture of finality. "Then I'm sorry, but you'll have to come back another time. Mr. Olin is a very busy man and he never sees anyone without an appointment. That's the rule."

"No exceptions?"

"Not unless you're somebody pretty special. Are you somebody pretty special, Mr. Gamble?"

"I like to think so."

Her eyes were cool; beautiful, but cool. "In that case, all you have to do is make me think so, too."

"What if I told you, I was his insurance agent and I urgently need his signature on a couple of policy endorsements."

She shook her head. "Not good enough. And not true, either. Dave Mitchell handles all Mr. Olin's insurance."

"Well, then, how about if I told you my real name is Dick Steele. I'm hung like a horse, I bat from both sides and if your boss doesn't see me right now, he'll miss signing his next star attraction?"

"Better," she allowed, warming a little this time. "But you haven't quite convinced me yet. Want another turn at bat, or should I go ahead and call security now?"

"Nope, best I can do," I said, "so let's try this." I took out one of my cards and wrote "Bobby Fury" on the back of it. "Give this to Mr. Olin, would you? Tell him I'll wait five minutes and then I'm going for the cops."

She looked at me and then at the card and then back at me and shook her head dubiously. "You're kidding me, right? I mean, this is a joke, isn't it?"

"Sure, it is, but play along anyway." I gave her a conspiratorial wink. "He'll get a big laugh out of it." I looked at my watch. "Four and a half minutes." She hesitated, then shrugged and disappeared through the door to the right of her desk, card in hand. I sat down on the couch and started thumbing through a year-old copy of *People*. Did anybody, I wondered, ever read *People* outside of a waiting room?

I was skimming through an article about how all the hottest celebrities were accessorizing their fall wardrobes when Arlene Olive emerged from behind the door and sat back down behind her desk, a little wide-eyed and red in the face. She didn't look at me and she didn't say anything; she just stared at the screen of her word processor.

"No trouble, I hope?"

"Nothing I haven't heard before," she said, her voice a little weak. "But if all this really is your idea of a joke, I better warn you, he wasn't laughing when I left just now."

Before I could reply to that, the com line on her phone buzzed. She picked it up and listened briefly, then hung up. "Mr. Olin will see you now, Mr. Gamble. Go through the door, then all the way down to the end of the hallway."

I could have found it without directions. Olin's office was as big as an aircraft hangar, and decorated just as elaborately as the waiting area, right down to the blue suede couch and the fancy sculpture on the glass pedestal. Nearest the door was a glass-topped conference table. Three of the walls were hung with modern art prints. The fourth wall, behind Olin's desk, held a large window that overlooked the southern part of the city. Eighteen stories up, it was quite a view. From where I stood, I could see Union Station, part of the Vanderbilt University campus on West End, and even the old office building on the corner of Sixteenth and Hayes where I hung out my shingle when I first started in the private detective business.

Olin was seated in front of the window at an executive model of the desk

Arlene Olive occupied in the waiting room. He was a big man, about fifty years old with a tan, craggy face that would probably need attention to remove melanoma lesions one day. He had bushy eyebrows and a full head of long, prematurely white hair that, together with the tan, made him look like an updated version of the late Charlie Rich. He wore a mint green sport coat and a white knit shirt that was open at the throat. An abundant growth of dark chest hair that reached all the way to his neck showed above his open collar.

On the other side of the office, sitting in a chair tilted back against the wall, was another man. He was younger than Olin, and me, for that matter, with the chiseled good looks of a Hollywood action hero and the muscular build of a WWE superstar. He was dressed in stylishly faded Levis, snakeskin cowboy boots, sunglasses, and a western-style shirt like the one worn by the old Marlboro Man. His arms and his neck, up to his jawline were covered with elaborate tattoos in bird-of-paradise shades of red, blue, and green. These, I knew were expensive and time-consuming to apply. He was picking at his teeth with the corner of a business card, probably mine, and trying his best to measure up to the image of a rough, tough, *hombre* who had seen it all before, and wasn't in the least impressed by me. It made the feeling mutual.

Since it didn't appear that an invitation was in the offing, I walked in and sat down in one of the visitor's chairs facing the desk. Olin just sat there, staring at me as if he expected me to sprout feathers and start flapping around the room. Finally, he cleared his throat.

"I got your message, Mr. Gamble. What do you want?"

"Just the usual," I said. "A three-picture deal, cable TV residuals, percentage points if I can get them. I won't insist on that, though."

A voice behind me, the Marlboro Man, said, "When Mr. Olin asks you a question, you need to give him a straight answer, Snoopy. Otherwise, you'll be walking out of here with your head tucked under your arm."

"Impressive. How long have you been practicing to use that line on somebody?"

Olin chuckled softly to himself. "I would advise you not to make the mistake of taking my associate too lightly, Mr. Gamble. Among his other attributes, Vincent holds a master's degree from the University of the South."

"He majored in what, *film noir* dialog?"

"Physical education, plus the United States Marine Corps."

"Right," I said. "So, then that makes him more powerful than a locomotive. But is he faster than a speeding bullet?"

"Excuse me?"

I flipped my jacket open so he could see the Colt .380 I had tucked into a shoulder rig hanging beneath my left armpit. "I asked you, is he faster than a speeding bullet? Because if he so much as looks like he's about to get out of that chair, we're all going to have the chance to find out. And before you think about reaching into your desk drawer for whatever you got stuck in there, if any shooting starts, the one that's going to get shot first is you."

"I see." His eyes flickered back and forth between me and the man seated across the room. "Vincent, I wonder if you'd mind letting Mr. Gamble and me have a bit of privacy, just for a minute."

"Are you sure, Mr. Olin?" Vincent, now that I knew his name, sounded disappointed. "It wouldn't be any problem for me to throw this nosy bastard back out on the street where he came from."

Olin shook his head. "No point in stirring the pot too much until we find out what's in the soup. Just don't wander off. I'll holler if I need you, thanks." He waited until Vincent was out of the office and shut the door behind him.

"Now, then, Mr. Gamble, you're sitting in my office right now because you led me to believe you had something you wanted to discuss that might be of interest to me. Well, here you are." He looked meaningfully at his watch. "And it's Friday afternoon and it's just about time for me to head for the barn, so if it's not too much trouble, maybe we could just get down to business." He leaned forward in his chair and folded his hands on his desk.

"So, I'll ask you again, sir. What can I do for you? And before you start, I assume it's got something to do with the name you've written on the back of your card."

"It does," I said. "He's got something I want. I thought you might want to help me get it."

"What makes you think I even know who this fella is?"

"Because if you didn't know him, why would I be sitting here?"

That bought me a smile. "Point taken. And just what is it you think I can do for you, Mr. Gamble?"

I said, "Do we really have to fuck around like this? Look, I know Bobby Furillo, or Fury if you prefer, has a financial arrangement with you, but that's not my issue. I also have a pretty good idea what business you're both in, and frankly, that's not my issue either. Hell, I might have even seen one or two of your pictures somewhere along the line. You're giving people what they want, and that's fine with me. But right now, I need to find Bobby Fury, and I think you have a pretty good idea where I should be looking."

He considered that. "And why do you need to find him?"

"As I said, he has something I want."

"And what would that be?"

"A fourteen-year-old girl who looks like she's eighteen. For all I know, she might even have Bobby believing she's eighteen. But the thing is, she's not, she's fourteen, going on fifteen, and her mother misses her badly."

When he didn't say anything to that, I said, "Look, Mr. Olin, here's the situation. I have no intention of causing any trouble for you. I've been asked to find this kid. The cops are looking for her too, but they're busy and for the moment, they seem to be spinning their wheels. Otherwise, they would have already paid you a visit. So, I can help them or I can help you. Either way, all I want is the girl. Once she's home safe, you'll never see me again."

A small smile flickered across his face. "So then, that's what you think I can do for you. What do you think you can do for me?"

"I can see to it this problem gets resolved right here, right now. You get hold of Bobby. Tell him I want the girl back. Her name is Gabrielle. Here's her picture." I took one of the copies I had made and slid it across Olin's desk.

"Either you or Bobby, I don't care who, gets in touch with me by Monday morning and tells me where she is. I'll go and pick her up, and if she's okay, that's the end of it. If she's not, or if I don't hear, I'll be back and I'll bring reinforcements."

"What do you think that will accomplish? What I'm doing is perfectly legal."

"As long as what you're doing only involves consenting adults, you're right. But if a minor child is involved, that's something else altogether. If it turns out you're planning to use her in one of your films, or if that's what Bobby Fury is doing, as long as he's working for you, you'll go down with him. And even if you have a good lawyer and no charges are filed, I wonder whether your friends at the country club know what you do for a living, not to mention the women at your wife's garden club. I'm guessing they all think you make inspirational films for Christian organizations."

"Sometimes we do. Did you know that?"

"I'm sure the Lord will bless you for it."

"How 'bout this?" he said. "How 'bout I just write you a check? Maybe pay you to go fishing down in Costa Rica for a week? Maybe get a little sunshine, maybe take an attractive companion with you?"

I said, "Look, Mr. Olin, I didn't come here to shake you down. I'm guessing you have nothing to do with this girl. I think you're way too smart for that. But it doesn't change the fact that she's missing and her mother wants her back. I think you're the man who can help me get it done. Now you have my number. I'll expect your call." When he didn't answer, I said, "Do we have a deal?"

He leaned back in his chair and propped one leg up on the top of his desk. He was enjoying himself now. "Let me ask you something, Mr. Gamble. Do you have a lot of friends?"

"A few, I guess."

"Are they good friends?"

"Some are, some not so much. Where are we going with this?"

"Friends are good to have," he said, rolling right past my question. "They can help you sometimes, when you have a problem. Other times you can help them right back. Take right now, for instance. From what I've been hearing, it sounds like to me we both have a problem. Your problem is you need to find this little girl, whoever she is. You want help from me, but I'm not your friend. On the other hand, my problem is you, so you can't help me, either. Means we're sort of stuck, if you see what I mean. You want me to help find this girl and I want you to go away and not come back.

He shifted in his chair. "Only thing is, I don't know where she is. I've never met her and I've never seen this picture before. You say she's with Bobby Fury, and okay, maybe she is. So, let's do this. Let's give it until Monday, like you said. I'll shake the trees a little and see if she falls out. If she does, I'll make it clear to Bobby he needs to turn her over to you. But if she doesn't, well then, you need to start looking someplace else. Does that seem reasonable?"

"It does," I said.

"Good. Because unlike you, I have lots of friends, and if I have any trouble from you down the road, I'll get in touch with one or two of them, and then your friends, if you have any, will have to hire somebody to try and find you. Understood?"

When I didn't say anything, he said, "I'll take that as a yes. Now, if there isn't anything else?"

"Just one more thing. If I see that idiot, excuse me, that Master of Arts Vincent in the lobby, or the elevator, or anywhere else on my way out of here, I will shoot him. Does that seem reasonable to you?"

"Mister Gamble, I think we have come to an understanding. I like that."

Backtracking through the lobby, I passed by Arlene Olive's desk. She had her phone to her ear and held up one finger indicating I should wait. I heard her say, "Will do," and then she hung up.

"Finished so soon? You only just got here."

"I didn't want to take up a lot of his time," I told her. "He seems like a busy man."

She gave me a look of mild amusement. "That he is."

"Tell me something, Arlene," I said, "because I'd really like to know. Why are you working here? You must know what this place is all about."

She gave a small shrug. "The pay is good, and it doesn't involve much real work. Just a little bit of typing. Plus, I meet people. Not all of them are in this business." She reached into her desk drawer and took out an unlabeled DVD tucked inside a plain paper sleeve. "Here, Mr. Olin said I should give this to you. His compliments."

"That's nice of him." I held up the DVD. "Will I be seeing you?"

"Not unless you come back here for some reason," she said. "Otherwise, I'm just front office eye candy."

I didn't know whether to thank her or just throw it into the wastebasket. Instead, I put it into my jacket pocket and walked out of the office. I held my breath all the way down the hall to the elevator stop. I half expected I would run into Olin's man Vincent, eager to show his boss that he was as tough as he made himself out to be. I didn't, though, and that left me with nothing to do on a Friday evening except go home and fall asleep in front of the television.

Chapter Fifteen

Maggie Totten lived in a townhouse complex in the Belle Meade area of the city, a community I wouldn't have thought she'd be able to afford on a teacher's salary. Unless, of course, she'd used her settlement from the school district—or perhaps the proceeds from her divorce. I wondered, but decided it might be better not to ask how she had managed it. It wasn't any of my business, and either answer would only have served to dredge up old, painful memories.

She must have been watching out the window when I drove up, because she was out the door and down her front steps before I was halfway out of the car. She looked terrific in a knee-length burgundy dress that revealed enough cleavage to create a traffic jam, black three-inch sling-back heels, and black stockings. The look was finished with a gray knit blazer. I wore a jacket and slacks, no tie. She was dressed for the prom. I should have rented a tux.

Since I wasn't sure what type of cuisine she favored, I picked a Cajun-themed spot that offered a fairly broad menu. It was a block or two off the beaten path and not usually frequented by celebrities, so I knew we would not be competing for a table with hordes of tourists hoping to get an autograph, or take a selfie with some country music bigfoot.

After we were seated with menus in hand, a waiter came and took our drink order. Maggie asked for an appletini, whatever that is. I ordered a Stella. While we waited, I filled her in on my conversations with Carl Sutton, Mickey Reddick, and Jack Olin. I left out any description of Mickey's condition, as well as my visit from Roberta Jeffries and my subsequent telephone conversation with Wanda Beaudry. At this early stage of our relationship, I had no wish to start things off talking about battered women. I also didn't want to have to explain my association with Wanda, nor how it was likely to involve me in very short order in a highly extralegal activity that was almost certain to leave Roberta Jeffries's husband with a lasting disability.

Maggie took a sip of her martini. The look on her face said it met expectations. "I'm interested in this Bobby Fury character. Do you really think he has Gabrielle with him?"

"Where else could she be," I said. "I think at a minimum, he has something to do with why she's gone. Maybe he listened to her story about how terrible things are at home and thought he could help her. Maybe he didn't do anything more than drive her to a runaway shelter and hasn't seen her since. It could be as innocent as that, but even so, he's the only real lead we have."

"But if you believe what his girlfriend said…"

"Ex-girlfriend," I corrected her.

"Ex-girlfriend, then. If you believe what she said, Bobby is not a nice guy. He takes advantage of women. And it sounds as if he's more than a little possessive. I mean, for all we know he could have told Gabrielle some sweet story and then headed off with her to God knows where. Have you thought about that?"

I took a swallow of my beer. "Yes."

"And if that's what happened, what do we do then?"

We were interrupted just then by the waiter who brought us fresh drinks and asked whether we were ready to order. Maggie chose Italian shrimp and grits, served over cheese polenta. I went for crawfish etouffee, and we decided to share an appetizer of calamari with remoulade sauce.

After the waiter had gone, Maggie said, "The question, in case you've forgotten, or if you're just avoiding it, was what do we do if he's taken her away?"

"You mean like out of state? Away that way?"

"Yes, like that. What then?"

"Well, if that's how it shakes out, the short answer is, there isn't much we

117

can do. At that point, it's a federal case and way over our heads. For the time being the police are doing what they can, and I'll follow up the leads I've developed on my own, but I don't have the resources to do anything more than that. There are other private investigative agencies with longer reaches, but they're expensive and there's no guarantee they'll get any better results. My guess, however, is that Bobby is still here in town. He wants to make movies, and his angel is here."

"Movies," she said. "As in pornographic movies?"

"Yes. It appears he wants to make pornographic movies, and he's got this guy Jack Olin who seems willing to back him. So, my thought is, he's apt to stay close to where the money's coming from."

I dipped a piece of calamari in the remoulade sauce and popped into my mouth. "I know this is going to sound funny, but I think that works in our favor."

She put her fork down and gave me a quizzical look. "You think it's good that Bobby is being given money to produce porn at the same time he's got an underaged girl strapped to his hip?"

"Not where I was going with this," I said. "I think it's to our advantage that he's found somebody like Jack Olin to give him financial backing."

"And that is because?"

"Because I don't think Bobby is likely to do anything to risk losing his financing. Look, I talked with Jack Olin. Starting off I gave him a little more smartass than I should have, but he didn't take the bait and he didn't have his sidekick throw me out on my ear. Instead, he listened to what I had to say. He wasn't happy, but he listened anyway. That tells me that, first, he doesn't see me as a danger to his business, which I would not be anyway since as far as I know, he isn't doing anything illegal. But it also told me he doesn't want any part of producing child pornography. Something like that could bring his whole enterprise crashing down around his ears. Not to mention what it would do to his standing, such as it is, within the business community.

"When I left his office yesterday, he made a point of having his receptionist hand me a DVD with a few of his videos on it. Last night I watched it. They're not going to win any Golden Globes, but they're actually better than a lot of the stuff you can find on the Internet."

She gave me a look of amusement. "And you would know about that, how?"

"Well," I said.

"Uh-huh, right. Lots of blow jobs?"

"Pretty much wall-to-wall."

"Well, don't get your hopes up too high on that score because it seems like a one-way proposition to me." She took a last swallow of her drink and set the glass down, hard. "I mean, think about it. In your entire life have you ever heard a woman say, 'You know, I'm looking forward, tonight, to having a dick in my mouth.'"

"I guess if that's the way you look at it."

"Okay, never mind that. What makes a Jack Olin porn film so good? I'd really like to know that."

"He uses multiple cameras. He shoots in high definition. The lighting is good. The audio is clear. I'd say he spends a lot of money to get these videos to look right."

"You seem well informed. Should I be worried about you?"

"Not where that's concerned. The point is, whether we approve of it or not, Jack Olin is running a legal business. But just the same, he knows he isn't likely to get invited to the annual Chamber of Commerce awards dinner. He also doesn't want his wife's friends or his kids' schoolmates knowing what he does to afford that big house he lives in out in Brentwood. And before you ask, I checked. He's got a wife and kids and it's a big house, in Brentwood."

"Do you seriously believe he cares what people think?"

I paused while the waiter brought our food, refilled our water glasses, and brought another basket of dinner rolls. Maggie pointed at her martini glass and nodded. That made three, at eight dollars a pop. The waiter said, "Of course," and hurried away.

I said, "If Jack Olin didn't care what people thought, he would have had his man throw me down a flight of stairs to make the point he wasn't somebody I should be messing with. Since then, I haven't gotten any threatening phone calls, or visits from leg-breakers delivering not-so-friendly warnings. That tells me that, first, he's probably not directly connected with organized crime, and second, that he's going to help us out, if only to make sure I go away. One way or the other, by Monday, we should know."

"What if he doesn't call?"

"Then I don't know, except that we're going to have to find Bobby the hard way. Meantime," I said, as our meal was served along with Maggie's martini, "let's enjoy dinner and talk about something else. After all, this is how you're compensating me for my services."

"Okay, then how about you tell me how you got into the private investigator business. I mean, as far as I know, PI firms don't send recruiters around to colleges to attract new talent. Or do they?"

"They don't. The FBI does, and the CIA used to, but I don't know if that's still a thing. Most of the operatives I know are ex-cops or ex-military intelligence or some such. They do their twenty years in government service, put in for their pensions, and then after a while get bored fishing or playing golf every day. So, they start doing security work or take on investigations for insurance companies. It gets them out of the house and makes them feel useful again."

"But that's not what you did."

"Well, no, not exactly. After college, I wanted to go to law school, but I didn't have the money and I didn't want to take out a big loan. I had an idea I'd get into police work until I could save up the tuition, which it never seemed like I was able to do. But it turned out I was a pretty good cop, and after I earned my detective's shield, I got assigned part-time to the district attorney's office as an investigator. Then, more or less by accident, I stumbled over a judge who was taking money to hand down favorable rulings for certain defendants. I didn't think that was right, so I started a freelance investigation of my own. It was an election year and the DA at the time didn't like what I was doing and told me I needed to back off. But I didn't, and so I was ticketed to get busted back to a patrolman. I didn't want to go back to a uniform so I quit. I tried my hand at a few other things and even thought about being a teacher, but that would have meant more school, and more tuition to get a teaching degree. In the end, I settled for being a PI."

"And that's enough?"

"It's something I can call my own. I get to set my own hours. I can take the cases that look interesting and pass on the ones that don't. Once in a while, I get to put things right. A lot of what I do is find people who have gone missing. It's usually not that difficult because most people who run away don't really want to be gone forever. They just need to get away from whatever's got them upset in the moment. I find them, talk to them, and if I can, try to convince them to go home."

"What do you do when you're not working for free chasing down lost little girls?"

"It varies." I took a forkful of etouffee. It was very hot, and more than a little on the spicy side. I took a swallow of my beer to return my internal temperature to normal.

"Sometimes I provide security for music industry celebrities in town for a recording session. That's a twenty-four-seven job and it pays very well. Once in a while I track down a blackmailer or a bail-jumper or deliver a ransom to buy back stolen property that its owner probably obtained illegally in the first place. Other times I investigate inventory shrinkage in retail stores or distribution centers. One time a guy tried to hire me to shoot his neighbor's dog because it kept him awake barking all night."

"I can't wait to hear how you put that right."

"I didn't have to. Somebody left the neighbor's gate open and the dog ran away all by itself. The client thought I must have seen to it and paid me a hundred dollars." I ate some more of my etouffee.

She tilted her head to one side and looked at me like she was seeing me for the first time. "Do you ever think about how what you do affects people's lives? I mean, do you even care a little bit about the ones who get hurt during the process, or is all this just a job to you?"

"I want to be careful how I answer this," I said. "First of all, the people you're talking about, the ones who sometimes get hurt, they come to me. I don't go around knocking on doors looking for clients. And yes, very often what I do ends up badly for at least some of the people involved. But then, there are cases like this one, where I can find a little girl who's gotten into what could be really bad trouble and bring her back to her family. I'd say that's a good thing, and I like to think it helps to balance off the bad."

When she didn't respond, I said, "How about you? Why did you give up teaching for guidance counseling?"

She was starting to slur her words just a bit, and her voice went up a level or two. "Order me one more drink and I'll tell you my life story. Never mind, I'll do it myself." She caught the waiter's eye and pointed to her glass. He was back almost immediately with her fourth cocktail. He made a slight bow as he set down the glass.

"Compliments of the management," he said, "for a lovely guest."

She gave him a smile that would have left any man gasping for air. Then she took a sip of her drink and ate another shrimp. When she put her fork down, she missed the edge of the table and it fell on the floor. When I reached down to pick it up, I caught an immodest glimpse of her thigh above the top of her stocking. She must have read my mind, because after I wiped off her fork with my napkin and handed it back, she said, "Ever watch a woman take off her stockings?"

"Yes, once or twice."

"Or maybe a hundred? It can be a very graceful act, very feminine. Think Anne Bancroft in *The Graduate.*"

"Okay..."

"On the other hand, watching someone taking off pantyhose is like watching a lizard trying to shed its skin. There's nothing erotic or elegant about it, do you think?"

"I think it depends on what happens next," I said.

"You men are so predictable. What were we talking about?"

"You were telling me the story of your life."

"Oh, right. Well, there's not much to tell. You already heard the exciting part. I grew up in Mansfield, Ohio. I had a few boyfriends and slept with one I thought I was in love with. After graduation, he went into the Marines. I went to college, in Memphis. I got a degree in psychology and a teaching certificate, and I wound up here. I taught for a few years, got married, got pushed down a flight of stairs, lost a baby, and then got divorced. When the district transferred me to Woodcrest, there was an opening in the guidance department. I decided to take the job, mostly because I found I was more comfortable talking to one kid at a time rather than a whole classroom full of them. Moving forward to the present day, and on a completely unrelated note, I haven't had sex for quite a while now, and now I just met some guy who says he's a private eye. I'm not sure about him, though. He works awful cheap to make much of a living at it."

While she was talking, she leaned forward just slightly, and I noticed a tattoo about the size of a dime on her right breast, just visible inside the top of her dress. It was a cherry with a stem and a single green leaf. I didn't notice it when she was sitting up straight, but now that I had, I couldn't take my eyes off it. She caught me staring, and I expected her to say something about her eyes being up here. Instead, she smiled and said, "It was a spring break thing, senior year. I think margaritas, or maybe tequila sunrises on the beach had something to do with it. After I got home and I had a chance to think about it, it embarrassed me a little, especially when I put on a bathing suit. Anymore, I don't even notice it.

"But," and here she paused for dramatic effect, "there's another one just like it that's much lower down. You can't see it unless I'm naked." She paused for a moment to let that sink in. "But if you want to come home with me, you can look at it all you want."

"That's a good offer, Maggie, but I think I'm hearing the martinis talking."

"You are," she said, reaching across the table and placing her hands over mine, "and all four of them are talking at the same time. But tonight, the drinks are for courage, not as a substitute for poor judgment.

"However," she reached for her glass and took another drink, "before I let myself get swept out to sea on a wave of alcohol, I need to know something. After we had our little talk in my office the other day, did you ask me out because you felt sorry for me?"

"I have no reason to feel sorry for you. I asked you out because I like you."

"Why?"

"Well, because you're smart and you seem to be good at what you do. You've had a couple of serious setbacks in your life, but I don't get the sense you waste time feeling sorry for yourself. Also, and this is the most important thing, you're pretty damn good looking."

"Is that so? Then why haven't you told me how drop-dead gorgeous I look tonight?"

Her tone was playful, but I knew I had dropped the ball. "I forgot to say that?"

"Let me clear this up for you. How did you get ready for our date this evening?"

"Well, I took a shower and shaved and put on a clean shirt. Clean underwear, too, if that's where you're going."

"Quite an effort," she said. "You should be proud. I, on the other hand, got a manicure. I got a pedi. I had my eyebrows done, and I got a wax. I even bought a new bra and panty set and believe me when I tell you it's a killer. But I swear," and here she paused for a tiny belch, "if you don't tell me how good I look, and I mean right this fucking minute, we'll just forget this whole night ever happened and I'll go home in a cab."

So, of course, I told her, at great length and in terms I hoped would make her overlook my earlier omission. It must have worked, because we decided to skip dessert. I paid the check and we left. Forty-five minutes later we were back at Maggie's townhouse and I got to see not only the bra and the panties, but also the other cherry she had talked about earlier. Two hours after that, I was still giving it my full attention.

Chapter Sixteen

The next morning, I was up early. Maggie was still sleeping, so I gathered my clothes, tiptoed down the hall, and showered in her guest bathroom. I found a toothbrush and deodorant in a drawer in the vanity, but nothing I could use to shave with. I didn't find anything like a comb either, so I patted down my hair the best way I could, got dressed, and went back to the bedroom to check on Maggie. When I walked in, she was awake and sitting up with her back propped against the headboard of the bed. She had the covers pulled all the way up to her chin. Disappointing, since the last time I saw her, she had on no clothes at all.

"Just like a man," she said, with the smallest hint of mock disapproval in her voice. "Here I was thinking you'd be on your way back for another lap around the track. Instead, I find you're dressed, and on your way out the door."

"Not at all," I said. "I have plans for us this morning."

"It's Sunday. Don't we deserve a day of rest?"

I sat down on the bed next to her and kissed her lightly on the forehead. She smelled good in a musky kind of way, with last night's perfume mixed with something a bit more primal. "After last night, I think we could both use more than just one day to recuperate. I know for sure I'm going to be sore for at least a week."

She wrapped her arms around my neck and kissed me fiercely on the mouth. "You know what they say about getting back on the horse." She pulled the covers down a short way and I got another look at one of the cherries.

125

"I do," I said, "and I'm foursquare behind it." I looked at the clock on the night table. "But it's seven-thirty now, and if we're going to make the nine o'clock service, you don't have much time to get yourself presentable."

"What are you talking about? What service? I know things went a little way into the weeds last night, but I don't remember talking about going to church this morning."

"We didn't. It's an idea I had while I was in the shower. This morning we are going to attend the worship service at the Divine Light Pentecostal Congregation. We are going to check out, up close and personal, the Reverend Jericho Hawkins, his orchestra and chorus, and his all-star rattlesnake revue."

She searched my face to see whether I was joking. "Why would we do that?"

"I don't know," I said. "I just want to see what goes on there. It's possible we might learn something. You don't have to come if you don't want to."

"Are you kidding? I wouldn't miss this for anything." She threw the covers back and hopped out of bed, indifferent to the fact she was naked. "Go pour yourself some orange juice and eat a piece of toast. I'll be down in half an hour."

"Wear something modest," I said. "That outfit you had on last night would send Christianity straight back to the days of the Inquisition."

"How about if I just wear this?" she turned and grinned. "That'll take us all the way back to the Garden of Eden." And with that, she disappeared into the bathroom. I went downstairs and dug out a Diet Coke from the refrigerator.

It actually took about thirty-five minutes before Maggie reappeared, wearing a plain blue print dress with a blue knit shrug and flat shoes. Her hair was tied back with a tortoise-shell barrette and her only makeup was a light shade of lipstick. "What do you think, Christian enough?"

"You look positively born again. Just don't tell anybody what you did last night."

"Any female over the age of fourteen will be able to take one look at me and know what I did last night."

126

"Does that mean you're glowing?"

"That would be one word for it, but don't give yourself too much credit. I thought I held up my end of things pretty well."

"No argument there," I told her.

It was about a twenty-minute drive from Maggie's townhouse to the Divine Light Congregation Church, and I noticed as we drove along that her disposition began to change. Earlier she had been excited about attending the service. Now she was quiet, as if in deep thought, and the playfulness that had marked her earlier mood was gone. I wondered if there was something I had said, but shouldn't have, and then I wondered whether there was something I should have said but didn't. Either way, nothing came to me. Knowing I might be asking for trouble, I decided to take a shot anyway.

"Is something wrong?"

"I don't know. Maybe we shouldn't do this."

"Do what? You mean be together?"

"No. I mean go to this church. This is not like attending Christmas mass with a thousand people at some cathedral. We're not going to be welcome. They're going to want to know what we're doing there."

I said, "There isn't anything to be afraid of. We're not going in with guns blazing. If they ask us to leave, we'll leave."

"What then?"

"Then we go to a Waffle House for breakfast. After that, we can go back to your place and see about getting back on the horse." When she didn't answer, I said, "Okay?"

"Okay," she said, but she didn't sound sold on the idea.

"What a relief. I was afraid you were going to want to have the talk about our relationship."

"Let's see how this goes first. There's still plenty of time for that."

And that was one thing I was afraid of.

The Divine Light church was located on a county lane that dead-ended at Blue Hole Road on the far southeast side of the city. The address was marked by a plywood sign cut in the shape of a cross. A rutted gravel driveway curved out of sight into the trees. When we got to the end of the driveway, we found an unpaved parking area that had been hacked out of the surrounding forest. Two dozen or so vehicles, most of them pickup trucks, were already there. At one end of the parking area was a structure the size of a two-car garage where a handful of children were visible through the open door. That, I supposed, was where Sunday school was held.

At the other end of the parking area was the church itself. It was a white prefabricated building not much bigger than a double-wide with paired doors in the front and a cross attached to the peak of the roof overhead. There were no windows. Ventilation came from a row of cyclone vents spinning lazily atop the roof and a large air conditioner that was clattering noisily from its mount on a concrete pad.

The church was set part ways back into the trees on two sides. On the third side was a clearing that held a small graveyard where I counted maybe thirty headstones. I wondered how many of the stones marked the final resting places of congregation members who had come to the end of the trail at the business end of a venomous snake.

I got out of the car and walked around to open the passenger door for Maggie. Two men wearing white shirts and black neckties stood near the steps leading into the church, greeting other members as they arrived. They were also paying careful attention to Maggie and me. Before she got out of the car, Maggie put her hand on my arm.

"I still don't like this, Gamble. We should just go."

"And miss what we came for? Where's your sense of adventure?" When that got no response, I said, "Seriously, it'll be okay. We'll sit in the back. If things start to get too crazy, we'll just leave. I promise."

I held her door and helped her out of the car. As we approached the front steps of the church, one of the men separated himself from his companion and walked over to meet us. "May I help you, folks? Are you here to worship the Lord?"

I said, "We're here to find truth. We believe we may find it here."

After a moment's hesitation, the man said, "Then you are welcome. However, since you are newcomers and not familiar with our service, I must ask that you kindly be respectful."

He held the door open for us and we entered. Inside there was a vestibule that ran the width of the building and another set of doors. On the other side of the doors was the sanctuary itself, which consisted of a double row of pews ten deep with a center aisle. The aisle was narrow, and each pew looked as if it could seat no more than six congregants comfortably. In the front was a raised platform with a podium that held a microphone. There was no altar similar to what might be found in a mainstream church. On one side of the platform was a drum kit, an electric guitar with an amplifier and speaker, a battered upright piano, and a tambourine. On the other side was a wooden box on top of a table. The box was painted black. It had a hinged lid and holes in the sides covered with heavy screen mesh.

Maggie and I took seats in a pew in the last row. Above our heads, ceiling fans rotated slowly, stirring the stale, sticky air. I caught sight of Delsey seated in a front pew. If she saw Maggie and me as we came in, she gave no indication.

After a few minutes, the men who had been waiting outside came in, shut the outside doors behind them, and took their seats. Counting the house, there were maybe forty people in all. I noticed all the men were dressed in dark pants and long-sleeved white or light blue shirts. Some wore neckties, others just collars buttoned at the neck. The women wore plain, ankle-length dresses, thick stockings, no jewelry other than wedding rings, and no makeup. Except that the women wore no bonnets, their style of dress was very similar to what you might find in a Mennonite community.

Once everyone was seated, someone closed the inside doors, and then the service began. There was a moment of expectant silence and then Reverend Hawkins entered from a door at the back of the platform and walked to the podium. He raised his hands as if in supplication and looked out over the congregation.

"Dear Lord," he began in a low voice, "we thank you for the opportunity to come together for worship on this day. We ask that you bless all our brothers and sisters and protect us from harm as we demonstrate our unwavering belief in your goodness and mercy." He bowed his head and the congregation shouted in unison, "Amen!"

He continued, "There are brothers and sisters among us who are in need of your merciful healing. One of us in particular is suffering the ravages of a wasting disease. Pray with me as I ask for the Lord's divine intervention on behalf of our brother David." Reverend Hawkins stepped down from the podium and approached a man seated in the front pew.

"Rise up, Brother David, and face your brothers and sisters. Feel their love and compassion." An individual of indeterminate age stood and turned toward the congregation. If concern and compassion could help him, he needed all he could get. He was very pale and his eyes were hollow and dark, like someone who had arrived at the end stage of some terrible cancer, one which had progressed beyond all but palliative treatment. Absent a miracle, it was clear that before long, he would be taking his final rest in the cemetery out back.

Reverend Hawkins placed his hands on the man's shoulders and said in a loud voice, "Father in heaven, our brother David is not well. He has a disease that has taken his strength. We ask, if it is your will, that he be healed so that he may be returned to the fullness of life to love and serve you and his family here on earth. In the name of Jesus, we pray," he finished, and again, the congregation shouted "Amen."

Reverend Hawkins then led his flock in another prayer, asking for grace and forgiveness in times of great troubles across the land. The congregation, accompanied by a soloist on piano, then sang "What a Friend We Have in Jesus," "Holy is the Lord" and "Ancient of Days." After that, Reverend Hawkins returned to the platform and nodded toward some additional musicians who had taken their place and picked up their instruments. They began to play a piece like nothing I had ever heard in any church, anywhere, any time. Minus the pianist, the drummer banged, the tambourinist rattled and the guitarist began to rip at his six-string like Pete Townsend on uppers. As the first notes began to shake the building, people in the pews jumped up from their seats and started dancing and writhing like a fraternity house toga party gone bat-shit crazy.

I looked at Maggie and she looked at me and said something I couldn't hear over the noise, but that I would have sworn was, "What the fuck?"

Amidst the commotion, one man went over to the box on the right side of the platform. He opened the lid, reached inside, and came out with two snakes that I recognized as timber rattlesnakes. He passed one each to two other men and then went back to the box to retrieve two more. By the time he was finished, there were six different venomous snakes being handed one to another by various congregants. Some held the reptiles above their heads while others draped them over their necks or wrapped them around their arms. While this was going on, other people lit rags that had been stuffed into glass bottles, like Molotov cocktails. The bottles were filled with a lamp oil of some sort, so they didn't explode, but the rags burned with bright blue and red flames. As the music, unrecognizable as it was, got louder, members of the congregation danced and clapped their hands, or just hopped up and down, threw their heads back, and shouted "Jesus!"

While we were watching all this going on, Jericho Hawkins approached me, and with both hands, held out a large snake for me to take. Not knowing what else to do, and thinking there was some point about to be made one way or the other, I stood up and took it into my hands. Out of the corner of my eye, I saw Maggie take two steps away from me. Her own eyes had gotten large as dessert plates and her mouth hung slightly open. After that, I lost sight of her as my attention was now firmly riveted on the basilisk-eyed reptile I had just been handed,

There is a common misconception that snakes are slippery, like fish. They are not. Because they are cold-blooded, they are cool to the touch. Otherwise, they have a dry, textured feel, somewhat like finely dressed leather.

The snake I was holding was a timber rattler, sometimes called a canebrake, about four feet long and weighing maybe two pounds. Its body color was brown, with chevron-shaped tan and black markings along its back and sides. With that protective coloration, it was easy to see why it would be almost invisible when hidden amongst fallen leaves on a forest floor. I held the snake with two hands, under the thickest part of its body. For its size, it had powerful muscles that I could feel flexing as it tried to crawl away, and I had to keep shifting my grip to keep it from dropping to the floor. I was extremely careful not to make any movements that might frighten or irritate the snake, so I handled it as gently as I could. I knew that the venom of a canebrake is seldom fatal to a healthy adult, but I also knew a bite would be extremely painful and could lead to serious complications. I was counting on the snake being accustomed to human handling and that it would tolerate my clumsy manipulations without striking.

With more assurance than I thought I would have possessed I lifted the snake over my head and let it drape itself around the back of my neck. As it crawled forward it turned its body so that it was looking directly at me. I knew if it chose that moment to strike my face or my neck, I would be in real trouble, as there would be no way to apply a tourniquet to stop the spread of the venom through my system. As I looked into its coal-black eyes, it flicked a forked tongue in my direction, tasting the air and apparently deciding that whatever it found was not to its liking. After a moment that seemed like a lifetime, it turned away and resumed its struggles to gain its freedom. I looked at Reverend Hawkins, who had been standing a couple of feet away during the entire encounter. He nodded his head as if he was satisfied with my efforts, and I passed the reptile back to him. I noted, somewhat foolishly, that during the time I held the snake nobody else in the church, other than Maggie and Jericho, had paid the slightest attention to me. The rest, except for those who were also making merry with rattlesnakes and copperheads, were completely absorbed with their dancing, praying, tambourine rattling, and holy rolling.

As soon as Reverend Hawkins had taken back the snake and turned away, Maggie punched me on the shoulder, hard enough to raise a bruise, and said, "We. Are. Leaving. Right the hell now." When I hesitated, she said, "I mean it, let's go. Now."

We walked outside and back to the car in silence. With some difficulty, because I seemed to be having trouble fitting the key into the ignition, I started the car and turned it around. The windows were down and we could hear the singing and banging still going on inside the church. I wondered, without really wanting to know, how long they would keep it up before calling it a day. Maggie gave me a look like she might give to one of her students who had just flushed a cherry bomb down a toilet.

"Are you going to tell me what that was all about?"

I stopped the car at the end of the driveway and turned off the engine. I leaned forward and rested my head on the rim of the steering wheel. My hands were shaking. My heart was pounding, and my shirt was soaked through with perspiration.

"I don't know," I said. "I think I just wanted to make a point."

"And what point might that be?"

I shrugged. "I don't know that either."

"I see." She shook her head slowly. "When you figure out what it was, tell me." She didn't say anything after that. She just looked out the window as we drove back to the city. When we pulled up in front of her condo, she got out, shut the door, and looked back at me through the window.

"You are an idiot," she said, with just the barest smile. "Call me tomorrow."

Chapter Seventeen

I spent the next morning moping around the office, waiting for something to happen. Nothing did. Nobody called. Nobody stopped in. When I walked down the hall to the restroom, nobody jumped out of a stall to beat me up or threaten to throw me down an elevator shaft if I didn't drop the case. At eleven forty-five I went to lunch. I walked around the block, just for the exercise. Then I went back to the office and did a crossword puzzle. When some of the clues proved too arcane for me to decipher, I wadded up the puzzle and threw it into the wastebasket.

The call finally came about one-thirty in the afternoon. A man's voice I hadn't remembered hearing before said, "You got a package waiting for you. You still want it, you need to come and pick it up right away. I ain't gonna wait all day."

I said, "Who is this?"

"Never you mind. You want the goods, then you best be where I tell you at three o'clock. I ain't gonna hang around."

I made a note of the location. "What condition is the package in?"

"Like brand new. Not a scratch on her," the voice said, and hung up.

After my meeting with Jack Olin on Friday, I was pretty sure who had made the call. I was also fairly confident the call was on the level, and that Gabrielle would be where Bobby Fury said she would be. On the other hand, I didn't think making the pickup alone was a good idea. For all Gabrielle, or anybody else looking might know, Bobby was selling her to some white slaver. The pickup was to be in a public place, and if Gabrielle threw some kind of an emotional fit, there was no telling what might happen. I had to take a woman with me who Gabrielle knew, and I hoped, trusted.

I thought about calling Delsey, then decided otherwise. After all, Delsey was exactly the person Gabrielle was running away from. However, to make sure Gabrielle was in mint condition, as Bobby had promised, I was going to need a female to look her over, get her cleaned up and, if necessary, take her to a hospital before her mother and father saw her. And I knew just the person for the job.

Half an hour later Maggie and I were in her silver Volvo station wagon, heading for a campground near Percy Priest Reservoir. She was driving. I decided we should take her car since it had four doors, and if things went to hell and we needed to get away quickly, it would be easier to get Gabrielle into the car and out of harm's way with an extra pair of doors.

When we got to the park entrance, a ranger came out of a small gatehouse to greet us. Maggie rolled down her window.

"Help you folks?"

I leaned toward the open window and said, "Can you point us toward Site Eleven?"

"You plan on spending the night?"

Without missing a beat, Maggie said, "No, we're just looking around. We've been thinking about doing some camping, and someone at work said she thought we might like this spot."

"Well, it's getting to be a little late in the season, but there're still a few good days left, I expect." He looked us both over and gave us a knowing grin. "Take the left fork up ahead and then just follow the road around. The sites are all marked. You won't have any trouble finding it." He handed a map of the park through Maggie's open window. "Long as you're here, you all might as well take your time looking around. There're plenty of good spots, and this time of year even on the weekends, the park isn't crowded."

As we pulled away from the entrance, Maggie said, "You think he figured us for a nooner?"

"Well, if this doesn't pan out, there are worse ways to spend the afternoon."

"It'll take more than one dinner, bub, but you're on the right track."

"What would you think about coffee and a donut from Dunkin?"

"That'd probably do."

We continued up the drive for a short distance before coming to where the road split, then followed the left fork for another hundred yards before coming to a place where it turned sharply back to the right. All around us, the trees, except for the evergreens, were a riot of color, with leaves of red, orange, yellow, and just enough green and brown mixed in to remind the observer that the end-of-the-season palette had both a beginning and an end-point. On another day, under other circumstances, I would have enjoyed just walking through the park with Maggie, holding hands like high school sweethearts and taking in the vista. But not today. Today held the threat of a very bad outcome, maybe for Gabrielle, maybe for Maggie and me, and no amount of fall color could make the burden of that knowledge any easier to ignore.

Just beyond the curve, I spotted a red pickup truck parked next to a campsite where there was a picnic table, a stone fireplace, and a shower house. If there was going to be trouble, I knew that's where it would come from.

"Stop here," I told Maggie. "This is as far as you go." I drew my Colt from the shoulder rig I was wearing and racked a round into the chamber. Then I gently let the hammer down so there would be no accidental discharges.

She gave me a look. "I thought we were here to retrieve Gabrielle, not to shoot somebody."

"I'm not planning to shoot anybody," I said, "but I have no idea whether this is on the up-and-up. For all I know, there are six guys waiting in the bushes with automatic weapons ready to blast away so this bastard can go back to playing house with Gabrielle. So, listen. I want you to stay in the car. If this starts to get noisy, you get the hell out of here. Don't wait for me. Don't try to get into the act. Just step on the gas and go. Do you understand?"

When she didn't answer, I said, "Look at me."

She turned toward me. I said, "This is important. I don't want you getting shot."

"I understand."

"All right, then. Just wait here and keep the engine running. Don't worry

136

about me. I'll be fine." I got out of the car and began walking toward where the truck was parked. I was holding the Colt behind my back, hammer down, safety off. When I got close to the shower house, I called out, "Gabrielle?"

Silence.

I called out again, "Gabrielle? Come on out. You're safe. Nobody is going to hurt you."

I heard a man's voice coming from inside the women's shower area. "Go on, get out there. He ain't gonna hurt you."

A girl's voice said, "I'm not going. I'm not leaving you."

The man said, "Get out there, you little bitch, or I'll break your arm."

"I have a better idea," I said. "Bobby, just so you know, I'm armed. I need you to come on out, real slow, and keep your hands where I can see them." When there was no answer, I said, "Do it now. Just do what I tell you and everybody's going to be fine." From behind me I heard a car door open and close and then the sound of footsteps approaching. That would be Maggie.

Change of plans.

She didn't understand.

I waved my free hand at her to indicate she should stay back.

I said, "Last chance, Bobby. Then I'm coming in."

There was a short silence while he thought about that, I supposed. Then he said, "All right I'm coming out. Don't shoot me."

"I'm not going to shoot you, just come on out. Keep your hands where I can see them. Gabrielle, you stay put."

The man I recognized from the photo I'd found in Gabrielle's bedroom as Bobby Fury walked out of the shower house, hands empty, arms held away from his sides. He was wearing sunglasses, same as in the photo, but even with them on I could see his face was bruised and his right ear, partly torn away, had been reattached with a dozen or so stitches. When he got to within about ten paces away from me, I motioned for him to stop.

"Did Vincent do that?" I asked.

"You put him on to me," Bobby said. "First chance I get, I'm gonna fuck you up. You and that bitch you brought with you."

"Okay," I said, "let's understand one another. I know right now you're pretty unhappy about what Vincent did to you, and you blame me for that. I get it, and if I were in your position, I'd feel the same way. But when we finish up here, I'm going to let you walk away from this. You can turn yourself in to the cops, or you can make a run for it. I don't care one way or the other. And if you want to come looking for me, I'm in the phone book. But if you go near either one of these women, and I have to come looking for you a second time, I will kill you. It's just that simple. I will kill you."

He just stared at me. I cocked the hammer back on my .380 and pointed it at the middle of his chest. "Is that clear?"

He nodded, once.

"Good. Now I want you to lay down on the ground, flat on your stomach, arms straight out at your sides, and don't move."

After he was down, I walked over and knelt over him with one knee in the middle of his back. I patted him down to make sure he didn't have a weapon. When I was satisfied that he was clean, I got back up and stepped away. Then I motioned for Maggie to go on into the shower house and retrieve Gabrielle. As she walked past Bobby, I heard her say "Pervert."

He lifted his head to look at me. "I didn't know, man. She told me she was eighteen."

"Maybe she did, but you met her girlfriend, and she doesn't look eighteen. That should have told you something wasn't right," I said. "So, here's the deal. Soon as we leave here, we're going to drive her home. After that, I expect her mother will take her to see a doctor. If it turns out she's been molested, or if she pops up later in some shitty porn video, I will hunt you down and I will not stop until I find you and they throw your sorry ass into a cell and weld the door shut."

I waited another minute and then Maggie came out of the shower house with Gabrielle in tow. And I had to admit, I could see how Bobby could have let himself believe Gabrielle was older than her actual age. Dressed as she was, in an ultra-short black leather miniskirt, skin-tight leggings, and a low-cut top, in the right light she could have fooled anybody.

I said, "Gabrielle, are you okay?"

She glared at me and said, "Fuck you. Just fuck you, okay?"

"I'll take that as a yes."

I said to Maggie, "Take her back to the car. If she gives you a hard time, smack her in the head. We've got to wrap this up and get out of here before that ranger shows up to see if we want to reserve a campsite."

As Gabrielle walked past where Bobby was lying on the ground, she gave him a vicious kick in the ribs. From the yelp of pain he gave, I guessed that Vincent must have done a little work of his own in that same spot.

"That's for letting these two find me. You were supposed to take care of me."

"I will, baby. I'll get you back. Don't you worry about that."

"Be a mistake," I said. "Where are the clothes she left home with? I can't bring her back looking like that."

"In the truck, in a bag behind the passenger seat. The door ain't locked."

"Okay. Give me your keys. Unless you want to die right here, you stay where you are."

I took the keys, then went over to Bobby's truck and collected Gabrielle's overnight bag. Then I walked back to where Bobby was still flat on his face on the ground.

"I'm going to leave your keys back at the ranger station. I'll tell him I found them outside the shower house. It shouldn't take you more than fifteen minutes to walk down there and back. Meantime you stay where you are until you see us drive off."

"What happens to me then?"

"It's like I told you. If she's in anything less than tip-top condition, I will make sure the cops come looking for you. Once they find you—and they will—you'll go away for a long time. If she's okay, then it'll be up to police and the county attorney to decide what to charge you with. When the dust settles, you'll probably get tagged with contributing to the delinquency of a minor. Worst case they'll call it unlawful restraint. Maybe they'll knock it down to some kind of a misdemeanor charge, but who knows? Either way, I suggest either you get out of town and don't come back, or else get a lawyer and turn yourself in."

"You're not going to bust me?"

"I'm not a cop. Far as I'm concerned, you can walk away from this. My job is to bring back the girl, that's all. After that, it'll be up to the police." I de-cocked my gun and dropped it into my coat pocket. "What were you hoping to accomplish with this stunt, anyway? You must have known that people would be looking for her."

"Can I sit up? It's cold just lying here on the ground."

"Go ahead."

When he got resettled, he said, "You want to know what I was hoping for? Man, have you looked at her? I mean, have you really looked? Have you ever seen a woman more beautiful?"

"What were you going to do, get married?" I shook my head. "You should have looked more closely, Bobby. She's not a woman. She's fourteen years old. And I will tell you again, if you somehow avoid prosecution and prison time, you need to stay away from her, or the next time I see you, you will be dead."

Chapter Eighteen

When I got back to the car, Maggie and Gabrielle were sitting in the back seat. Gabrielle was crying noisily. She had wedged herself against the passenger side door as far from Maggie as she could get. I opened the front door on the driver's side and handed Gabrielle's overnight bag to Maggie. "See if there's something else in there she can put on. We can't take her home dressed the way she is now."

"What did you say to him back there?"

"I suggested strongly that he should consider dating someone his own age."

"That was it?"

"I was very persuasive," I said.

"You hurt him, didn't you?" Gabrielle said between sobs.

I had to laugh at that. "You kicked him, not me. I told him we're taking you home and he should stay away from you."

"I'm not going home. If you make me, I'll just run away again first chance I get."

"Gabrielle...," Maggie began.

I said, "Look, you obviously have issues with your mother and father, but I don't have a dog in that fight. I was hired to find you and bring you home, and that's what I'm going to do. What happens after that is up to you and your parents."

"You don't understand," she said, wiping a tear from her cheek. "If you make me go home, my father will kill me the minute I walk in the door."

"No, he won't. He won't because Ms. Totten and I are going to walk in the

141

door with you and talk to your parents. My guess is they'll be so relieved to have you back safe they'll forget all about how you got gone in the first place. If I'm wrong, and if it looks like things are going to get ugly, we'll take you someplace else where you'll be safe until everybody can cool off some."

I could see she was already working on a way to avoid the trip home.

"And another thing. I've got the keys to Bobby's truck. I'm going to leave them with the ranger when we leave the park. Now, I know what you're thinking, but if you make a stink at the ranger station, he'll call the police and hold us there until they get here. If that happens, we'll all end up going downtown, but the only one who won't end up in his own bed tonight will be Bobby, because the police are already looking for him. So, you just sit there and keep quiet, and if you feel like running away again, do it on your own time, understand?"

When we got to the park entrance, I stopped at the ranger gatehouse and handed him the set of keys I took from Bobby Fury.

"We found these next to the campsite near the shower house. I think they might go with a red pickup truck parked up there, but there was nobody around, so I thought I'd leave them with you if that's okay."

"Sure, no problem," he said. "I'll be on the lookout."

I said thanks and gunned it the hell out of the park before it came to him that when Maggie and I first arrived we didn't have a teenaged girl sitting in the back seat. Fortunately, Gabrielle kept her mouth shut during the exchange, so I didn't have to think of an explanation for what she was doing there now.

On the way back into the city I stopped at a Texaco station, so Maggie could take Gabrielle into the women's washroom and get her clothes changed. While they were gone, I got on my cell and called the number Delsey had given me for the admissions office at Baptist Hospital. It took a minute or two before she came to the phone.

"Delsey, this is Jackson Gamble. I've got Gabrielle. She's ready to come home. Can you get the rest of the afternoon off, or do you want me to bring her to the hospital?"

"The hospital?" There was a note of panic in her voice. "Is she all right?"

"I'm sorry," I said. "I shouldn't have said it that way. Yes, she's fine, or at least, she's fine as far as I can tell. What I meant was, are you able to get home by yourself, or do you need to wait for a ride?"

"I have my car. I'll be there in fifteen minutes."

"Okay. I have Ms. Totten with me. It might take us a little longer. Give us half an hour." I paused. "Will your husband be there? We'd like to be able to talk with you both."

"He's home now, probably working on his sermon for next Sunday."

"Good. Let's hope his topic will be forgiveness."

As I ended the call, Maggie came out of the restroom with Gabrielle. Minus the leather mini and the low-cut top and now wearing jeans and a sweatshirt, she looked like a normal high school kid and not the teenaged hooker, Iris, from *Taxi Driver*. I noticed also that Maggie had wiped most of the heavy makeup from Gabrielle's face.

When they got back into the car I said to Maggie, "Do we have a problem?"

"I couldn't do anything about the thong, but other than that I think we're okay. She says they didn't have sex, and I didn't see anything to indicate she's been physically hurt."

I tried to imagine Maggie in a thong. "Then let's go."

Heading back to Jacktown, Maggie tried talking to Gabrielle, to reassure her things were going to be okay once she got back home. It was pretty much a one-way discussion, however, as Gabrielle didn't seem to have anything to say except "I don't care," and "Go to hell."

Delsey was waiting on the front porch as we drove up. I told Maggie to wait in the car for just a moment while I went to talk with Delsey. She gave me an anxious look when I got out of the car and approached her alone.

"Where's Gabrielle? You said she's all right."

"Far as I can tell, she is. She doesn't seem to have suffered any harm, but I want to warn you, she's very angry and frightened, and I don't get the impression she's too happy about coming home. I don't have any idea what she's been doing since she left, but you should understand she wasn't kidnapped. Wherever she went and whatever she did, it was what she wanted to do. Do you think you can deal with that?"

"Gabrielle is my daughter. I love her more than anything."

"How about Jericho? Is he going to be okay with her?"

She nodded. "He's been praying on it. I believe he'll come around."

"Okay." I waved for Maggie to bring Gabrielle up to the house. As they approached, Delsey opened her arms to embrace her daughter. Gabrielle wasn't having any of it, however. She walked right past her mother without so much as a look and went into the house. A moment later, I heard a door slam. Gabrielle's bedroom door, no doubt.

Maggie said, "Give her a day or two. She's been on quite a ride. It's a lot for a girl her age to process."

Delsey didn't say anything, but Maggie read the question in her eyes. "She says nothing happened, and I have no reason to disbelieve her. But all the same, I think you should take her to a doctor, just to be sure."

There didn't seem to be anything more to talk about after that. Delsey said, "Mr. Gamble, thank you again for what you done. You too, Miss Totten. Send me a bill for whatever I owe you and I'll see you get paid."

"Don't worry about it," I said. "We'll figure something out."

Maggie said, "Call me if either of you need some help, or just somebody to talk to. I'm always available."

Delsey went into the house and Maggie and I walked back to the car. As we were getting set to go, Jericho came out the front door and walked slowly toward the car. I got out to meet him, not sure what to expect. For all I could tell, he was getting ready to shoot me. But to my surprise, he held out his hand for me to shake.

"I owe you an apology, Mr. Gamble. After yesterday at church, I now see that you are a righteous man, and I misjudged you badly. I hope you'll accept my apology. And we will send you fair payment for your services."

"Done," I said, shaking his hand. "Be good to your daughter. Love her like never before. She's going to need some time."

And that, I thought, was the end of that. And for a while, it was.

Chapter Nineteen

I went into the office on Tuesday and spent the morning playing games on my computer. I thought the phone might start ringing right away, but when it got to be noontime and I still hadn't heard from anybody, I locked the door to the inner office and went to lunch. Afterward, just for the exercise, I walked over to the state capitol building and back. By that time, it was after two o'clock, and I decided that if there were no calls while I was out, I might as well call it a day. I was just getting ready to close up shop when the phone finally did ring. It was Delsey.

"I wanted to let you know, I took Gabrielle to the doctor this morning, you know, to see if...to see if she was all right."

I didn't ask what kind of doctor. "You mean to find out if she's still a virgin."

There was a pause. "Well, I guess that's straight enough to the point for just about anybody."

"I know. I'm sorry. It's a bad habit I have. Let me try this again. How is she?"

"Doctor says nothing happened between her and that boyfriend, so I guess we're done with him for a time."

"We can hope so, anyway," I said. "Did you notify the police she's back? I expect they're going to want to talk to her, and then they're going to go looking for Bobby."

"I did. I called Lieutenant Sutton first thing this morning, just like I been doing right along, only this time I said I had good news for him. He said he was glad to hear and that he'd stop by after supper today just to make

145

sure everything was all right. And you're right. He did ask me if I had any information that would help him find Bobby."

"And?"

"And I told him I didn't have any idea, but that he should talk to you because you're the one brought her back." Then, quickly she added, "Oh, my. I shouldn't have told him that, should I? Did I get you into trouble?"

"Don't worry about it. He would have gotten the whole story anyway when he talked to Gabrielle. Besides," I lied, "I was just getting ready to call him."

"Well, that's good, then. I don't want him to be mad at you after all the good you done. But he did say that if I talked to you before he did, to tell you that you should come by his office soon as you could. He said he wanted to clear up a few details."

"I'm sure he does," I said.

"Do you think the police are going to arrest Bobby?"

"If they locate him, there isn't any doubt about it. They'll find something to charge him with. My guess is when he's arraigned the judge will set his bail high enough that unless he's got a friend with deep pockets, he won't be able to post it, so he'll end up sitting in the county lockup until he goes to trial. That could be a year or more. I don't think he'll be coming around looking for Gabrielle any time soon."

She was quiet for a moment. "The Lord says we should be quick to forgive, so I'm sorry for him. Maybe some good will come out of this for him. Also, I noticed you and Ms. Totten at services on Sunday. I saw what happened when my husband passed you the serpent. You were very brave."

"More like very foolish, I think. I'm just glad it was in a good mood."

"Snakes don't have moods, Mr. Gamble. They are just dumb creatures put on earth to help fulfill God's purpose. It was the same God as protected you. He knew you were getting close to bringing my Gabrielle back home to us. He wasn't going to let anything happen to prevent that."

It was as good an explanation as any, and she seemed firmly enough convinced of it that I couldn't see anything to be gained by arguing. I told her she should call any time if she needed help. She thanked me again for finding Gabrielle and said she'd remember me in her prayers. Then we said goodbye.

After I hung up the phone, I started thinking that now that Carl Sutton knew Gabrielle was back home and it was me that brought her there, I should maybe lay low for the rest of the day. I knew he was going to have some questions for me and that he probably wasn't going to like some of the answers. That seemed like a conversation that could wait for another day.

Before leaving the office, I called Maggie to let her know Gabrielle had seen a doctor and that she was unmolested. I also had an idea about getting together with her that evening.

"Then she's okay?"

"Delsey says she's fine, or at least, she's still a virgin, if that term still carries any weight."

"If she is, she's in a distinct minority, at least at this school. Sex education is a required course for freshmen here at Woodcrest, but a lot of these kids could teach the class just as well as the faculty getting paid to do it." While she was talking, I heard a voice in the background saying something, and then Maggie said, "Yeah, I'm all set." To me, she said, "Listen, I'm glad you called because I forgot to tell you about this yesterday. I'm signed up to be at a guidance and counseling conference at UT in Knoxville tomorrow and Thursday. Three of us are carpooling up there right after school today. There's a dinner Thursday night and then we're coming back the next morning, so I can't see you until Friday night at the soonest." When I didn't say anything right away, she said, "Or am I being presumptuous?"

"Not presumptuous, but I am disappointed. I was hoping for tonight."

"Sorry, buster, no can do. But if you can wait, I'll make it up to you when I get back. Come by my place around six and I'll whip something up for us to eat. And be sure to bring the video."

"I like the way you think."

"That isn't all you'll like. And just to make sure you're not late, there's some free time during the conference for me to run out and buy something scandalous to wear after dinner. Do you think that will hold you until Friday?"

"I think it will do nicely," I said, and we hung up.

Not more than thirty seconds passed before the phone rang again. It was a familiar voice; one I had heard just a few days earlier.

"Mister Gamble, do you know who this is?"

"I recognize your voice, Mr. Olin. What can I do for you?"

"I understand you got your little gal back home safe and sound. I was thinking you might be grateful and you'd want to call and say thanks."

"You're right, where are my manners? Well, then, I appreciate what you did. I'm sure we're both better off for the effort. Guess I can't say the same for Bobby Fury, though. Looks like your man leaned on him a little bit."

"Sometimes you need to reason with folks a bit to get 'em to see their way through the problem. The way I heard it, Bobby had a hard time coming around. I expect he won't make that mistake again."

"One would hope not," I said.

"And I also expect I won't be seeing you again, so I'll just say it was a pleasure doing business with you."

"Same to you," I said. And with that, my day came to an end.

Chapter Twenty

With Gabrielle Hawkins back at home, Maggie at UT until the weekend, and no other investigations pending at the moment, I figured I had a couple of free days to spend any way I wanted. For lack of anything better to do, I called my across-the-street neighbor, Klein, to see whether he'd be interested in some late-season fishing. A few years back he had inherited a hefty chunk of cash from a cousin he thought was already dead, and bought himself a top-notch Ranger bass boat with all the trimmings. Most weekends he found an excuse to get out on the water, usually by himself. He said it was a way to get away from all the noise, though I couldn't imagine what he was talking about, since he lived alone, and since nothing made more of a racket than the two-hundred horsepower outboard that came with his boat. I had a standing invitation to come along, and once in a while I did, even though I am not nearly as committed to drowning bait as he is.

Turned out, my timing was bad. "I'm scheduled for a colonoscopy tomorrow, so I expect you can pretty well guess what I'm doing today."

"Another time," I said. "There's still a few weeks left before cold weather sets in." And so, with no better option on the horizon, I drove downtown to the office just in case something interesting walked through the door.

They didn't walk in. They were already there in the outer office, waiting. And they didn't look pleased to see me.

The tall one was somebody I knew. His name was Spillner, Detective Sergeant John Spillner. He was about fifty years old, dressed in a brown suit that needed pressing, a white shirt, and a blue and red striped necktie pulled loose at the collar. His hair had been red once but was now going to gray, and his face bore the tired expression of a man who had seen too much, too often. His partner was an attractive black woman who looked to be hovering right around forty. She wore gray slacks, a white top, and an off-white jacket with three-quarter length sleeves. Her dark hair was cut medium length, and except for a light shade of lipstick, no other makeup. She had a detective's badge clipped to the left side of her belt near the buckle and a holster with a Smith & Wesson .40 caliber autoloader on her right hip. When I came through the door, the two were already standing.

"It's ten-thirty, Gamble. What kind of hours do you keep?"

Spillner was a homicide cop, but since I had no idea what he and his partner wanted with me, I decided to wait and let whatever they wanted come to me. "It varies," I said. "I had some errands to run this morning. You should have called first. It would have saved you the wait."

"Not a problem. We're on city time." He nodded in the direction of his partner. "Gamble, this is Lorraine Proctor. She came over from narcotics a couple months ago. You can call her Detective Proctor."

"Right, got it," I said, taking his meaning. "Pleased to meet you, Detective."

"Likewise, Mr. Gamble," she said, and we shook hands.

"Now that we're all friends, what brings you around?"

Spillner said, "How about let's go inside where we can talk."

I unlocked the door to the inner office and steered the two detectives into my visitor's chairs. "I don't have any coffee, but there's water, and I think some Diet Cokes in the refrigerator. Help yourselves if you want."

"We'll pass, thank you." Spillner waited until I sat down behind my desk. Some kind of signal passed between the two cops, and then Lorraine Proctor spoke up. "Mr. Gamble, Sergeant Spillner has told me you're an okay guy. He says you used to be on the job, so I'll assume you'll be willing to cooperate."

"I might. I could tell you better if I knew what I'm cooperating with."

"Then I'll get right to it." She removed a small notebook from her jacket pocket and flipped it open. "Are you acquainted with a woman named Michelle Reddick? I believe she also goes by the name Mickey Reddick?"

Alarm bells began jangling in my head. "Suppose I am. What then?"

"What then is, maybe you can tell us why we found your business card on the kitchen counter in her apartment at the same time that we found her dead on the floor not three feet away. And before you ask, a neighbor phoned it in. She was walking down the hall, on her way to work, and noticed Miss Reddick's door was open. She looked inside, saw the deceased, and called 911."

"Any point in saying I don't know what you're talking about?"

"None at all. And please, let's not waste time having you tell us about how you hand out business cards all over town and she could have gotten it from anybody. Since we had your card, we figured you knew the dead woman, so we traced your movements over the last week or so. We know you asked about Miss Reddick from one of your old girlfriends at some strip club down on Lower Broad. Nice company you keep, by the way."

I looked at Spillner. "She's good, isn't she?"

"Good as they come, I'd say."

Lorraine Proctor raised her eyebrows just slightly. "Mr. Gamble?"

I had to give it to her. She wasn't threatening or accusatory. She spoke without any discernable accent, as if she had recently stepped off the set of a network news program or talk show. She kept her voice pleasant and even, like a doctor updating a patient's medical history.

"She had one of my cards because I left it with her. We spoke last week in connection with a missing person investigation I was conducting."

"And that would be," she paused again to check her notebook, "a young girl named Gabrielle Hawkins. I understand you returned her to her parents on Monday. Good job on that, by the way. Is she okay?"

"Far as I know, she's good."

"Glad to hear it. And of course, you notified missing persons?"

"I wasn't being paid by missing persons. Her mother talked to Carl Sutton."

Proctor drummed her fingernails on the arm of her chair. "So that's a no. Keep that in mind that next time you need a favor. Why did you need to talk to Miss Reddick?"

"I interviewed Mickey Reddick because I had learned she was a sometime girlfriend of a man believed to have abducted Gabrielle, only Gabrielle wasn't

151

abducted. She had gone with that someone by choice."

"Someone named Robert Furillo?" When I didn't answer right away, she said, "Oh wait, maybe you know him as Bobby Fury."

I had a feeling Lorraine Proctor was leading me in small steps to the edge of a precipice and was about to give me a shove. I just couldn't see a way to step back away from it.

"If you already know all this, why are we having this conversation?"

"Because when we found Mickey Reddick's body, it was clear she had been beaten up pretty badly. Sergeant Spillner doesn't think you would do something like that. Me, I don't know you well enough to know what I think, but just the same, we have to ask if you know anything about how she got dead."

"Excuse me. Didn't you just say she was beaten to death?"

"No. There was a syringe next to the body. We think she died from an overdose."

"Then it could have been an accident or a suicide."

"Maybe, but when the crime scene folks examined the syringe, there were no fingerprints on it. Now you tell me, who injects herself with an overdose either accidentally or on purpose and then wipes the syringe clean?"

"Then it was a hotshot."

"It looks that way, yes. Best guess is it was a combination of heroin and fentanyl."

"And you like Bobby Fury for it?"

She looked at Spillner. Spillner said to me, "Don't you?"

I leaned back in my chair. "Off the top of my head, I wouldn't know who else you should be looking for. A couple days before I talked to her, Bobby had been to see her. They got into some kind of an argument and Bobby ended up burning her hand with a lighted cigarette."

Spillner nodded. "We saw the burn mark. We wondered about that."

"I gave Mickey my card and told her I could put her in touch with some people who could help her, not just to get away from Bobby, but also to help get herself cleaned up, which I'm sure from her general appearance you must have suspected was a problem for her. I'm guessing that after I retrieved

Gabrielle, Bobby figured Mickey put me on to him and decided to get a little payback. Only for one reason or another, things got out of hand and she ended up getting killed."

Lorraine Proctor said, "Yep, that's pretty much the way it looked to us. So now that we're agreed as to what happened to the late Ms. Reddick, where do we find Bobby?"

"No idea," I said. "He was renting a place over on Antioch Pike, but the word is he's moved out. Mickey said he was looking for an apartment in the city somewhere, but I don't know where it is, or if he did."

"Then how did you find him to get the girl back?" It was the question I'd been waiting for them to ask since the moment they both sat down. It was the one question I was not willing to answer. Not that I had any particular feelings of warmth toward Jack Olin, but he'd held up his end of our agreement and I couldn't see any reason to sell him out to the cops.

"I asked around. And before you ask, that's all I can tell you."

"You mean you won't."

"If that way sounds better to you, then no, I won't. But think of it this way. When I was looking for Bobby, all I wanted to do was retrieve a runaway teenaged girl. Plus, he didn't know I was on his trail. It wasn't the easiest thing, but I was able to persuade my source to help me find him. You two are looking for a suspected killer, and that same source is not at all likely to want to get involved in a homicide investigation."

"If you want, we could go downtown and talk about this some more at our house."

"You could," I said. "But then you'd have to read me my rights, and then I'd invoke, and you wouldn't learn anything more than you know right now."

Spillner appeared to give that some thought. "Okay, then let's think about this. When you had him, after you got the girl, why didn't you just bring him in? You could have done that, you know."

"Bring him in how? I'm not on the job. The city doesn't pay me. My assignment was to find the girl and take her home, which I did."

"Yes, you did," he said, as the two cops got up to leave, "and now we'll go and find Bobby Fury. That's our job. But the thing is, you had the ball first and goal on the one-yard line and you punted instead of running it in. If you'd handed him over when you had the chance, Mickey Reddick might still be alive. And that's on you."

After they were gone, I thought about what Spillner had said at the end. I turned his words upside down. I pulled them inside out. I tried to spin them another way. And in the end, I realized he was right. I'd fucked up. I'd cut Bobby slack when there was no reason to do so, except that I thought maybe he had learned a lesson from his encounter with Vincent. He hadn't. He'd gone from being a pedophile and a potential child molester to a killer in less than twenty-four hours. And while I wasn't particularly worried about him for myself, my fear was that now that he had nothing to lose, he'd be coming back for Gabrielle, and possibly for Maggie as well.

I couldn't let that happen. And the more I thought about it, the more convinced I became that unless the cops found him quickly, or he turned himself in, there was only one thing left for me to do.

I would have to find him myself. And when I did, I would have to kill him.

Chapter Twenty-One

T hing is, when you come right down to it, if you have the nerve and the will, killing somebody isn't difficult. That's true whether you're talking about a king, a prime minister, a significant other, or a scumbag like Bobby Fury. All you have to do is get close to your target, pull the trigger and, boom! Job done.

Think about it. Two guys get into an argument in a bar over a woman or a football game or some other damn thing. It doesn't end on friendly terms. They're both drunk. Words get said, maybe punches get thrown. One of them goes home, gets his gun, comes back, and shoots the other one. A dozen people see him do it. The shooter, now filled with remorse, sits tight, maybe has another couple of beers. The cops arrive, make the arrest, and that's the end of it. If you want to take the route of a suicide bomber, it's even easier, plus you'll never have to worry about having to explain a felony conviction on a job application.

What makes killing someone infinitely more difficult is getting away with it, particularly when the killer and the victim are known to one another, like the two guys in the bar, or a husband and a wife. That's why serial killers are so difficult to apprehend. Their victims are complete strangers, chosen at random, and the killers have no obvious motive other than an irresistible urge to take a life. What finally gets them caught, if they get caught at all, is that they get sloppy. They become arrogant and start playing cat-and-mouse games with the cops, or they get overconfident and a pattern to their crimes emerges. Sometimes it takes years before they make a critical mistake that leads to their capture. Other times they don't get caught at all. They move to another city, or they die themselves, or, for whatever reason, they just stop the killing. Finding Bobby Fury was not going to present that kind of a challenge. The police knew who they were looking for, and so did I. One of us was bound to find him. The only question was whether he would survive the encounter.

I began making a mental list of what I knew about Bobby. It was not very much. He wanted to make movies and perhaps saw porn films as either a real career path or as a stepping stone to more mainstream cinema. He had a connection with Jack Olin, who apparently was willing to give him financial support, for reasons that were not yet clear. I wondered how long that had been going on. Bobby had been renting a house, and even though it was in a relatively down-market area, he wasn't living there for free. That meant he was getting money for doing something, but what?

And then there was that truck. I know next to nothing about pickup trucks, having never owned one, but I did recognize that Bobby's ride was both new and expensive, like BMW bucks expensive. It had a crew cab, an eight-foot bed, a camper shell, dual rear wheels, and four-wheel drive. Where did he get the money to pay for it? I live in a place where big pickups are common, and I get the shit-kicker mindset that says the bigger the truck, the more testosterone it takes to fuel it. But even so, trucks like Bobby's cost serious money. So again, where was he getting it?

Finally, I thought about something Delsey had told me, namely that Gabrielle had not had sex with Bobby. I wondered, why not? She had been with him for two weeks, and she certainly didn't seem to be in any particular hurry to get away from him. I had no evidence to support the idea, but I took her willingness to stay put to mean that if he had wanted to have sex with her, she very likely would have jumped in with both feet. That suggested that either Bobby wasn't interested in Gabrielle as a sexual partner-slash-fantasy dream girl, or else he had an overriding reason to abstain.

The expensive truck. The financial backing from Jack Olin. Gabrielle still a virgin. Was there a connection?

An idea began to form in a dark corner of my brain. It was an unpleasant thought, and I was not pleased to have come up with it, but I was going to need something more to go on before I could be sure. That meant going at least partway back to the beginning of the search for Gabrielle, to try to connect the dots in a different sequence. Unless he made a move, settling the score with Bobby Fury would have to take a back seat for a while.

I didn't think I needed to have another conversation with Carly Barrett at the Rhinestone Cowgirl. Mickey was dead, and unless Bobby had gone back to his old haunts on Lower Broad, there was no reason to expect Carly would know anything more than what she had previously told me. Besides, if he had turned back up at the Cowgirl, I was pretty sure I would have gotten a call from Carly. With the cops on his trail, he had most likely gone to ground someplace where he wouldn't attract any attention. Failing that, he was in the wind, probably a thousand miles away. But just to be sure, and to have a place to start, I decided to take a look at Bobby's rental house on Antioch Pike. Maybe he had left something behind when he moved out that would tell me what direction he was heading now.

I didn't have a street address for Bobby's rental, but I did have a general familiarity with the area Mickey Reddick had described when I talked to her. And as it turned out, finding Bobby's former residence was no problem at all. On a street where all the homes were modest, but well-maintained, with neatly trimmed lawns, some with late-season flowers still blooming, I spotted one with a front yard that appeared not to have been mowed since sometime around Labor Day. And since the front windows covered with bedsheets instead of drapes or shutters, I was pretty sure I had found *chez* Furillo. I cruised slowly past the house, looking for any indication that somebody might be at home. Seeing no vehicles and no activity, I turned my car around and parked in the narrow driveway, like somebody who had every right to be there. All the same, and just to make doubly sure no one was watching, I got out of my car and walked slowly around the entire property. I figured if any of the neighbors noticed me and asked what I was doing, I could claim to be working for the leasing agent and was making an inspection before the house went back on the market. I needn't have worried. Either the folks on both sides were not at home, or else they were, and didn't notice me or didn't care.

I waited a couple more minutes to make sure I was alone, and then went around to the rear and kicked in the basement window closest to the back porch, where I figured it would be least likely to be noticed. I took off my shoe and used the heel to knock the remaining glass out of the frame so I wouldn't cut myself getting inside. It was a tight fit, but I managed to squeeze feet-first through the opening and dropped down onto the basement floor.

It took a few moments for my eyes to get acclimated to the near-total darkness in the basement, and a moment longer to find a light socket with a bulb and a chain attached to a floor joist. I turned the light on and saw an almost completely empty space, except for an empty plastic trash container and a photographer's backdrop sweep leaning in one corner.

I went upstairs and made a quick first pass through the house. It wasn't a hot day, but the sun was out and the windows were buttoned up tight. I began to sweat almost immediately. Bobby's residence was a postwar starter home, very basic, with two bedrooms, a kitchen, one bathroom, and a living room. No dining room, no family room, no walk-in closets. No pictures on the walls. No carpets on the floor.

I wasn't sure what I was looking for, and even less sure there would be anything to find. Still, considering that Bobby Fury was now an accused murderer who represented a danger to Gabrielle, and maybe Maggie as well, looking for anything at all that might help me find him seemed like a sensible thing to do. I began my search in the bathroom. I found nothing in the medicine cabinet except a bottle of aspirin, a half-used-up tube of toothpaste, and a can of spray deodorant. There was a dark ring around the toilet bowl and a robust growth of mold in the bathtub. Bobby definitely did not subscribe to *Martha Stewart Living*.

The first bedroom was no more promising. Except for a heavily stained mattress on the floor and some empty wire coat hangers in the closet, the room had been cleaned out. I supposed the mattress was where Bobby's homeboys crashed when they stayed over. I couldn't imagine Gabrielle willingly sleeping on it.

The second bedroom had a cleaner, somewhat more lived-in appearance. There was a queen-sized bed, no mattress or box spring, a dresser, a nightstand with a table lamp, and a ceiling fan with a burned-out bulb in the light attachment. I riffled quickly through the drawers in the dresser and nightstand without finding anything at all, not even dirty underwear. And then I remembered something.

Gabrielle had hidden the photos she wanted to keep secret by taping them to the bottom of a drawer in her bedroom. Maybe she wasn't as inventive as I had first thought. Maybe she learned the trick from Bobby. With that in mind, I went back through the dresser, this time feeling underneath the drawers. My fingers touched something securely fastened underneath the second drawer from the bottom. I reached in with both hands and pulled it free. It was a manila envelope containing photographs of young girls, a dozen images in all. Except for one girl, I had no idea who I was looking at. On the other hand, I thought I knew what.

There were six girls, six pairs of photos, each eight-by-ten. For each girl there was a headshot, showing carefully arranged hair and artfully applied makeup. The second photo was full-length. In each, the girl was standing in front of the sweep wearing a sleeveless knee-length black dress, no shoes, with her hair combed out straight and her hands held stiffly at her sides as if she were standing in a police lineup. All were in their early teens, slender and clear-skinned. Five of the girls I didn't recognize.

The sixth girl was Gabrielle. And I wasn't looking at prom photos, pinups, or publicity stills. I was looking at inventory.

Chapter Twenty-Two

I replaced the photos in the envelope and got out of Bobby Fury's house as fast as I could, which meant leaving by the front door rather that crawling back through the broken basement window. Bad luck. Just as I was leaving, an across-the-street neighbor sweeping her front sidewalk noticed me coming out. She stopped what she was doing and stared as if she were trying to memorize my face for a later description. I made a big show of pretending to lock the door behind me and then waved to her like somebody who'd finished whatever was his legitimate business there. I didn't think she was fooled.

I knew I should take the photos directly to the cops and dump whatever evidence they represented into their laps. Clearly, if the photos in Bobby's bedroom meant what I thought they did, then the situation was too big and too hot for me to tackle on my own. Still, I had some questions that needed answers, and I knew the only way to get them was to first talk to Gabrielle.

When I arrived at the house on Newsome Street, I found Jericho's Dodge in the driveway. More bad luck. That meant the first thing I would have to do was talk my way past him. I parked my car on the street, tucked the envelope with the photos under my arm, and walked up to the front door. I remembered that the doorbell wasn't working, and knocked on the screen door. In a moment or two, Jericho appeared. He didn't invite me in, but he didn't punch me in the nose either. Instead, he stepped out onto the front stoop.

"Mr. Gamble. What can I do for you?"

"Just a couple things, Reverend," I said. "I wanted to come by and see how

Gabrielle is getting along after—well, now that she's back home."

"She's fine. We been praying together a lot and I think she'll be coming around to seeing what she did was wrong in the eyes of God." I wasn't so sure about that, but I didn't pursue it. Instead, I nodded like I understood just what he was talking about.

"By the way," he reached into his jacket pocket and extracted a thick wad of cash secured with a rubber band. "Long as you're here, I have something for you."

"What's this for?"

"To compensate you for your troubles," he answered. "The wife and I are grateful to you and to the good Lord for bringing our little girl back home safe. I don't know if this'll cover all your expenses, but just the same we wanted to give you what we could. The congregation put most of it up at Wednesday night services after they found out what you did for us."

I thought about declining, then decided, what the hell, take the money. I thanked him and put the cash in my pocket. "Also, before I go, I'd like to ask Gabrielle one or two questions."

"About what?" A note of suspicion crept into his voice. "Mind you, I'm not one to be telling you your business, and the wife and I both appreciate all you done, but I'm thinking you asking her a lot of questions might not be such a good idea. You already know, she's been through a lot. Besides, she's home now and safe. What more could you want to ask her about?"

I had a story made up and ready to go, but then I decided it might be better just to lay my cards on the table. "Reverend, the man your daughter was with during those two weeks she was gone has been implicated in a murder. Understand, I'm not suggesting Gabrielle had anything to do with that, or that she even knows anything about it, but she may still have some idea where we can find him. He's dangerous, and if we don't find him, he may well hurt somebody else." I left the question of just who that might be to his imagination.

"There's another thing." I reached into the envelope I had brought with me and removed the two photos of Gabrielle. I held them up so he could see them. "I found these pictures in the house where Bobby Fury was living, and where Gabrielle was probably staying while she was with him. There were others, just like these, six girls in all, including Gabrielle. That makes me think whatever was going on, it wasn't just some teenaged romance gone haywire. I think this guy might be involved in procuring young girls for sex traffickers. I also think that if we hadn't gotten Gabrielle back when we did, you and Delsey might never have seen her again. Along with the possibility that he's a killer, that's why we have to find this guy and either put him away or put him down."

When he hesitated, I said, "There's no way of knowing how many families have lost their daughters to whatever he's involved with. Right now, our best hope of finding him is finding out what Gabrielle knows."

There was sadness in his voice. "Her mother and I have tried talkin' to her. She won't tell us anything. Why do you think you'll do any better?"

"I don't know, maybe I won't. But when you talked to her, we didn't know what we know now about Bobby. I'm hoping if she's the kind of kid you and Delsey raised her to be, she's got a conscience and she'll want to help these other girls." I paused. "And sir, with respect, I'm hoping you do, too."

He nodded. "You make it hard to say no, Mr. Gamble. Guess you better come on inside."

Jericho seated me at the dining room table and went to fetch Gabrielle. From the sound of things, she was sitting tight in her bedroom and had no wish to talk to me. Words were exchanged, many that I thought both might regret later, and then Jericho said something in a low voice that I wasn't able to make out. A minute later he reappeared, walking behind Gabrielle with a hand on each of her shoulders. She took a seat on the side of the table across from me; Jericho sat at the head. "Ask your questions, Mr. Gamble. My daughter will tell you whatever you need to know."

The Gabrielle seated across from me was a far cry from the Gabrielle Maggie and I had rescued only a few days earlier. Gone was the makeup, the carefully arranged hair, and the micro-mini skirt she had been wearing that day at the park. Instead, she was dressed in blue jeans and a shapeless gray sweatshirt. Her face was scrubbed clean of even a hint of cosmetics and her hair was combed out straight and tied in a ponytail. Her expression, however, was defiant and her eyes burned with an intensity that said, given half a chance, she'd plunge a kitchen knife into her father's heart and be out the door without so much as a backward look. I wondered what Jericho had said to her to get her to come to the table. But the fury in her eyes told me there was no point in trying to start off with small talk, so I came straight to the point.

I said, "Gabrielle, I promise I won't keep you long. I just need to ask you one or two things about Bobby and then we'll be done here, okay?"

No response.

"Fine. When you were staying with him, were you at his house over on Antioch?"

"Yes." She shot me a venomous look. "Now are you going to ask if he fucked me?"

I expected that remark would send Jericho flying out of his chair like a human cannonball, but he said nothing.

"No. That's none of my business. What I was going to ask is while you were there if you met any of his friends."

"Like who?"

"I'm thinking of a woman named Michelle Reddick. You might know her as Mickey. She was in one of the pictures I found in your bedroom back when your mother first asked me to start looking for you."

No answer.

"Gabrielle, did you meet Mickey or not?"

"Okay, I met her, so what?"

"This is what. She's dead, Gabrielle. The police have evidence Bobby killed her."

She shook her head from side to side. "No! Bobby wouldn't do that. He's not—he wouldn't hurt anybody."

"Then he should turn himself in so the police can clear him and get started looking for the real killer. Have you been in touch with Bobby since you've been back home? Or do you know where he might be? Because as long as he stays on the run, there's a chance he might get hurt."

"No, and if I did know, I wouldn't tell you." She turned to give her father a poisonous look. "Or him."

"I understand how you feel, but just the same, think about it in case he does try to get in touch. People have been known to get hurt running from the police." I put the envelope with the photographs on the table and removed the pictures of Gabrielle. I spread them in front of her, keeping them just out of her reach. "I wonder what you can tell me about these two pictures."

She seemed genuinely surprised. "Where did those come from?"

"You tell me. This is you, isn't it? Did Bobby take these?"

"Yes. Where did you get them?"

I decided there was no point in holding out. "Bobby had them hidden in his bedroom. Did he show them to you?"

"He said he was going to show them around. He said they would help me find parts in movies, or maybe if I wanted to do some modeling. He said he had helped some other girls, but that I was prettier than any of them and I would be sure to get some calls. There was another man there when he took the pictures, and that man said Bobby was right, that he had never seen anyone as...what's the word?"

"Photogenic," I suggested.

"Yes, that's it, photogenic. He said I was photogenic. The camera loved me." She brightened a bit at the recollection, then, noticing that her father was staring at her disapprovingly, let her face fall again.

"The other man, did you happen to hear his name?"

"No, but I didn't like him. He acted like he was all tough or something, and he had a lot of tattoos on his arms and his neck. I think Bobby was afraid of him."

Vincent. Bobby was right to be afraid of him, I thought. "What happened after they were finished taking pictures?"

"We all went back upstairs. I changed back into my regular clothes and then we drank some wine."

There was the magic word. Jericho's eyes flew fully open and there was a look of horror on his face. "You drank wine?"

"You drink wine at your stupid services every Sunday. That doesn't seem to bother you any."

CHAPTER TWENTY-TWO

"You're a child!" he thundered.

"And you're a…" She let the sentence trail off. "Anyway, if it makes you feel any better, the wine made me throw up. They had to take me to a doctor."

I said, "What doctor?"

"I don't know. I wasn't feeling good. I didn't hear his name."

"Was this during the day, or at night?"

"It was at night. It was a yellow building around the corner from the college library. It had lights on in the front."

"Do you remember what the doctor looked like?"

She shook her head. "He had on a mask—what do you call it—like if he was going to do an operation."

"You mean a surgical mask?" She nodded. "What did the doctor do to you?"

"He gave me a shot and I went to sleep. After that, I don't know. When I woke up, it was morning and I was back at Bobby's house in bed. It was like nothing ever happened. I felt a little dizzy at first, but then it went away, and that was it. After that, I took a bath and got dressed Bobby made me breakfast, and then we watched TV for the rest of the day. Two days after that he told me we were going to the park for the day. Instead, he handed me over to you and Miss Totten and now here I am."

"Okay," I said. "Just one more thing and then we'll be through. At any time when you were with Bobby, did you meet any other girls around your age, or did Bobby talk about any other girls he might have also photographed?"

"No. There aren't any other girls. Bobby loves me. He said he did. He never talked about anybody else. He just said we'd be going away soon, just as soon as it was time. He said he needed to work out a few things and then we'd be gone forever."

"You're home and you're safe now," Jericho said. "You're not going to be going anywhere with that man or anybody else until you're old enough to make better decisions. In the meantime, your mother and I will make sure nothing like this ever happens to you again. I promise you that."

"And I promise you," she spat back at him, "that when Bobby comes back for me, and he said he would, I'll make sure this time after I'm gone, you'll never see me again. Not either one of you, not ever. Not in a million years." And with that, she got up from the table and left the room. From the back of the house came the noise of a door slamming shut. I looked at Jericho. He folded his hands on the table, making no move to follow his angry daughter, and the look on his face was one of deep and unmistakable sadness.

It was time for me to leave. I had gotten the answers I came for. I said goodbye to Jericho and walked out into the afternoon sunlight of a late October day.

Chapter Twenty-Three

After leaving Jericho and Gabrielle to sort out their issues, I drove out West End once again, this time to the Vanderbilt campus, and started cruising the side streets looking for a doctor's office located in a yellow building. I felt okay leaving the two of them alone. I didn't know Jericho very well, but I had seen enough of him to believe that he had enough self-control not to do violence to his daughter. I hoped that he also had enough empathy to understand the feelings she was experiencing and that the things she had said to him were nothing more than angry words that could be forgiven in time.

It took fifteen or twenty minutes of driving around before I spotted the doctor's office where Gabrielle said Bobby had taken her after her photoshoot and subsequent glass, or glasses, of wine. It was located in the middle of the block on Louise Avenue, around the corner from the Vanderbilt campus. As she had remembered, it was a single-story office, painted a muddy yellow color with a black door and black shutters. Along one side was a parking lot that held half a dozen cars. A discreet sign attached to a signpost in front of the building read "Dr. Dexter Morse, Obstetrics and Gynecology." I made a note of the address and the doctor's name and then drove downtown to police headquarters. My plan was to show the photos to the two homicide cops who had visited me earlier to see whether they could help figure out who were the girls pictured and whether they might now have some connection to Gabrielle. I was also curious about why a fourteen-year-old girl apparently made queasy from a glass of wine would need to be seen by a gynecologist.

I parked my car on the street outside police headquarters and rode the elevator up to the detective division on the second floor. I found Lorraine Proctor seated at her desk with her feet propped up on an open drawer, eating either a late lunch or a mid-afternoon snack. When she spotted me, she waved me over and pointed to a visitor's chair next to her desk.

"Back so soon? Tell me you've brought in Bobby Fury and I'll give you half my sandwich."

"Sorry, nothing doing there, but I'm beginning to wonder whether he's not the only one we should be looking for."

"So now what, you're telling me you don't think he did it?" She put down her sandwich and took a drink from a can of orange soda. As she had during our meeting earlier in the day, she kept her voice neutral. I suspected it was a technique she employed as a way to persuade reluctant witnesses and uncooperative suspects to tell her what she wanted to know. The real threat was in her eyes, which had narrowed slightly as she began drilling down. It gave them a look just hard enough to let you know she wasn't fucking around.

I said, "I'm telling you I'm not sure anymore. I think this case might be about something else. And Bobby Fury might be just a small part of it."

"Something else such as what?"

"Such as sex trafficking. I think it's possible—no, I think it's more than possible that Bobby didn't grab Gabrielle Hawkins because he has some creepy kind of crush on her. I think he grabbed her because he intended to sell her to the highest bidder. By the way, where's Spillner?"

"Court. Some old case of his finally came to trial. He's been tied up there since right after we talked to you. Hence you find me here at my desk, late-lunching on the best chicken salad on white our vending machine has to offer." She leaned back in her chair and took another swallow of her orange soda. "Let's get back to your deal, here. Say I buy this. You got anything at all to support your hypothesis if I take it upstairs?"

"I got these." I tossed the envelope I retrieved from Bobby Fury's bedroom onto her desk. She opened it and studied each of the photos.

"Who am I looking at?

168

"This is Gabrielle," I said, pointing. "The other five, I don't know."

She narrowed her eyes again. "Where did you get these?"

"Does it matter?"

"Yeah," she said, "it kind of does."

"Well, then, I found them in a house that Bobby Fury was renting, but he's now moving out of. I went in, just to see if I could find anything that might give me an idea what his next move was going to be. I found these taped to the bottom of a dresser drawer, the same way Gabrielle had hidden some photos in her bedroom."

"In other words, you committed a burglary."

"Well...I rang the doorbell, but there was nobody home."

"Right. Across-the-street neighbor reported a broken window. She wrote down your license plate number, too." She gave me a mirthless smile. "Never a dull moment with you, is there Mr. Gamble? I would have thought after you found the girl, you'd be on to something else."

"I would have been. I thought when I took Gabrielle back home that was the end as far as this case was concerned. But then, after you and your partner told me Mickey Reddick had been murdered, I began thinking that maybe Bobby was getting back at everybody who had fucked things up for him and Gabrielle. I was worried he might try to contact her again, and I was worried there might be other people he might want to hurt."

"Are we talking about Margaret Totten? You're involved?"

Again, I had to hand it to her. She had game. I wondered if there was anything about this case that she didn't already know.

She said, "And since you're involved, you're worried about her, and you've gone riding to the rescue."

"That's how it started out. But then I began thinking maybe I had things all wrong. I mean if Bobby had just snatched Gabrielle off the street that would be one thing. But she didn't want to go back to her parents. She wanted to stay with him, so there must have been an attraction. But then, why hadn't they had sex? That suggested to me that for whatever reason, she was worth more as a virgin than as a sex partner."

"Maybe he's just some kind of freak. Maybe he can't get it up, or maybe he wanted to preserve her in an unblemished state for all time, like a fly in amber."

"Sure, and maybe Bobby found religion and they were saving it for their wedding night. Come on, Detective, look at these pictures. These weren't pasted up all over Bobby's bedroom like he was some kind of fetishist. They look more like sale items in a catalog. The only thing missing is the price tags. The question is, who might be willing to pay more for a girl who's still a virgin? Not ordinary sex traffickers. They don't give a shit. They just grab runaways at the bus station. They beat them up, drug them up, and force them into the life. I think somebody decided these girls are more valuable than that."

"All right say all this is true. How does that get Bobby off the hook for the Reddick kill?"

"I don't know, maybe it doesn't. But if this is really about high-end sex trafficking and not just some half-assed Romeo and Juliet thing, we need to find out who these other girls are."

She raised her eyebrows at that. "We? Who's we?"

"All right then, you need to find out. If all five of them are alive and well and home with their parents, then fine, I'm wrong and we're back to just looking for Bobby. However, if my hunch is right, then Bobby could be mixed up with some people who have a lot more skin in the game than he does, and I'm thinking they could be the people who killed Mickey Reddick."

She turned her palms out, interlaced her fingers, and cracked her knuckles. "I don't suppose when you were conducting your, what shall we call it, your reconnaissance, you happened to run across a forwarding address for Mr. Fury?"

"Afraid not. He could be anywhere. He's got that truck he could live in if he had to. He could be parked at the airport, in a Wal-Mart lot, anyplace where there are lots of vehicles. He could also be a thousand miles away, where nobody is looking for him."

"Or he could be in a shallow grave or at the bottom of the Cumberland River."

"Could be," I said. "That would solve at least one of our problems. But somehow. I think he's still around, and I could be way off base here, but somehow I think there's more to Mickey's murder than just a lovers' quarrel gone wrong."

"That doesn't sound promising." She took a last bite of her sandwich and threw the rest into the wastebasket. "You got anything else?"

"One more thing. There's a doctor I think you should take a look at. His name is Dexter Morse. He's got an OB practice over on Louise. I spoke with Gabrielle earlier and she told me Bobby took her to see this doc right after he took these pictures."

"And what did the doctor do for her? Or should I ask what he did to her?"

"She didn't know. She said he gave her an injection and when she woke up, she was back at Bobby's house."

"Okay." She wrote the name down on her notepad. "We'll take a look at him."

"While you're at it, see if you can find a connection between Bobby, the good doctor, and a guy named Jack Olin."

"Jack Olin? We're talking the porn king of the mid-South?"

"That's the one. According to the late Michelle Reddick, Olin had promised to bankroll some of Bobby Fury's adventures in filmmaking. I think there's a connection between Bobby, Jack Olin, Doctor Morse, and the girls in these photographs."

"You think. But you don't know."

"I figured that was your job. Also, Jack Olin's sidekick, a body-builder type named Vincent, last name unknown, was on hand when Bobby took these pictures."

This time she didn't write anything down. "Okay, is that really it this time, or is there somebody else? Johnny Cash, maybe?"

"This isn't enough? Aren't you at least curious?"

"Curious, yes, but I'm still not sure I like it. I'll talk to Spillner when he gets through with court and see what he thinks. We'll also look into this guy Vincent and see if anything pops up. Meantime, I'll try to find out who these other girls are, but I don't think this case is going to turn out to be anything more than what it looks like, which is that Bobby Fury killed his old girlfriend because she talked to you. Which, speaking on behalf of the public at large, seems not to be a particularly good idea."

I started to say something to that, but she cut me off. "Look, I don't know how many homicides you worked when you were on the job, but last year we had more than eighty here in the metro area, so even in the short time since I came over from narcotics, I've seen quite a few. Most of the time, they were pretty simple. The killers didn't have alibis, and there were no alternative theories that made any sense.

"But just the same, leave the photos with me and I'll see what I can come up with. And I'll let you know if there's anything more to it than what's right out in plain sight. Meantime, why don't you go back to doing whatever it is you do, or better yet, take your Miss Totten to dinner and a movie? That's what my partner and I do when one of us has had a bad day. She's an ADA, and believe me, she has lots of them."

I looked at her and nodded. "Seen anything good lately?"

A wide smile spread across her face. I said, "What?"

"Congratulations, Mr. Gamble, you're not an asshole."

"You lost me."

"When I said I had a partner, you didn't look at me like I was some kind of a flaming lesbian deviant."

"What would make you a deviant?" I asked. "You've made a commitment to somebody you care about, and who evidently cares about you. What could be wrong with that?"

Chapter Twenty-Four

Maggie's silver Volvo was parked in front of her townhouse when I rolled up, in full daylight this time. Before parking my own car, I took a drive around her complex, paying closer attention to the layout than I had during my previous visit. I took serious notice of where the parking areas were and how many exits there were to the street.

Facing the front of Maggie's quad, from left to right, her unit was the second of four. I liked that because it meant she had only two outside walls. That would make it somewhat more secure in the event somebody was trying to break in. What I didn't like was that the units were constructed with three levels, with the lower-level windows in the front at garden height. The front door was reached by a set of four concrete stairs. There were windows on both the main and upper levels as well, but someone wanting to break in would need at least a six-foot ladder to reach those.

I parked my car in an open space and walked around to the back. All the units had walk-out basements with French doors leading out to individual patios. Each patio was partly shaded by a deck that had a set of stairs leading down to the lower level. Entry to the unit from the deck was through a sliding glass door. Beyond the patio were a common greenbelt and an aerated detention pond, to catch the runoff after a heavy rain. Bordering the pond was a row of evergreen trees which acted as a noise barrier for the roadway on the other side. I estimated fifty yards from the tree line to the back of Maggie's unit.

From a security standpoint, the biggest problem I could see was that the bedrooms were on the upper level. That location meant that if someone tried to break in through a garden-level window during the night, it would be almost impossible to hear from the upstairs bedrooms. I hoped the units had been equipped by the builder with an alarm system. In a high-end complex like this one, that was at least a possibility.

I walked back to where my car was parked. I unlocked the glove compartment and took out a short-barreled Smith & Wesson .32 caliber revolver. I emptied the cartridges from the cylinder and put the gun into my jacket pocket. Then I climbed Maggie's front steps and rang her doorbell. In a minute she came and opened the door, I noticed, without having to unlock it first. That was another security problem. I knew she was expecting me, but I hadn't called ahead to let her know that I was on my way. Leaving her door unlocked meant anyone could have gotten inside without any trouble at all. Not that the lock she did have was likely to provide much security anyway. Although the door was metal-clad, the frame was wood and the lock consisted of a single through-bolt that I doubted would present much of an obstacle to a determined housebreaker.

She greeted me wearing a short terrycloth bathrobe and a towel wrapped around her hair. She kissed me and said, "As you can see, I'm not ready."

I hooked my finger in her robe and pulled her toward me. "That depends upon what we're doing, doesn't it?"

"You are such a pig," she said, disengaging my finger and taking a step back. "Wait here."

I sat down on the couch. Maggie disappeared up the stairs. I heard paper rattling, and when she came back down, she was carrying a pink shopping bag from a store I didn't recognize.

"We were late getting away from the conference this morning. I didn't have time to stop on the way for groceries because I wanted to be home when you got here, so we're going to have to eat out. It'll be my treat this time. You don't mind, do you?"

"Not at all."

She opened the shopping bag and took out a short, sheer, rose-colored negligee. Holding it up in front of her, she said "What do you think?"

"I think if the last thing I saw on this earth before I was suddenly struck blind was you wearing whatever you call that thing, I could die happy."

"You're sweet." She showed me a wide smile that turned into a laugh. "So, what'll it be, EF or FF? Either way, I can be good to go in just a minute."

"I think TF, talk first. There're some things I need to tell you and I don't think you're going to like it."

"Shit," she said, "and me with a brand-new nightie. Please don't tell me you've got an ex-wife who's decided to take you back."

"No, it's nothing like that," I said and sat her down on the couch. "You need to hear this."

I told her about Mickey Reddick and how the police thought that it was Bobby Fury who had killed her, maybe for revenge, because he thought it was Mickey who had pointed me in his direction when I was looking for Gabrielle Hawkins.

She listened closely and then said, "You say that's what the police think, but you didn't say what you think. Do you believe somebody besides Bobby might have killed her?"

"I'd say it's at least a possibility. When the police told me she had been murdered, I came to the same conclusion they did, which was that Bobby did it. She had been beaten up, which, from what I got from the cops, seems to be a usual outcome for women who get close to him. In this case, though, she apparently died from an injection of heroin mixed with fentanyl."

"So then, it could have been an accidental overdose."

"Maybe, but then there were no prints on the syringe. If you're going to inject yourself, why wipe your prints?" I shook my head. "No, it's pretty clear somebody killed her. And it probably was Bobby who did it, but then there might be something more to this case than him losing Gabrielle and taking it out on Mickey."

I went on to tell Maggie about the photos I had found hidden in Bobby's house and how they suggested he might be involved in some kind of sex trafficking operation that specialized in underage teenaged girls.

"But," I said, "what makes Gabrielle special is that she's a virgin. Bobby may not have known that when he first took her away. He may have genuinely had a crush on her, but then when she told him she'd never had sex before, she suddenly became much more valuable. There are people who will pay a premium for untouched girls. Bobby even took her to a doctor to make sure she was telling the truth.

"Here's how I think this works. Bobby finds girls, maybe at the bus station or at a mall or the park or wherever. He picks them up, promises he'll put them in a movie, and then when the time is right, passes them along to whoever he's working with. The girls end up forced into prostitution in Atlanta or New York or some other big city, and Bobby gets paid a finder's fee.

"With Gabrielle, though, he saw something special, and either he decided to keep her for himself, or else he was stringing her along until arrangements could be made to sell her to the highest bidder. Either way, the shit hit the fan when I connected him back to Jack Olin. Olin wasn't ready to risk his porn empire to take on a sideline selling underage girls, so he sent his guy Vincent to tell Bobby to turn over the girl if he wanted to keep on getting money to finance his movies. Bobby balked at letting go of Gabrielle, so Vincent scuffed him up a little to help him see the bigger picture. When I talked to Olin, I told him I wanted to hear from him or from Bobby no later than Monday. I didn't know anything for sure. I was just running a bluff. But then Monday came and so did Bobby's call. You with me so far?"

"Yes."

"The question then becomes, did Bobby kill Mickey Reddick because she was indirectly responsible for him losing the girl of his dreams, or because she caused him to miss out on a big payday when the time came to put her on the block? Either way, I don't think we've seen the last of Bobby Fury."

"Then Gabrielle could still be in danger."

"That depends on what kind of danger we're talking about. Gabrielle doesn't think she has anything to fear, at least not from Bobby. She wants to be with him. She made that clear enough when we took her home the other day."

She nodded. "You're worried they'll try to get back together again, and she'll end up walking into a nightmare."

"I am," I said. "If this is just some misguided romance, that's one thing. But for all we know, Bobby still has plans to put her up for auction."

I could tell she was thinking about that.

"It doesn't matter what his intentions are, Gamble, we can't let them reconnect. Even if they are in love and they somehow manage to run off and make babies on some tropical island, it would be the worst possible outcome for Gabrielle."

Before I could answer her, the telephone rang. Maggie answered, listened for a moment, and then handed the phone to me. "It's some woman. She says her name is Lorraine Proctor and she's with the police." She gave me a quizzical look. "Gamble, what's going on? Why are the police calling you here?"

I put my hand over the mouthpiece. "This may take a minute. Why don't you go put some clothes on, and then we'll talk about it."

On the phone, Lorraine Proctor said, "That sounds hot. Am I interrupting something?"

"In another minute you might have. How did you find me?"

"I called your cell number first, but your phone is turned off, so I thought I'd try your lady friend. After all, you did imply you two were an item."

"Okay, more good police work. What can I do for you?"

"Well, actually I'm calling to tell you that you did some pretty good work yourself, even if you did conduct an illegal search, which, by the way, I wouldn't mention to anyone else. It's inadmissible evidence, in case you forgot how putting a case together is supposed to work."

"I remember."

"Good. Anyhow, after you left, I ran those photos through R-and-I, and right away I came up with a match, a girl called Bethany DiPaolo. Turns out she's fifteen years old and she went missing about six months ago. So far, we haven't been able to turn anything up on her whereabouts. Then I thought maybe the other girls might also be missing, but not from our jurisdiction, so I got hold of TBI and asked them to run a statewide check."

"And?"

"And it's bad, really bad. You went five for five."

"Let's have it."

"Okay. Leading off we've got Rayanne Dean, age thirteen-and-a-half, gone missing from Jackson last December, no further information. Next up, Jessica Mather, age sixteen, this time missing from Clarksville in February. After that, Kelsey Boyd and Ariel Carbonara, ages fifteen and sixteen. They were best friends. Both disappeared while on a shopping trip to a mall in Chattanooga during spring break. And there may be more. TBI is going back through their records now to see how many other missing girls fit the profile."

"The Mather girl," I said. "Any chance she just upped and ran off with some Screaming Eagle from Fort Campbell?"

"Military is checking to see whether any soldier boys either went AWOL or turned up with surprise spouses about the same time. But even if they get a hit on this one, those other four girls didn't take a stroll down the aisle with some guy in khaki unless they were boy scouts." She paused, and then I heard a voice saying something in the background. "Listen, I've got to go. I'll call you back if I find out anything else."

I hung up the phone. Maggie had seated herself on the couch with her hands folded in her lap. "You said there were six sets of photos. We know where Gabrielle is. The other five girls are gone, too, aren't they? That's what the detective was telling you."

"Yes, that's what she was telling me. Maybe they'll be lucky and get arrested for prostitution or shoplifting, or turn up in a runaway shelter. At least then they'll be alive and have a chance to get back home."

"What about Gabrielle? She's home, and she's still not safe."

"Maybe, maybe not, but just to be sure I think she needs to be on a fairly short leash, at least until Bobby is taken into custody. Tomorrow I'll get hold of Delsey and Jericho and make it clear that they're going to need to know where Gabrielle is 24-7. How does she get to school every day?"

"She doesn't live far. I think she walks."

"Then one of her parents will have to drive her. It doesn't have to be forever, just until this Bobby thing is settled." I took a breath before moving on to what I was going to say next.

"That goes for you, too. We have to find a way to make sure you're protected."

"Me? Protected from Bobby, or from you?" She uncrossed and crossed her legs, exposing a tantalizing expanse of thigh and a bit more in the process. A playful look crossed her face. "Maybe the better question is who's going to protect you from me?"

"Keep that up and you'll find out. Look," I said, "I hate to spoil the mood, but just for a minute here, we need to take this seriously. If it was Bobby who killed Mickey, then he knows the cops are looking for him. In that case, he'll be keeping his head low until he can make a getaway if he hasn't already. He won't be thinking about you. But if he didn't kill Mickey, even though it's been in the news, it's possible he doesn't even know she's dead. He'll believe he's got nothing to worry about, and if Gabrielle still wants to be with him, they'll try to figure out a way to get back together. In that case, he might threaten you as a way of making sure I don't interfere with his plans all over again."

"So, what are you suggesting?"

I took the Smith & Wesson out of my jacket pocket and set it on the sofa cushion between us. She stared at it as if it were one of Jericho's snakes, coiled to strike.

I said, "Have you ever fired a handgun?"

"What, you think I'm going to shoot him?"

"You shouldn't have to. But if something goes wrong, you need to be able to defend yourself. Does your unit have an alarm system?"

She shook her head, "No."

I was afraid of that. "Okay, I don't think you'll have any problems during the day, but at night when you're here by yourself you should have some protection." I picked up the gun and held it where she could see it. "This is a .32 caliber revolver. It's very simple to use, you just point and pull the trigger. No safety to worry about and not much recoil. Right now, it's not loaded. Tomorrow I'll take you to a range so you can learn to use it. The main thing is, if you hear somebody trying to break in, fire one shot into the ceiling. That will make enough noise to scare off an intruder."

"And what if just noise isn't enough?"

"Then lock yourself in the bathroom. If the knob rattles, fire the other five rounds through the middle of the door and hope one of them hits whoever's on the other side."

"This isn't a joke," she said softly. "You're serious, aren't you?"

"Serious, yes," I agreed, "and selfish. I don't want anything to happen to you."

"Because?"

"Because when I see you my heart beats a little faster."

"You're sweet. Are you sure it's unloaded?"

"I'm sure."

"Okay." She took the .32 from me and dry-fired several times at the wall before handing it back to me. "Listen, if you're really worried, how about if you just move in with me for a while? Maybe see how you like it?"

I said, "That might be complicated."

"Complicated how? Listen, can I tell you something? When I first met you, back when you showed up in my office the first time, I thought you were just some con man, trying to squeeze a few dollars out of a mother desperate to get her daughter back."

"And now?"

"And now," she said, "I know better. You're a good guy, and if we keep going like we are, I think I'm going to fall in love with you. The question is, on those terms, do you want me in your life?"

"On those terms," I said, "you couldn't be more welcome."

Chapter Twenty-Five

Saturday morning arrived after a very short Friday night, which included an attentive viewing of the DVD given to me on the way out of Jack Olin's office. For me, it was a rerun, but Maggie seemed inspired by some of what she saw and challenged me to a foot race up two flights of stairs to the bedroom. I wouldn't have guessed she could move that fast, but she passed me on the first-floor landing and never looked back.

Despite my lack of sleep, I was up at daybreak. I got cleaned up the best way I could in Maggie's downstairs half-bath and crept out, I hoped, without waking her. I left a note on the kitchen counter saying that I had loaded the .32 revolver and placed it behind the middle cushion on the couch and that I would call later. I knew that between leaving her a loaded gun and her declaration of blossoming love, there was sure to be a long discussion to follow and I needed time to think about what I wanted to say in response.

Before heading home, I stopped by the office to pick up any messages left over from the day before and to lock the door to the outer office, since I had failed to do that the previous afternoon. Because it was a Saturday, I wasn't expecting to see anybody, but when I got there, I found a surprise waiting for me. It was Douglas Dahlberg, the aspiring songwriter, sitting on the couch flipping through an outdated magazine. He stood up when he saw me come in.

"Mr. Gamble," he greeted me, extending his hand. "Remember me?"

"Mr. Dahlberg," I said, shaking his hand. "What can I do for you?"

"I was downtown. I took a chance you'd be here. When I found your door open, I thought I'd wait for a few minutes." He took out his wallet and handed me a twenty-dollar bill. "I wanted to pay you the money I owe you."

It took me a second to realize what he was talking about. "You sold one of your songs?"

"I did." He was beaming now. "Big Sky Records. They paid me five thousand dollars for 'Blue Moon over Kentucky.' Of course, they said that name was taken so they changed it to 'Broken-Hearted Moon,' but they gave me an option for three more songs."

"Mr. Dahlberg, you don't owe me any money." I tried to hand the twenty back to him. "I'm just glad things are working out for you."

"But I do owe you," he insisted. "You told me I should pay you when I sold a song." I understood then that this was an important moment for him. I folded the bill and put it in my pocket. "I'm going to get a frame for this and hang it on my wall."

"I'd like that," he said, "and I'm grateful."

"You wrote the song. I didn't do anything."

"You didn't laugh. That was enough." We shook hands again and then he left, no doubt with a song in his heart.

The double sawbuck reminded me I had the roll of cash I got from Jericho Hawkins in my jacket pocket. I took the money out and counted it: nine hundred and sixty-seven dollars. I wondered how a congregation like Jericho Hawkins's managed to come up with that much money, but then these days it's hard to tell by looking who has money and who doesn't.

The small wave of euphoria washing over me as a result of my newly acquired wealth lasted about as long as it took me to walk down the hall to the washroom and back. That was when the phone rang. It was Wanda.

"I'm thinking it's tonight, Gamble," she said, skipping the preliminaries. "William Jeffries, remember? That work for you?"

"What's the play, Wanda?"

"Tell you when I pick you up. I've still got a couple of details to work out. Your place around eleven, okay? Wear gloves and dark clothes. And make sure you're dressed for the occasion." That last was a reference to being armed. None of it sounded good.

I locked Douglas Dahlberg's double sawbuck and the money I got from

Jericho Hawkins in my desk drawer and headed for home. When I got there, I picked up the phone and called Maggie's number. I got no answer, so I left a message that I would try again later. I then called the Hawkins' number and wound up talking to Jericho. I briefed him on what I had learned about the girls in the photos I had found and told him it would be a good idea to keep Gabrielle close until further notice. He said he understood, and we hung up.

After that, I took a long shower and sat down in front of the television to watch a college football game, Georgia versus Florida. Called the "World's Largest Outdoor Cocktail Party," the game is a big deal in that part of the South, a rivalry game that's been played every year since 1915 except for one year during World War II. To keep things friendly, most years the teams play the game on a neutral field in Jacksonville. This year's game promised to be a real barnburner. It turned out to be so exciting that I dozed off before the end of the first half.

When I woke up the game was over. The six o'clock news was on and the light outside had all but dissolved into darkness. I had been sleeping for nearly four hours. I went into the kitchen and got a Diet Coke from the refrigerator, then tried calling Maggie again. She answered on the second ring.

"So, I give you a few rolls in the hay, and now you think you can just sneak out? Is that all I have to look forward to with you?"

I wasn't sure if she was kidding, so I held my response to a question. "Is this something you're worried about?"

"No," she said, her voice softening. "I'm worried about what I told you last night. I think I might have said too much too soon."

"When you said it, did you mean it?"

"I did."

"Then what you said was perfect. The thing you should really be worrying about is getting involved with somebody like me who does what I do for a living. I can't promise you a normal relationship. I don't keep regular hours and I don't deal with regular people. You need to understand that."

"There's a song," she said after a pause. "It goes, 'You don't have to say you love me, just be close at hand.' Do you know that song?"

"Dusty Springfield," I said. "It's a good song."

"That's the one. Do you think you can be close at hand, Gamble?"

"I can be as close as you want and as far away as you need me to be."

"That's a perfect answer, too. Will I see you later?"

"Not tonight, I'm afraid. There's something I have to do. It's a promise I made to a friend a long time ago."

"Are you going to tell me what it is?"

"Depends on how things go. Ask me in the morning."

"That reptile church doesn't have a Saturday service, does it?"

"No. It's something else."

The line went quiet for a moment. "See that you don't get killed, okay?"

"I'll see you tomorrow," I said, but she had already hung up.

As promised, Wanda showed up at eleven. I asked her if she wanted to come in, but she said no, we could talk on the way.

"On the way where?" I asked.

"We are paying a visit to William Jeffries. He isn't home just now, but he will be later. We'll have to wait." She looked at me. "You carrying?"

I said I was.

"You probably won't need it. If there's any shooting, I've got a throw-down piece I picked up a few years ago. We can toss it into the river on the way back. It'll be gone for good."

It had been almost a year since I had seen Wanda last, at a fundraiser for her shelter. At that time, she looked happy and excited about the prospects of securing reliable funding for her operation, and spent much of the evening giving hugs to women and handshakes to men, and schmoozing animatedly with anyone who showed up with a checkbook in his pocket. A couple of large, well-funded charities had given tentative approval to her grant applications, and the city was willing to give partial property tax abatement on the building she was using. Several well-heeled private contributors had also stepped forward with pledges.

I was invited, mostly to provide security, since there were any number of angry husbands and boyfriends, both past and present, who might be expected to show up and cause trouble. Fortunately, nothing like that happened, and the evening passed without incident. In lieu of my usual fee, which when I was helping Wanda was zero, I was granted unlimited access to the *hors d'oeuvres* table and the open bar.

Tonight, though, was different. The Wanda I was riding with at that moment manifested none of the joy she had radiated the previous year. Her expression was deadly serious. Her eyes were fixed on the road ahead, as if she were running a lap or two behind in a NASCAR race and was determined to make up ground. The flaming red, yellow, and orange ensemble she wore at the fundraiser had given way to an all-black outfit including calf-height boots, leather pants, and motorcycle jacket. She had topped that off with an Oakland Raiders watch cap pulled down low, at least partly to conceal her hair, which was chestnut brown accented with a fire-engine-red streak. The black getup, I knew, was not some Goth fashion statement. It was protective coloration in case we needed to become invisible to neighbors or late-night dog-walkers. For my part, I had picked out black denim pants and a navy-blue hooded sweatshirt. I thought that might come in handy anyhow, as the October nights had gotten chilly.

We had been driving for close to twenty minutes and Wanda still hadn't said anything about what was her plan for William Jeffries. I said, "You going to tell me what we're doing, or is the idea just to kick the door and go in with guns blazing?"

For the first time since I'd gotten into her car, she showed the barest hint of a smile. "Nothing so obvious as that. I'm going to talk to him and try to persuade him to mend his ways as he continues down the pathways of his life."

"A speech fit for the pulpit. And if that doesn't work?"

"Then his path will be considerably rockier. And perhaps shorter."

I shook my head. "I'm not doing murder, Wanda.

"Nobody said anything about murder. He didn't kill anybody, so he doesn't have that coming. I have other ways to make my point. You're just here to hold the fort in case this character turns out to be scrappier than what I've been led to believe."

Wanda's route took us north of the city towards Goodlettsville. After we passed Brick Church Pike, she made a left on a street whose name I didn't catch, and then another left and we found ourselves in a neighborhood of small bungalow-style houses, built right after World War II. It was near midnight and most of the residences were already dark. Except for a streetlight at the corner and a few front yards with gas lamps glowing softly, there was practically no illumination.

"Jeffries lives two houses down, on the other side of the street. It's the one with the 'For Sale' sign in the yard. I checked it out during the week. I pretended to be house hunting and got the listing estate agent to take me through."

"How much is he asking for the place?" I asked, just to be saying something.

"A buck seventy-five, can you believe it? It's not worth more than one and a half, tops. There's a living room that runs the width of the house in front, a dining room on the right, and a kitchen behind that. On the left is a hallway with two bedrooms and a bathroom. I figure we can take care of business in the hallway. It'll be quieter there because there are no outside walls."

It sounded a lot like my own house on the opposite side of the city. "You still haven't told me the plan, Wanda."

"Saturday nights he stays out late, drinking with his shithead buddies at some legion hall. The hall closes at one, and then he comes home and sleeps most of the day Sunday." She checked the time on her watch. "When he gets here, which should be in just about forty-five minutes, I'm going to approach him like my car's broken down. Then I'll pop him with my stun gun and throw a pillowcase over his head. Once he's down you can help me drag him into the house."

"What happens after that?"

"Unless you want to get into the act, you go back and sit in the car. I'll finish my business with him and then we'll get out of here and go have pancakes at an all-night Waffle House. That okay with you?"

"It's your play, Wanda. But I'm going in with you, just in case." Just in case, that is, he said or did the wrong thing and she decided to finish him after all. I didn't think she would actually do that, since she had already pointed out that he had stopped short of killing his wife. But in situations like this, it's better to be careful.

William Jeffries was running late that night. Wanda and I sat in her car until nearly two-thirty. Eventually, she got around to asking me what I was working on. I told her about Bobby Fury and Gabrielle and the photos of the other five girls I had found in Bobby's rental house. I also mentioned that there might be a connection between Gabrielle's disappearance and a pornographer named Jack Olin.

"So, you're thinking," she said, "that this Olin character and your man Bobby Fury might be involved in grabbing young girls off the street and selling them into the sex trade. What about that doctor, what's his name, Morse? Does he have a part in this?"

"If he is involved, it's to make sure that these girls are in fact virgins, or maybe just to check for STDs. If they are virgins, they bring a higher price when they're sold outside the country."

"And you told all this to the cops?"

"I did. They're looking into it. We'll see what they come up with."

"What are the odds," she said, and I could tell she was thinking about adding a couple more names to her appointment list. After that we ran out of things to talk about. She rolled down her window and smoked. I dozed off, drifting in and out of a dreamless sleep. Finally, a car came down the street, high beams blazing. Wanda nudged me awake and we both ducked down in our seats until the car passed and turned into Jeffries's driveway.

"Give it a minute," she said. Then she got out of the car, pulled her hat down low over her eyes, and crossed the street as Jeffries was approaching his front door.

"Excuse me, sir, could you help me?" I heard her say. Jeffries turned to see what she wanted. I couldn't see his face, but he was a big-bellied man, probably weighing around a deuce and a half. For a moment, the two seemed to be talking, and then Wanda reached into her purse, took out her stun gun, and pressed it against William Jeffries's belly. I heard him yelp and then he fell down on his porch like a sack of cornmeal dropping off the back of a truck. Because of his size, I supposed, she popped him again for good measure. That was my cue to get moving.

I ran to the porch and helped Wanda roll Jeffries over onto his stomach. I held his arms while she bound his wrists together with two long zip ties and then did the same with his ankles. I picked his keys up from where he had dropped them, unlocked the front door and we dragged him inside the house and into the hallway leading to the bedrooms. The house was just the way Wanda described it, but she hadn't mentioned the smell, which was a combination of unremoved kitchen trash, unwashed laundry, and a moldy odor that seemed to be coming up from the basement.

After we got Jeffries settled in the hallway, Wanda took a dark pillowcase out of the bag she was carrying and pulled it over Jeffries's head, securing it with a length of duct tape from a roll she had in her bag. I wondered, without really wanting to know, what else was in there. As I would find out shortly, she had much more.

While Jeffries was on the floor, I patted him down and found a .25 caliber autoloader in the pocket of his sweatshirt. Nice, I thought, just the thing to have handy when you're out for a night of heavy-duty drinking. As he was coming around, I removed the clip from the little pistol and thumbed the cartridges out. I left them on the floor where they fell and put the gun in my own pocket. Wanda, meantime, pulled a .44 caliber Bulldog revolver from a holster clipped to her belt.

From beneath the pillowcase, Jeffries moaned and started to say something that sounded like "Wuthafug?" Wanda pressed the .44 to the side of Jeffries's head and twisted the barrel like she was trying to screw it into his ear.

"Mister Jeffries," she began in a heavily accented voice that made her sound like Scarlett O'Hara, "I have a gun pointed at your head, and if you make so much as a move or a sound without my permission, I will pull the trigger and you will be history. Do you understand? You may speak now."

Jeffries began to thrash around on the floor. "Who the fuck..." he began, but Wanda cut him off with a solid rap to his head with the side of her gun. "Sir, what you felt there is what they call in golf a mulligan. It means you get another try, but it's the last one you're going to get." She smacked him again on the other side of his head. "The last mulligan, I mean. Now, let's try this one more time. Do you understand?"

From under the pillowcase, "Yes."

"Okay, good," she continued in her honey-dripped accent. "The reason I'm spending this time with you is we need to discuss what you did to your wife a few weeks ago. Do you remember that incident and what took place?"

The man in the pillowcase said, "Are you gonna hit me again?"

"I'm sorry, I forgot. No, you may speak."

"Okay, then, yeah, I remember."

"Good. Now can you tell me what you did? You can speak."

"I...I smacked her around a little bit. I guess I might've hurt her more'n I was meanin' to, but, well, we got to arguin' a bit and she pissed me off."

"About what?"

When he didn't answer, she rapped him on the head again. "I asked you, what about?"

"I'm sorry, I don't remember."

"So then, were you intoxicated?"

He hesitated. "I guess maybe I was, a little, but God damn it, sometimes she just needs a little straightening out."

Wrong thing to say, I thought. *That's going to cost you.*

"So then, you admit what you did?" She cocked the hammer on the .44, which in the otherwise quiet house sounded as loud as a two-pound sledgehammer striking an anvil.

"I do. God forgive me, I know I done wrong. I promise, if you let me go, I'll never lay another hand on Bobbie as long as I live. I swear, I'll never do nothing like that ever again."

And then he started to sob. I couldn't tell if it was genuine remorse or fright from the sound made by Wanda's revolver. Probably both. Either way, I wasn't buying one word of it, and I knew Wanda wasn't, either. Still, she remained steadfastly polite.

"Mister Jeffries, I have no doubt you feel really bad right now, either because of what you did, or because you're worried what's going to happen to you next." He started to say something, but she cut him off with another sharp rap to the head. I still hadn't said a word since we'd gotten inside the house. I thought it would be better if Jeffries didn't know how many people he was dealing with.

Wanda continued, "I'd bet anything right now that your head is starting to hurt, what with all the reminders I've had to keep giving you, so I'm going to give you a shot of something to make you sleepy. It will start to work in a minute or so and last about half an hour. I promise you; you won't feel a thing."

She reached into her bag one more time and came up with a syringe and a vial filled with clear liquid. She pierced the rubber stopper in the vial and drew out the liquid. "Little stick," she said and injected the sedative into Jeffries's neck. He convulsed once. I pressed down on his shoulders while Wanda applied her weight to his knees.

"Goodnight, sweet prince," she said, and in almost no time at all he went limp.

"What did you give him?" I said, surprised that it worked as quickly as it did.

"Special K," she said, dropping the accent. "Some people use it in lower doses as a recreational drug because it brings on hallucinations. Now and then we see users at the shelter. Generally, they're pretty fucked up when they get there."

She was talking about ketamine, a powerful but short-acting sedative used as an animal tranquilizer, and as an anesthetic used in connection with emergency surgery. I didn't know much about it, although I was aware it could cause respiratory complications, so before we left, we would need to make sure Jeffries was breathing normally—that is, if he was still breathing at all. I was particularly concerned because the injection worked as quickly as it did. I wondered how large the dose she gave Jeffries was.

She seemed to read my mind. "He'll be okay. He's a big guy." She went fishing around in her bag one more time and came out with a pair of surgical shears. "Okay," she said, "let's do this," and began tugging at Jeffries's belt. It was made of thick leather, and she said, "I wonder if this is what he used to beat his wife."

I took a firm grip on her arm. "If you're about to cut off this guy's nuts,

190

it's not what I came for, and I'm not going to let you do it, either."

"Why not? You saw what this son of a bitch did."

"Yes, I did, and like you said earlier, he didn't kill her. Plus, for all we know, they could kiss and make up tomorrow or next week, and if he's running around with no balls or with half a pecker, she's going to figure out who did it and you'll take the fall for it. Worse yet, if you fuck this up and he bleeds out, you'll go away forever."

I said, "Look, you want to put a hit out on this guy, we both know where to find somebody to do it, but you'd better be on a Caribbean cruise or someplace else far away when it goes down. You got away with this once, but that was personal. You were on the job at the time, and the police and the D.A. were willing to give you a pass. They won't let it go this time, Wanda. And besides, your job is looking after the women who trust you. You can't do that from a prison cell."

"We planned this," she started. "Don't tell me you're going to back out now."

"No. You planned this. I said I'd help you, but I'm not going to be involved in mutilating this guy or whatever else you're thinking about. You'll have to get somebody else to help you with that."

"And what if he kills her next time, what then?"

"Then I expect he'll spend the rest of his life in prison. But worrying about what he might do doesn't justify what you're about to do."

She thought about that for a moment before making up her mind. "You're right," she said. "Maybe we put the fear of God into him and that's enough. Go wait for me in the car. I'll clean up in here and be with you in a minute. I just want to make sure he's breathing okay before we leave."

I knew she was lying so she could get rid of me, but I said okay and went back to the car to wait. I hoped that none of the neighbors noticed there was an unfamiliar car parked at the curb and decided to call the cops.

It took about fifteen minutes before Wanda came out, longer than it seemed like it should, but since I didn't hear any gunshots or blood-curdling screams, I told myself, without really believing it, that she was just doing what she had said, making sure Jeffries was breathing normally. I did not, however,

191

ask her about it, and she did not invite any questions.

We didn't talk much on the way back into the city. We decided it was too late for pancakes, so we skipped the Waffle House. Instead, she dumped me at the curb in front of my place and drove off to wherever she was headed next.

A week or so went by and then there was a story on the television news about how a man named William Jeffries, armed with an AR-15 semiautomatic rifle and a .45 caliber pistol, had tried to force his way into a women's shelter where he believed his wife had taken refuge. The police were immediately summoned. They arrived while Jeffries was still pounding and kicking at the heavy steel security door that protected the shelter. There was a confrontation, shots were fired, and William Jeffries was killed in the exchange. The responding officers were unhurt.

As it turned out, Jeffries had chosen the wrong shelter to try retrieving his wife. Wanda's shelter was clear on the other side of town. Out of curiosity, I wandered down to the coroner's office and talked my way into a look at the autopsy report. Sure enough, the cause of death was multiple gunshot wounds. The report also noted that about half an inch had been severed from the end of the victim's penis. No explanation was offered as to the origin of that wound.

Chapter Twenty-Six

After Wanda drove away, I grabbed a few hours sleep, got cleaned up, and drove over to see Maggie. I got there just before noon. I hoped she wouldn't be annoyed I hadn't called first. More than that, I hoped she wouldn't ask a lot of questions about where I went and what I had done the night before. At first, it looked as if luck would be with me. If she was put out, she gave no indication. Instead, she greeted me at the door with a hug and a quick kiss. "I'm ready," she said. "Let's go."

"Ready for what? Where are we going?"

"You said you were going to teach me how to shoot, so unless you've changed your mind we're going to a range."

"Right, I did say that. Where's the gun now?"

She picked up her bag and patted it. "In here."

I nodded. "Leave it where it is and keep the bag shut until we get where we're going. Unless you have a permit, which I doubt, you can't carry a firearm outside your home or your car."

Our time at the range turned out to be something of a surprise. Maggie didn't pull off any trick shots like Annie Oakley or fan the hammer like a Wild West gunfighter, but she did turn out to be a proficient shooter, and at seven yards on the handgun range, she managed to put most of her rounds through the vital areas on the silhouette targets we were using. After she'd blasted her way through four thirty-five-dollar boxes of ammunition, I wasn't worried about whether she'd be able to handle the gun. My concern was whether she'd be able to use it to defend herself if she had to.

"What do you think?" she said when we were back in the car. She sounded excited, like she was ready to shoot the next guy who stared too long at her ass. I didn't like that.

"You did well. You're a pretty good shot."

"Do you mean that, really?"

"I do, absolutely."

"But," she said, catching my tone.

"But there's a difference between shooting at a target and shooting at a person. For one thing, a person is not likely to stand still while you take aim. For another, a target doesn't shoot back. A person might, if he's armed. Or he might come straight at you. The real question is, are you willing to shoot to kill? Because the one thing you must not do, and I can't emphasize this enough, is this. If you believe someone is going to harm you, if someone uninvited is in your home, and threatening to harm you, do not stand there and talk. Don't say something like, 'Take one more step and I'll shoot.' Just shoot. You might feel guilty, and probably have nightmares, but at least you'll be alive to deal with those feelings. Do you understand?"

"Yes."

"If you want to practice some more, we can do that. But when it comes down to it, the difference between whether you live or die is your own willingness to do what you have to do." I took her face in my hands. "I want you safe and alive. My reasons are entirely selfish."

"You're sweet for saying that. Do you have any other come-hither lines?"

"I do, but I'm saving those for when I try to convince you to take your clothes off."

She laughed. "In case you haven't noticed, I don't require much convincing."

From the range we drove to a restaurant for a late lunch. I ordered a BLT sandwich on whole-grain bread and a bottle of beer. Maggie had a Caesar salad with blackened chicken and a glass of iced tea, unsweetened. Over our meals, we laughed, flirted a little, and talked about the things that people talk about at the beginning of a new relationship.

We finished lunch and the waitress had cleared the table. I decided to have one more beer. Maggie stuck with a refill for her iced tea. It was then that she got around to asking the question I had hoped to avoid.

"Did you take care of what you needed to do last night?"

"Yes."

"Are you going to tell me what it was?"

I said, "Ask me what you want to know, Maggie. I won't lie to you."

"All right, I will. Whatever you were doing, did it involve a woman?"

"Yes."

"And," she paused to swirl around the ice in her glass, "how do I ask this? Did it involve sex?"

"It did not." I told her about Wanda Beaudry and Roberta Jeffries and her husband William and Wanda's plan to teach him a life-changing lesson.

"I see. And is that what happened? Did you cut off his testicles?"

"No."

She considered for a moment, apparently hearing something in my tone that begged another question. "Are you saying Wanda did it by herself?"

"I'm not saying that, either. I don't know what she did." I said, "Look, Maggie, you've seen just a little bit of what I do for a living. And you know now that my cases don't play out like Hallmark Mysteries. I help people who are in trouble. Sometimes they operate outside the boundaries of normal behavior, and more often than I'd like, I have to color outside the lines myself. But that's what I do and I'm going to keep right on doing it because I'm good at it. The other day when we took Gabrielle home, it was like a small part of the world changed for the better. It wasn't the storybook ending we both hoped for, but I felt good about it just the same.

"I'm telling you this as plainly as I can because you said you're falling in love with me. I want that to be true, but it won't work if we go into this relationship with any illusions about who we really are. I guess what I'm saying is that I don't want you to fall in love with somebody I'm not, because sooner or later you will be disappointed, and I don't want that to happen. If we have to turn back, it's better to do it now rather than down the road when the pain will be that much worse. Does that make any sense, or am I just talking to hear my head rattle?"

"What would you say," she answered, "if I told you I want us to go home right this minute and spend the rest of the day making love?"

I signaled the waiter and asked for the check.

Chapter Twenty-Seven

The next few weeks passed more or less uneventfully, and the disappearance and subsequent return of Gabrielle Hawkins became just another file in the drawer. The coroner's inquest into the death of Mickey Reddick revealed that she had died from a massive overdose of fentanyl, but there was no conclusive evidence as to whether the dose was self-administered or injected by a person or persons unknown. As such, the case could not be ruled a homicide, so it remained an open investigation, with Bobby Fury identified as a person of interest. For his part, Bobby seemed to have vanished from the face of the earth. For all anyone knew, he might have taken up residence in South America, or Jack Olin may have asked one of the many friends he claimed to have to find him a home at the bottom of Old Hickory Reservoir.

Gabrielle, meanwhile, was back in school, and after a flurry of attention from curious classmates, settled back into her accustomed C-plus routine. To be on the safe side, until Bobby either turned up dead or in custody, her parents were keeping her on a short leash. Delsey drove her to school each morning and Jericho scooped her up every afternoon. I'd had no contact with Gabrielle or her parents since the day I called to put them on their guard regarding Bobby.

I did keep in occasional touch with Lorraine Proctor to find out whether the police had made any progress into the investigation of the five missing girls whose photos I had found when I searched Bobby Fury's residence. The best she could tell me was that the case had been turned over to the Tennessee Bureau of Investigation, which in turn had requested assistance from the FBI. Both agencies were working on it but neither had been able to establish any connection to Jack Olin. And despite the continuing efforts of the FBI, the TBI, and the Metro police, none of the girls except for Gabrielle had resurfaced, alive or dead. The working hypothesis was that they had either been spirited somewhere far away, possibly out of the country, or that they were the victims of a serial killer of young girls. As in the case of the death of Mickey Reddick, Bobby Fury had once again been identified as a person of interest.

I had picked up a couple of new cases, neither of which required much work, but which paid me well. In the first, I was hired to bodyguard a graying-at-the-temples Welsh actor who had lately found unlikely late-career success as an action hero, and who was in town to film a couple of location scenes for an upcoming movie.

He proved to be an amiable sort, interesting to talk to, and willing to dish endlessly about many of the co-stars with whom he had shared top billing, and sometimes a bedroom. I wanted to surprise Maggie and ask her to join us for dinner in some out-of-the-way restaurant, but then decided that might not be a good idea since the studio was insisting that he keep his presence in town under wraps.

He did, however, have an enormous appetite for cocaine. I wasn't able to determine how he got it, although I assumed it was available in limitless quantities on the set. To his credit, he had a solid work ethic, and since my agreement with his employers only required me to make sure he was ready to go when needed, I didn't need to waste any time trying to keep him straight or rousting him out in the morning. He seemed to appreciate my live-and-let-live approach and spiffed me a thick wad of cash before I put him on his flight back to California. On top of my regular rate plus overtime for being on duty twenty-four-seven, it was a very profitable week's work.

The other assignment was a simple case of tracking down a bail skipper. Fat Wally Sadler, a bonding agent who was a regular customer, had a client who had slipped his tether and missed a court appearance. That required Wally to forfeit a $50,000 bond he had posted, refundable only if the client could be found and returned to custody. Turned out, the subject in question had simply taken a trip to his family home in Corinth, Mississippi, to attend the funeral of some relative or other. In his grief, the client had forgotten his obligation to appear. After a few phone calls, I was able to discover his whereabouts and drove down to Corinth to pick him up. He returned without a fuss and even sprung for meals on the drive back to Nashville. Once back in town, his bail was revoked and he was remanded pending a new hearing date.

Maggie and I began spending more of our free time together. To my surprise, she had taken an avid interest in shooting sports and had returned my Smith & Wesson .32, complaining that the long trigger pull was interfering with her accuracy. In its place, she bought a small Remington .380 which she kept in her purse, and a 9MM Ruger with a 15-round magazine. I knew that, for some goofy reason, these came in a variety of colors, and asked her why she chose basic black instead.

"It's a weapon, Gamble, not a fashion accessory." She also obtained a concealed carry permit. In short, if it came to a shootout, she had me out-gunned.

We had not exactly moved in together, but a piece at a time, it seemed, items of each other's clothing and toiletries began to appear in the drawers, closets, and bathrooms of our homes. Not entire wardrobes, but enough to provide a fresh change of clothes for the next day's work or play after an overnight sleepover. In that area of our relationship, Maggie had me outgunned as well. My contribution to her residence consisted of underwear, socks, a clean shirt, deodorant, toothbrush, and a razor. At my house, she kept, well, a lot more than that. Between the bedroom and the bathroom, there were hair care and feminine hygiene products, a makeup kit, nightgowns, a robe, packages of pantyhose in assorted shades, shoes, and underwear in a variety of colors. She also bought a coffee maker, a necessity for Maggie-in-the-morning, since I don't drink coffee and didn't own one. From time to time, I teased her about it, but I was gentle with my observations. Keeping our stuff at each others' homes made our relationship feel more secure, and since that seemed to make her happy, I was foursquare behind it.

Thanksgiving weekend, I had to be out of town to investigate a worker's comp claim that an insurance company, Mid-South Mutual, was disputing. Rodney Bowles, a factory worker, claimed he had slipped and fallen on a spot of oil that had been spilled on the shop floor. And although two doctors had examined him and found nothing wrong, he had lined up a weapons-grade attorney and had filed a lawsuit. The problem for Mid-South Mutual was that claimed back and neck injuries are very difficult to disprove, and juries are often sympathetic to injured parties, especially those working in low-paying jobs for companies with hefty liability policies. In situations like that, insurance companies are inclined to settle to avoid protracted and expensive litigation, especially when the outcome of a trial is uncertain and damages can be astronomical.

In this instance, however, the adjuster decided to invest in a little due diligence before breaking out his checkbook, and so I found myself in Huntsville, Alabama, where Rodney had gone to visit his sister and her husband over the long weekend. I didn't mind being away since Maggie had traveled back to Ohio to spend the long weekend with her family. She had invited me to come along, but I wasn't sure I was ready for a meet-the-parents visit and so used the Mid-South assignment as an excuse not to go with her. She said she understood, but I could tell she was disappointed. I partly restored her spirits by promising I would make it up at Christmas.

First thing Friday morning, I got a seat on an American Airlines flight to Carl T. Jones Field in Huntsville. I rented a car and tracked down the sister's address, which Rodney had listed in the box for next-of-kin on his employment application. The address was in nearby Decatur. I cruised the neighborhood just to get the lay of the land and then parked the rental in a far corner of a church lot across the street from the sister's residence to settle in and wait. I was outfitted with binoculars, a six-pack of Diet Dr. Pepper, a couple bags of pork rinds, a book of crossword puzzles, and a digital camera with an assortment of lenses provided by the insurance company. I sat there all afternoon and into the evening without seeing so much as a movement, either inside or outside the house. By eleven o'clock it was lights out, so I headed for a nearby motel for the night.

Next morning, I was back in my rental car in the church lot. The day was cold, but the sun was shining, so the inside of the car stayed fairly warm. I noticed that the message board in front of the church, which yesterday had read "Have A Blessed Thanksgiving" now announced "Potluck Supper and Social 7:00 P.M Today." At about three o'clock in the afternoon, a woman carrying a foil-covered roasting pan emerged from the sister's house, crossed the road, and entered the side door of the church. Watching her, I had an "a-ha" moment and figured that if Rodney was going to blow his cover, tonight might be the night. Pleased with what I considered to be good detective work I drove back to the motel to watch some late-season college football rivalry games until it was time to head back to the church.

I returned about six-thirty, by which time the parking lot was already filling up. By seven a band had arrived, and shortly after began playing line-dancing tunes. A few minutes later, Rodney Bowles, his sister, and another man, his brother-in-law, I supposed, walked across the street and went inside the church. I waited a few minutes before entering myself. For a ten-dollar "donation," I dined on a hot turkey sandwich with mashed potatoes, gravy, pork sausage stuffing, and green beans, plus my choice of lemonade or sweet tea.

After a while, Rodney's sister dragged him over to another table and introduced him to a woman sitting by herself. They visited for a few minutes and then Rodney asked her to dance. I used the camera in my phone to grab a few videos of Rodney busting some tricky moves on the dance floor and emailed them back to Mid-South Mutual. Sunday afternoon, I was on a United Airlines flight back to Nashville.

I retrieved my car from long-term parking and, on a whim and because I missed her, decided to drive over to Maggie's condo to see whether she had gotten back from Ohio. I would have called first, but I had forgotten to turn off my phone after I left the church social the night before, and the battery was dead. That meant my visit would be a surprise. I wondered as I drove from the airport to Belle Meade whether I should stop and pick up a bottle of wine as a welcome back gift. Then I decided I'd just take her to dinner and drove straight through. It was a decision that saved her life.

As I pulled into Maggie's parking area, the first thing I noticed was that the lights were on in her living room. Good. She was home. The second thing I noticed was the red truck. My blood froze, and in that moment, instinct and my former cop training took over. I reached inside my coat for my .380 before remembering that I had not taken it with me when I went to the airport on Friday. I did, however, still have the .32 Maggie returned to me locked in the glove compartment. I retrieved that, checked to make sure it was loaded, and headed for her front door on the dead run. Without breaking stride, I climbed her front steps and hit the door with my shoulder. As expected, the lock yielded without much resistance.

The scene that greeted me was straight out of my worst nightmare. Bobby was there with Maggie. She was seated in one of her dining room chairs. Her wrists and ankles were fastened to the arms and legs of the chair with duct tape. Her mouth and eyes were covered with the same tape. The right side of her face was red and swollen and her blouse and bra were torn open to the waist. Angry-looking cigarette burns covered the exposed part of her body.

When I came through the door, Bobby Fury was standing over her. In the last physical act of his time on this earth, he heard the door frame splinter and turned in time to see me take aim at the center of his chest.

"Wait!" he shouted and held up his hands in a gesture of surrender. I did not wait. I fired three times. The first round penetrated the open palm of his left hand. The second hit him in his left shoulder, knocking him back a step. When the impact registered, he dropped his eyes to look at the wound. Then he lifted his head again, looked straight at me, and said, "Please." That gave me time to take more careful aim and place the shot that ended his life just above his right eyebrow. He was dead before he hit the floor.

Chapter Twenty-Eight

Before the EMTs and the cops arrived, I cut Maggie loose from her chair, removed the tape from her eyes and mouth, and carried her over to the couch. I found some antiseptic cream in the upstairs bathroom and liberally applied it to her burns. Then I covered her with a blanket from her linen closet.

She looked at me uncomprehendingly. "How did you...where did you?"

"I was coming from the airport. I wanted to surprise you." I brushed an errant strand of hair away from her face and kissed her lightly on her forehead. "You're going to be okay. I don't see anything here that won't heal."

"Is he...?"

"That was me. Bobby's dead."

There was a pause, and the barest of a smile. "It took you three shots?"

We waited about ten minutes before the medics arrived, followed almost immediately after by a pair of uniformed cops. I held Maggie's hand while the techs checked her out. They took her vitals and gave her a shot of pain killer. Then, with their preliminaries completed, they placed her on a gurney and rolled her out to the waiting ambulance. By that time a small crowd of neighbors had gathered on the sidewalk outside, hoping, no doubt, to get a glimpse of the real or imagined carnage.

In the minutes that followed, the uniforms checked my ID, took my statement, secured the .32, and called for a second ambulance Code 1, DOA, and detectives from the homicide detail. I suggested they contact John Spillner since Bobby was a suspect in an earlier homicide that he and his partner had been working.

It took about ten minutes for Spillner to arrive, flying solo, dressed for the four-day weekend in jeans and a pullover sweater. He took a quick look around before focusing his attention first on the dead man on the floor and then on me.

"This yours?"

"Nobody else."

"Was it a righteous shoot?"

"It's in the report. He would have killed her. Your guys have got my gun. I'm going to want it back."

"We'll see. Meantime, I need you to come down and make a full statement."

"In the morning," I said. "Where's Proctor?"

"She's at Baptist, with your lady friend. And right now, that's where you're going."

I must have looked like I hadn't heard him right, because he said, "Go ahead and go. We'll secure the lady's place. Come by the department tomorrow morning. We'll take your statement, and unless there's something more to this than what I can see here, that'll be the end of it."

And so, I left. But it still wasn't the end. And it was about to get worse.

Chapter Twenty-Nine

When I walked into Maggie's hospital room, I found Lorraine Proctor settled comfortably in the visitor's chair. Lorraine was chatting away like Maggie was her best gal pal, in the hospital for some minor surgical procedure rather than for treatment following a sadistic attack by a man who would have continued to torture her until he had killed her.

Maggie, meanwhile, was propped up in bed with a couple of pillows and an IV drip attached to her left hand. She looked a little drowsy from the painkiller she had been given, and the side of her face where Bobby had struck her was bruised and swollen. When she heard me come in, she turned and gave me a lopsided smile.

"So, Mister Gamble," Lorraine Proctor said, grinning. "Or should I call you Mister Excitement? We were just talking about you. Your lady friend here thinks you're some kind of superhero. Me, I'd say that last shot you took was one too many. We would have enjoyed talking to the late Mister Furillo about that other investigation you so generously dumped into our laps."

"I'm sure," I said. "But considering all the time you've had to find him, I'd say I did you a favor. Looks like now you'll have to do some real police work, however burdensome that may seem. If it were me, I'd lean hard on that doctor. I'd say he's the one most likely to crack."

"Gosh, thanks," she said, "We never would have thought of that. Only don't shoot him before we get a chance to bring him in, will you?" Then, to Maggie, she said, "Unless something else comes up, I think I've got everything I need from you. Get some rest and I'll check back tomorrow to see how you're getting along."

To me, she said, "You know, Mister Gamble, kidding aside, you're not such a bad guy. Despite what I said earlier, if it had been me, I'd have shot that son of a bitch three more times, just to make sure he was down for the count." She got up to leave and motioned with her head for me to follow her out into the corridor.

"Okay," she said when we were out of Maggie's earshot, "the doctor says the bruise on her face will calm down in a week or ten days, and the burns will heal over time. There may be some scarring, but they won't look too bad." She was using her no-bullshit voice again, and her eyes bored directly into mine.

"That's good news," I said.

"Good of you to say so. The other part of this you need to be aware of, and you were a cop so you should already know it, is that she just went through the most terrifying experience of her life. She doesn't blame you, but it's still going to be a long time before her life gets back to normal, if it ever does. She also says she loves you, and although I can't imagine why," and here she gave me a knowing look, "I believe she means it. But the question for you is, do you love her, and are you in this for the long haul? Because right now, you're all she's got."

"I'm there all the way."

"I hope so. And I'll expect you in my office, tomorrow morning, ten o'clock."

After she was gone, I went back and sat down on the edge of Maggie's bed. I kissed her gently. I held her hand. And I wondered when I looked into her eyes, would I see accusation or absolution. She read my thoughts.

"We can talk about this later. I'm very tired and there are some things I want to say to you, but that can wait for now. Right now, all you need to know is that I love you and I don't blame you for anything that happened tonight. But before you go, I have to ask you, do you still want me in your life?"

"That might be something I should be asking you. After all this, are you sure my life is a place you want to be?"

"Kiss me again," she said, "but better this time. Maybe that will answer your question."

I didn't go home that night. Instead, I parked myself in the chair recently occupied by Lorraine Proctor and waited until Maggie drifted off to sleep. A couple of times during the night a nurse came in, once to change Maggie's IV, and once to check her vitals. During those times I excused myself and went down the hall to a vending machine for a soda and a package of peanut butter crackers. Eventually, I dozed off myself.

By the time Maggie opened her eyes Monday morning I was wide awake, roused earlier by the wheels of the breakfast cart clattering down the hallway.

"You still here? You didn't go home?"

"Just being close at hand. That was our agreement, remember?"

"What time is it?" she asked me.

"It's almost eight. You slept thirteen hours. A doctor came by earlier this morning. He said they're going to give you some prescriptions, and then this afternoon you can go home." I paused. "I think you should figure on staying with me for a day or two, at least until we can get your door fixed. I sort of busted it up last night."

She nodded her head and then her hand went to the side of her face. She felt the area where Bobby had hit her.

"It's going to be tender, and it doesn't look too good right now, so you might want to steer clear of mirrors for a few days. You've got a world-class black eye and a pretty good bruise. In fact," I handed her an ice bag the nurse had dropped off earlier, "doctor says he wants you to keep ice on it fifteen minutes every hour."

She nodded and held the bag against the side of her face.

"There's something else. They'll go over all this with you when you're discharged, but they're going to recommend counseling to help you get through this. I think you should do it." I thought she might give me an argument about that, but she just nodded and closed her eyes.

I said, "I have to go down to police headquarters and give a statement, but I'd like to ask you something before I go. How did Bobby get into your house? You didn't open the door for him, did you?"

"No. The police said the sliding door on the lower level had been forced. He was already inside waiting for me when I got home from visiting my parents. I had some leftovers from Thanksgiving dinner I brought back in a cooler bag." She half smiled at the recollection. "Everybody sitting around me on the plane could smell the turkey. I think it was making them hungry.

"Anyway, I left the bag on the kitchen counter. I took my suitcase upstairs. Then I came back down to put everything away in the refrigerator. I heard a sound behind me, and when I turned to see what it was, he hit me." She paused, gathering her thoughts.

"When I woke up, I was in that chair, the way you found me. He had put that tape over my eyes. He ripped my blouse open and then he started… he began hurting me." She started to cry, softly at first, and then she began sobbing and somehow talking at the same time.

"He put his hand over my mouth. He kept asking me the same question. Over and over, he kept asking, where is Gabrielle? And then he'd take his hand away, and I told him, she's at home with her parents. And then he'd say, you're lying, I already checked on that, and I know you know where she is, and then he'd put his hand over my mouth and burn me again. After a while, he gave up asking and put the tape over my mouth. I guess by then he'd made up his mind he was going to kill me. He just was going to take his time doing it. And he would have if you hadn't…thank you, Gamble. I'm sorry you had to shoot him, but thank you for my life."

I stayed with Maggie a while longer, until she had cried herself out. At about eight-thirty a nurse came in and gave her a shot of something to help her calm down. I waited another few minutes until she got drowsy. Before I left, I told her I'd be back to take her home as soon as I finished giving a statement to the police.

At ten sharp I was seated on a hard, wooden chair in an interview room at police headquarters. Seated at the table with me were Detective Lorraine Proctor, Detective Sergeant John Spillner, and Davidson County Assistant District Attorney Floyd Healy, whom I had met when we worked together on another investigation. Healy was a short, powerfully built man who wore wire-rimmed glasses and sported a bushy mustache. He had a bottle of water in front of him and an open briefcase on the table next to where he was sitting.

Under the circumstances, I had no reason to think the meeting would go badly for me. I knew the two homicide cops weren't going to be a problem, but I wasn't sure about Healy. He wasn't a headhunter, and he had no axe to grind with me, but he did have a knack for asking tough questions that didn't always have simple answers. At that moment he was reading over the statement I had given to Spillner and which was missing only my signature.

"So," he said, looking at me over to rims of his glasses. "You shot Mr. Furillo three times, is that right?"

"Yes."

"Once in the hand, once in the shoulder, and once in the head, is that correct?"

"Yes."

"Because you felt it was necessary to kill him in order to save Ms. Totten."

"I didn't immediately know her condition, or how close she might have been to death. I shot him because I felt it was necessary to stop him from harming her any more than he already had. At that moment I didn't care whether he lived or died."

"That's clear enough. And was it also because you observed that he had a gun, and he fired a shot at you?"

I hesitated at that. I didn't remember any guns. Spillner spoke up. "We found a .22 caliber semi-automatic pistol behind the couch in the living room. He evidently dropped it when Gamble shot him. It had been fired, but so far, we haven't been able to locate the slug. Probably it sailed out through the open door. It could be anywhere. Also, the grip had been taped, so no prints. Sorry."

"Let me guess. Nobody tested his hands for GSR."

"No. We didn't find the gun until after the coroner's people had removed the body. Again, sorry, no excuse."

"I see." Healy put the statement down on the table and looked at each of us. "Detective Proctor, is that your recollection as well?"

"I wasn't present, Mr. Healy. On my way to the scene, I learned that the victim was being transported to the hospital, so I drove directly there to see if I could get a statement."

"And did she say anything about a gun?"

She made a sound that could have been a sigh. "Mister Healy, by the time I finally spoke with Ms. Totten, she had been given a pain killer and a tranquilizer. Her memory of the details, other than what she told me the suspect had done to her, was pretty sketchy. Also, and you can read this in both statements, Ms. Totten's eyes were covered with tape during much of the incident, so she would not have been aware of a gun in any case."

"So then, she actually didn't see the shooting take place, is that right?"

"That would be correct."

"And did she mention hearing three shots fired, or four?"

"Wish I could tell you. She said she couldn't remember."

Healy sat with his hands folded on the table for what seemed like an eternity. Finally, he said, "Okay then, I guess that about covers it." To Spillner, he said, "After you get this signed, send a copy over to my office. And Gamble, it was good seeing you. Stay out of trouble, will you?" And with that, he got up, closed his briefcase, and left the room, leaving us all wondering what just happened.

I said, "I don't remember any guns."

"I don't remember finding one," said Spillner, "and yet, if you check the evidence locker, you'll find a .22 autoloader just like the one I described."

"Okay, so then what happens now?"

"Look, you didn't bring your A-game last night, but you did us all a favor getting rid of this bastard. Either he killed Michelle Reddick or he didn't, and maybe we'll never know, but one way or the other, the world is better off without him. We're not going to close the Reddick case, and if we find out somebody else did her, we'll get him. Meantime, TBI is looking into those girls who went missing, and who knows what they'll turn up. Either way, Bobby Fury is off the board, and that's good enough for one night's work."

I looked at Lorraine Proctor. "You okay with this?"

She shrugged and pushed my statement across the table. "Sign here," she said.

I signed it and then I got up and left. I was in a hurry to get back to Maggie. But I wondered, with Bobby Fury dead, how could Gabrielle Hawkins have gone missing all over again?

Chapter Thirty

Maggie was discharged from the hospital right after lunchtime. They sent her off with a handful of prescriptions and the name of a counselor whom she could call when she needed to. I took her home to my house, where she spent what was left of the day sleeping and watching daytime television. Occasionally, something would trigger her memory and she would flash back to Sunday night and start crying again. Toward evening, she said she was hungry. I offered to go for carryout, but she said no, she didn't want to be alone, so I whipped up the same amateurish egg concoction I had made for Delsey the night I took on the job of finding her daughter.

And that got me wondering all over again. With Bobby out of the picture, where was Gabrielle? Then I realized I was probably worried about nothing, that maybe the Hawkins family had decided, like Maggie, to go visit relatives for the long weekend. That's why Bobby couldn't find her. She was stuck visiting family back in east Tennessee, no doubt complaining the whole time about how boring it all was. Tomorrow I would call Delsey at the hospital, just to make sure Gabrielle was home and safe. I also wanted to let her and Jericho know that Bobby Fury would not present any further threat to Gabrielle.

After I got Maggie settled in, she wanted to know how my interview with the police had gone.

"Are they going to charge you with anything?"

"No. I think the general feeling around the table was that it was a public service killing. They would have liked to have questioned Bobby about

Mickey Reddick, but I think they're okay with how things turned out."

"And how about you?" she asked. "You killed somebody last night. Are you okay with that, too?"

It was a good question, and I didn't have a good answer. "It's not nothing," I said, "and I won't pretend it is. But I did what I had to, given the circumstances. I don't feel good about killing him, but I would do it again to protect you. I'm only sorry I wasn't there to keep it from happening in the first place. Other than that, I don't know what else I can tell you."

That night was a bad one for Maggie. She decided she would try to stretch out the intervals between the times she took her medications, insisting she did not want to become dependent on the hydrocodone and valium the hospital had prescribed. That decision caused the pain to return sooner and with greater intensity, and made the memory of what Bobby Fury had done to her seem more vivid. She did, however, allow me to apply lidocaine ointment to the burn spots on her abdomen.

It took some doing, but I finally convinced her she should take her meds and then go to bed. I asked whether she wanted me to join her in bed or sleep by herself.

"Maybe by myself, just for tonight. Do you mind?"

"Not at all," I told her. "We've got lots of time when you're feeling better."

Tuesday morning, I was out of bed before Maggie. I got cleaned up and then got on the telephone. The first call was to Woodcrest High School. I told the secretary that I was a friend of Ms. Totten. I explained that she had been the victim of a criminal assault and would not be back at work for at least the rest of the week, possibly longer. I gave her the name of Detective Lorraine Proctor at Metro Police Headquarters if the school needed to verify the information.

My second call was to the admissions office at Baptist Hospital. When I asked to speak to Delsey Hawkins, I was informed that she had not been at work on Monday, nor had she come in that morning. That set alarm bells jangling in my head.

I told Maggie I needed to go out for a while. The weather had turned quite chilly, so before I left, I turned up the thermostat to be sure she'd be comfortable. I waited until she took her meds, then warmed up a can of soup and gave her a quick tutorial on how the TV remote worked. After that, I drove over to talk to Delsey, but not before taking a detour past Maggie's place to make certain her broken doors had been repaired.

When I arrived at the Newsome Street address, I found Jericho's crap-wagon Dodge parked on the street as it had been the first night that I visited the Hawkins home. Delsey's car was in the driveway. Both cars being there gave me hope that perhaps Delsey's absence from work and Gabrielle's evident disappearance was nothing more than a case of the whole family holed up in the house with the flu.

I had to knock several times before Delsey came to the door. In a word, she looked awful, and at first, I thought my idea that the whole family had taken sick was a correct one. But when I looked closer, I saw that she had been crying, and her posture suggested that whatever energy she possessed had been all but drained out of her. I also noticed the way she was dressed, in a simple white dress like the ones the women wore at the service Maggie and I had attended a few weeks earlier.

And I knew. Something was very wrong.

I said, "Can I come in?"

She nodded and unhooked the screen door.

I entered the front room and looked around. Everything looked the same as the last time I had visited, except that the picture of Gabrielle that hung on the wall next to the picture of Jericho, Junior, had been turned toward the wall.

Once, when I was a kid, I was walking with some friends through a cemetery. We weren't there to upend any tombstones or to smoke some dope. It was daylight, and it was just a shortcut to get where we were going. One of my friends, or maybe it was me, I don't remember, noticed that the door to one of the private mausoleums was open. Evidently, the groundskeepers were performing some maintenance and had left the doors open while they went to lunch. It was a perfect opportunity to take a look inside a place where none of us had ever been.

The interior of the mausoleum was quite confined, about half the size of a single-car garage. The overhead lights were extinguished, so it was partly dark, and although it was a hot day, it was cool inside. There were crypts set into the walls with bronze plaques indicating the names and the birth and death dates of the occupants. It wasn't a frightening place, but being inside left me with the unmistakable feeling that this was a place where only the dead could find comfort. It was the same feeling that I got now, standing in Delsey's front room.

I was unsure how to begin. "I wanted to come by to talk to you because there have been some developments. I won't call it good news, but the young man who Gabrielle was planning to run away with has died. He won't threaten your family ever again."

"I know." Her voice sounded flat and empty of feeling. "The police called yesterday. They said he was shot. Was that you?"

"I'm afraid it was. He didn't leave me any choice." I waited to see whether she would react. After a moment I said, "Does Gabrielle know?"

"She knows, and she understands. She understands everything now."

"Is she here now? I'd like to talk to her if it's all right."

"She isn't here. She's at church, with Jericho."

I said, "You look as though you're dressed for church yourself. Do you want to go there now? I'll drive you if you'd like."

She nodded. "That would be nice, thank you. I'm not feeling quite myself today. Just let me get my coat."

Delsey had nothing else to say to me on the drive to the Divine Light Pentecostal Congregation Church. What speaking she did was with her eyes closed, praying quietly to herself. When we got to our destination, I drove into the lot and parked the car next to the front steps. I saw that there was a length of heavy chain looped around the doorknobs and fastened with a padlock. A handwritten cardboard sign taped to one of the doors said Sunday services were canceled on account of a family emergency.

Delsey got out of the car first. She walked up to the doors and turned a key in the lock. Then we went inside. The scene that greeted us when we went through the inner doors was like a tableau such as might be found in a wax museum. The first thing I saw was Gabrielle. She was laid out on a long table, surrounded by flowers. She was dressed in a long-sleeved white, full-length gown. Her hands, which held a crucifix, were folded across her stomach. Her feet were bare, and her hair was brushed out and arranged like flowing water around her face. On her head, she wore a halo of delicate white flowers. Baby's breath, I thought, or perhaps jasmine. Her face had been washed clean of any makeup, and her skin was pale and waxy. Dark circles were beginning to form around her eyes. From her appearance, I estimated she had died sometime late Saturday night or early Sunday morning.

Next, I saw Jericho, on the floor in front of the table. Like Gabrielle, his pose in death had been carefully arranged, except that instead of a crucifix, his hands were wrapped around a Bible. His suit jacket was buttoned, as was the collar of his shirt. However, unlike Gabrielle, who had been lovingly prepared, he was dressed in the clothes he was wearing at the moment of his death. I noticed there were still-damp bloodstains in three different spots on the front of his coat. Three shots, just like Bobby Fury, only all three were in his chest. He had been dead for only a short time, perhaps no more than a few hours.

Not knowing what to say or do, and feeling weak in the knees, I sat down in one of the front-row pews. I tried to take it all in, but it was too much, and words failed me. And although it had been decades since I last practiced the Catholic faith I had been baptized into, I bowed my head and said a silent prayer for Jericho and Gabrielle, asking a God whom I barely knew any longer to mercifully receive into a peaceful and eternal rest the souls of a sadly misguided father, and his beautiful, unhappy daughter.

At last, I said to Delsey, "Do you want to tell me what happened?"

She walked to the front of the room and stood with her hands folded. "Not much to tell, and I expect you can work it out for yourself."

"Tell me anyway. I'd rather hear it from you."

There was a long pause, and when she spoke her voice was flat and lifeless, as if it was already coming from beyond the grave.

"It was Saturday afternoon. Gabrielle was in her room, as usual, with the door closed. It was getting near time for supper, so I knocked on her door, and when she didn't answer I went in. She had a suitcase on her bed. I asked her where she thought she was going and she said she was leaving for good, that she was meeting Bobby and that they were going off together. She said there was nothing I could do to stop her.

"Well, things heated up, and we got to shouting. Jericho was in the next room reading his Good Book and he came in to find out what all the ruckus was. Gabrielle told Jericho what she told me. He said, no, that she wasn't going anywhere and that they were going to pray to Jesus on it. Gabrielle said there wasn't going to be any praying that Jericho and Jesus could both… well, you know.

"Then Jericho said there was no call to blaspheme the Lord, and that a demon must have gotten into her soul, like it talks about in the Book of Matthew. He told her to get her coat. He was going to take her to church and pray over her all night if that's what it would take to drive it out."

And that answered the question that had been bothering me since yesterday morning.

I said, "Bobby was waiting for her on Saturday night, wasn't he? Gabrielle was going to sneak out and meet up with him someplace. He waited, but she didn't show up. Maybe he drove by your house and figured out she wasn't there, either. And when she still hadn't turned up the next day, he went looking for Maggie Totten. He had it in his head that she might know where Gabrielle was. Only Maggie was visiting her family in Ohio, so it wasn't until that night that Bobby was able to get to her."

Delsey said, "I'm right sorry if he hurt Miss Totten. I wouldn't have wanted anything like that to happen to her. She was good to Gabrielle."

"She'll be all right. He hurt her some, but she'll be all right. He won't hurt anybody ever again."

"Well then, I'm glad for that. At least something good's come out of all this."

I said, "Let's get back to Jericho and Gabrielle. You said he took her to church? Did you go along with them?"

She shook her head sadly. "I see now I should have. But Jericho said no, that the prayers he was fixing to say were special ones and that I should stay here and do my praying from home."

And then it came to me what had happened. "He decided to test her faith, didn't he? He made her take hold of one of those snakes, and it bit her."

A tear ran down her cheek. "She was just a little girl. She must have been so afraid. I should have been there to comfort her."

"What happened then?"

"Jericho came home very early Sunday morning. He told me what happened. He said he turned off the heat, except for the lamp in the box where the snakes were kept. He put a chain lock on the doors of the church and a sign saying there would be no services on Sunday. That way nobody would find Gabrielle or disturb her until it was time to come back and resurrect her."

"Wait, what? He said he was going to resurrect her?" I thought I hadn't heard her correctly.

"Yes. He said just as Jesus had resurrected Lazarus, he was going to resurrect Gabrielle. He said it was all there in the Bible. We had to wait four days, just as Lazarus waited before he was resurrected. He said it was God's will that he try."

"And you believed him?"

"What else could I do? It was the only hope I had. Jericho and I went back to the church and we set up the table where you see her now. I brought her a clean gown and I washed her body and brushed her hair. I bought some flowers. I thought that if Jericho couldn't bring her back to life, at least I wanted her to look pretty when she arrived to meet the Lord."

"And then you waited all day Sunday and yesterday."

"The Bible says four days. This morning, we came back early, and Jericho read from the Book of John, verses eleven through forty-four."

I remembered. "'I am the resurrection and the life. Whosoever believes in me shall not die but shall live.' But Jericho couldn't bring Gabrielle back."

"No, he couldn't. Jericho said she did not live because she did not believe. He said the venom killed her, and she did not rise because her faith was not strong enough to overcome death."

Talitha cumi, spoken in Aramaic, in the Book of Mark. "Little girl, I say unto you, arise." It worked for Jesus, but not for Jericho Hawkins.

I remembered the gun she'd had in her purse. "And that's when you shot him."

She nodded. "If he had said even one time that he was sorry, or that he loved her, or if he had cried a single tear, maybe then I could have forgiven him. But as it was, the only thing he could find it in him to say was that my baby girl was dead and that it was her own fault. So yes, I shot him. I shot him because at that moment I hated him. I hadn't loved him for a very long time, but I always thought, well, this is where love goes when people grow old together. But I could not allow him to put one of them snakes in the hands of our daughter like it was just another Sunday service. Because make no mistake, it wasn't that snake that murdered my baby, it was Jericho."

I noticed while she was talking that she had been moving a step at a time toward the box where the reptiles were confined. She looked at me with the saddest eyes I have ever seen.

"You don't think Gabrielle was a bad girl, Mister Gamble, do you? Do you think she deserved to die like this, frightened and in pain?"

"Nobody deserves to die like that. I think Gabrielle was just a little girl who was having trouble finding her place in the world. I think she deserved to grow up and have lots of friends and enjoy all the things that pretty girls enjoy. She deserved to live a long life with a husband who would love her and give her children. But I also believe that you are making a big mistake if you do what I think you're about to do."

I said, "We need to call the police. You need to tell them what happened. They'll arrest you, and although I doubt it, there might be a trial. But either way, the law will not punish you. It will be hard, and you will never be able to put this behind you, but you can still do something good with your life."

"I don't think so. I don't think there are any good things left for me."

I don't know why I let her do it. I know that I should have stopped her, but for reasons that I cannot explain, I did not. Instead, I sat, transfixed as she opened the enclosure and lifted out a rattlesnake that must have been five feet long. She held the huge snake close to her face, and it seemed as though, as they stared into each other's eyes, an understanding had been reached.

So quickly that I almost missed it, the snake struck Delsey in the neck.

The bite must have hit a critical spot, as blood spurted from the wound. She jerked her head once, and the snake struck again, this time sinking its fangs into her cheek. And then the obscene moment was over.

She sighed and then returned the rattler to the box where the snakes were kept. She placed it inside and closed the lid. Then she turned and took a step toward me before she stumbled and dropped to her knees. I helped her to her feet and sat her down in a pew. I knew from the location of the bites that a tourniquet would be no use and that there would be no hope of sucking the venom out before it did its deadly work.

I got on my phone and called for help. I requested that the medics bring antivenin, knowing that in all probability it was already too late. I also asked that the police be dispatched. I knew it would take them longer to get there since the call would have to be relayed through the rescue team. I wanted it that way. Whether Delsey lived or died, I didn't want a bunch of clumsy cops asking her a lot of questions in what might well be the final moments of her life. Then I sat down in the pew next to her to wait.

She leaned over and rested her head on my shoulder.

"I'm afraid, Mister Gamble. I know I'll be leaving this life shortly, and I'm fearing when the Lord sees me, he will turn me away, and then I'll never see Gabrielle again, not in all eternity."

"He won't turn you away. If you ask, you'll be forgiven. I know you believe that."

Her breathing was getting shallow, and faster, and when she spoke it was with great effort. "Will you stay with me until…until it's over? I don't want to be alone, and it won't be long."

I put my arm over her shoulder and held her close. "Just rest now, and don't be afraid. I'm not going anywhere. No matter what happens, I'll be with you all the way."

She began to pray. "The Lord is my shepherd. I shall not want…" And that was as far as she got before she faded into unconsciousness.

Chapter Thirty-One

Several minutes passed and then I heard the wail of sirens in the distance, growing closer until finally a fire engine and a rescue squad truck skittered to a stop outside the church. By the time they arrived, I had laid Delsey down in the pew where we had been sitting. I was afraid at first that she had simply died on the spot, but she continued to breathe, though more and more laboriously.

I explained to the medical techs what had happened and watched as they administered antivenin and adrenaline and slipped an oxygen mask over Delsey's face. The two techs got her into the rescue truck, and within minutes after they arrived, they were gone. I asked them to take Delsey to Baptist, explaining that she was employed there and that she would likely be more closely cared for if she were among people who knew her.

That left me with the job of explaining to the fire department captain and a pair of sheriff's deputies, who showed up on the heels of the fire department, what the hell had been going on at the Divine Light Pentecostal Congregation. I went over it three times without any of it seeming to sink in.

One of the deputies, a very large man with a very loud voice said, "You know that snake handling in churches is illegal in the state of Tennessee, don't you Mr. Gamble?"

"I do, but this is not my church. How should I know what goes on here?"

"You admitted you were here when the lady was bitten, didn't you? You could have stopped her from doing that. Why didn't you?"

"I'm afraid of snakes." When that got no response other than a stony stare,

I said, "Look, this all happened very fast. I had no idea what she was going to do. The only way I could have stopped her would have been to shoot her, and where would that have left us?"

By then a Sheriff's Department detective had arrived and started asking questions of his own. "Tell us about the two bodies up there," he said. So, I went over it again, and then one more time.

"Okay, the father killed the little girl and the wife killed the father, is that what you're telling us?"

"Well, when you come right down to it, the snakes did most of the killing, but yes, that's pretty much the way it happened." I was getting tired of answering the same questions over and over and finally said so.

"Now, if you have any questions that I haven't heard yet, I'll be happy to answer them later, but right now I'd like to head for the hospital. The lady you're probably going to arrest for murder is my client, and I'd like to be there when she comes around. She's going to need a friend to help her get through this."

But as it turned out, Delsey didn't need a friend because she didn't come around. She died in the emergency room at the same hospital where she worked. The ER doc said there was simply too much venom in her system, and help had arrived too late.

In the end, a little girl had run away from home because she thought she was in love, and five people were dead.

The next day somebody from the county went out to Antioch and shut down the church, as it turned out, for good. About a week later there was a fire that consumed the entire structure. Nobody was inside at the time.

Speculation was that the oil used in the makeshift lamps like the ones used during the service Maggie and I attended had contributed to the speed with which the blaze progressed. However, the specific cause of the fire, the fire marshal determined, was definitely arson. Since he couldn't find anyone else, and given my involvement with the Hawkins family, the investigator liked me for the job, but Maggie swore I was with her the night the fire started. That was true, but only because it was Maggie who actually struck the match.

Luckily for them, the snakes escaped the conflagration. Before the fire, agents from the conservation department came and removed them, and since winter was already upon us, they were taken to a rescue facility until they could be released into the wild when warmer weather arrived.

There was a memorial service held for Gabrielle and her parents, but for obvious reasons, it did not take place at the Divine Light Pentecostal Congregation Church. Instead, the high school where Gabrielle had been a student offered its auditorium, and a quiet and dignified gathering was held on a Sunday afternoon in mid-December. The school said later it did not expect much of a crowd, but as it turned out the hall was packed with teachers and classmates, members of the hospital staff, and a few folks from the Divine Light Congregation. Jericho, Junior, was also in attendance, having been given compassionate leave from the Army.

Maggie and I were there, too, seated in the back. As the service progressed, and Scriptures were read, I saw tears forming in the corners of her eyes. None of the deceased were present. Their remains had been returned to Jericho and Delsey's hometown in east Tennessee where they were buried following a separate service for family only.

Maggie's recovery from her ordeal at the hands of Bobby Fury was going well. The bruises on her face disappeared after a couple of weeks, and to outward appearances, she looked good as new. The burn marks were healing as well, although it looked as if there might be some slight scarring. Her psychological recovery, however, was taking longer. With both of us back working, our sleepovers had become less frequent, although we tried to make up for the missed nights on the weekends. But sometimes I would get an agitated call from her in the small hours of the morning after she had been startled awake by a nightmare. Those times I would drive to her house and stay until the darkness dissolved into daylight, holding her close and reassuring her that she was safe, and that as long as I lived no one would ever hurt her again.

A few days after Christmas, I got a call from Lorraine Proctor. She got right to the point, informing me that despite the continuing efforts of the Metro police and the TBI, no further information had turned up regarding the five missing girls and no evidence had come to light connecting their disappearances to Jack Olin.

"Best guess is that Robert Furillo was not just a child abductor, he was also a serial murderer. I think he kept those girls around for a while and then when the moon was full or some other damn thing set him off, he killed them. We can't prove it, and those cases will stay open. But so far, that's the best we can do."

There were a couple of other interesting sidelights, however. "We checked up on a guy named Vincent Panetta. You might know who he is. He worked for Jack Olin."

"Past tense?" I asked.

"Very much so, from the look of things. His name came up when we were tearing Olin's life apart. It seems he'd spent a few years inside for multiple assault charges. Spillner and I looked him up to find out whether there was anything he could tell us, but he was gone. He seems to have disappeared from the face of the planet."

"Or maybe underneath it."

"That could be. We may never know. Moving on, there's that Doctor Morse you mentioned. We got security footage from the university's CCTV. It shows Bobby Fury walking into the doctor's office with a young girl who we assume is Gabrielle Hawkins. We can't say for sure because we can't see her face.

"The doctor says Bobby told him she was his sister and that she got carsick while they were driving around. He said he told them they should go to the ER, but she started throwing up, so he gave her something to settle her stomach, and then he sent them on their way. Again, we can't prove any different, although we did report him to the state medical board for not making a record of the treatment. Best guess, he'll get a strongly worded letter in the mail."

"So that's it then."

"I'm afraid so. Unless something else pops up, we're done. Of course, it's just possible that there really isn't anything more to it." There was a pause at her end of the line. "How's your lady, Mr. Gamble? She doing okay?"

CHAPTER THIRTY-ONE

"She's okay. She has good days and bad ones. It's going to take some time."

"You know she loves you, don't you? My advice, don't fuck this up."

After she hung up, I thought about what Lorraine Proctor had said, not just about Maggie, but all of it. And I knew she was right. Sometimes you never really find out the truth. Or maybe you already know, but you want there to be more, if only so that it all makes sense. Sometimes the bad ones get away with it, at least for a while. And then all you can do is acknowledge that you've done your best, and move on.

I thought about Maggie, and what she had been through, and I was amazed that after all that had happened, she didn't blame me for any of it. I decided I would take her to dinner, to the place we had gone the night of our first date. And I hoped she might wear that same burgundy dress, because this time I would show up appropriately dressed for an evening out with a beautiful woman. Maybe she would order an appletini or two, and we would enjoy a special dinner. And then, when the time was just right, I would tell her that everything was going to be all right, and that I would always be close at hand.

A Note from the Author

One of the central elements of this story, and one with which many readers may not be familiar, is the very real practice of handling venomous snakes (normally rattlesnakes, copperheads, and water moccasins) as part of a religious service. According to several recent online articles, as well as an article I retrieved from the *Chicago Tribune* in the early 1980s, handling snakes as part of a service more often occurs in rural churches in that part of the country known as Appalachia. Among such denominations that have adopted this practice are those identified as Pentecostal, Evangelical, Charismatic and Holiness. Briefly, the Holiness movement originated within the Methodist Church in the 19th century. The teachings emphasize the doctrine of a "second work of grace" in the quest for Christian perfection. With respect to the story, the practice of handling snakes during religious services was outlawed in the State of Tennessee in 1947 (though it still exists), and the author takes no position, faith-based or otherwise, on the practice.

https://en.wikipedia.org/wiki/Holiness_movement

https://en.wikipedia.org/wiki/Snake_handling_in_religion

"Praise-the-Lord-and-pass-the-snake service is a trip if you can handle it"
Chicago Tribune, April 3, 1983

Acknowledgements

At the top of my list of individuals to whom I am indebted for their support in seeing *Lost Little Girl* through to publication are the self-described "Dames of Detection," Verena Rose, Harriette Sackler and Shawn Reilly Simmons, the proprietors of Level Best Books who were willing to take me on as a new member of the LBB family. I am indeed honored to be a part of this highly regarded number.

Thanks must also go to my friends and colleagues at the Southeast Missouri Writers Guild and the Heartland Writers Guild, both of which are located in my adopted hometown of Cape Girardeau, Missouri. Writing for publication can be a lonely proposition, especially for a work of fiction, and the support and encouragement of others similarly engaged in creative writing goes a long way to helping keep a challenging project on track.

I also want to thank several individuals who provided both critical and proofreading support as well as the occasional pep-talk as the project ground its way to completion. These include writers and friends William Wade, Barry Pfanstiel, Barbara Barbre, Tom Neumeyer, David Kwinn, Chris Rellim, "Level Bestie" Mark Levenson, and my wife and best friend Carol, who stuck with me through innumerable edits and re-writes on the way to finalization.

About the Author

Lost Little Girl is Gregory Stout's debut mystery in the Jackson Gamble series. He is also the author of *Gideon's Ghost*, a young adult novel which takes place in small-town America in the mid-1960s. He has also written 21 books on the history of American railroads. His first title, *Route of the Eagles*, was released in 1995 and his most recent effort, now in production, will be in print in late 2021. A complete listing of Greg Stout's published works can be found at www.gregorystoutauthor.com. He resides with his wife, Carol, and two cats, Wallace and Gromit, in Cape Girardeau, Missouri, where he is a member of the Heartland Writers Guild and the Southeast Missouri Writers Guild.

Twitter:@GregStout16

Also by Gregory Stout

Gideon's Ghost (Beacon Publishing Group, 2018), various railroad history titles, 1996-2021.

www.gregorystoutauthor.com